CHEERS ~~FOR THE~~

WHISKEY MATTIMOE MYSTERY SERIES

"A few days with Whiskey Mattimoe and friends will give you the wildest ride you ever took from your armchair! Mystery fans will appreciate the clever clues, plot and suspects, but hang on to your sleuthing cap because things change right up until the end in true cliffhanger style. *Whiskey Straight Up* is a delight and you'll be anxious for your next visit to Magnet Springs. Wright has delivered a great cocktail for series fans."

—Julie Obermiller, *Mysterical-E*

"Delving into the second book in the series is like catching up with old friends. Wright keeps things light and fun; readers will want another round of Whiskey."

—*Toledo Alumni Magazine*

January/February 2007 Staff Pick

—*Creature and Crooks Bookshoppe,* www.cncbooks.com

Whiskey
and
Tonic

ALSO BY NINA WRIGHT FROM MIDNIGHT INK

Whiskey on the Rocks
Whiskey Straight Up

FORTHCOMING

Whiskey and Water

YOUNG ADULT BOOKS BY NINA WRIGHT

Homefree

FORTHCOMING

Sensitive

Whiskey and Tonic

A Whiskey Mattimoe Mystery

Nina Wright

MIDNIGHT INK
WOODBURY, MINNESOTA

First Edition
First Printing, 2007

Book design by Donna Burch
Cover design by Lisa Novak
Cover illustration © 2006 by Bunky Hurter   FR

Midnight Ink, an imprint of Llewellyn Publications

Library of Congress Cataloging-in-Publication Data
Wright, Nina.
  Whiskey and tonic : a Whiskey Mattimoe mystery / Nina Wright.
    p. cm.
  ISBN-13: 978-0-7387-1055-6
  ISBN-10: 0-7387-1055-5
    1. Mattimoe, Whiskey (Fictitious character)—Fiction. 2. Women real estate agents—Fiction. 3. Michigan—Fiction. 4. beauty contests—Fiction. 5. Domestic fiction. I. Title.

PS3623.R56W47   2007
813'.6—dc22   2007061150

Midnight Ink
Llewellyn Publications
2143 Wooddale Drive, Dept. 0-7387-1055-5
Woodbury, MN 55125-2989, U.S.A.
www.midnightinkbooks.com

Printed in the United States of America

For Rewind and Go . . . with fond memories of the tonic.

ACKNOWLEDGMENTS

Love to my father for his good humor. No doubt he taught me to laugh.

Many thanks to the wise and wonderful writers who critiqued my drafts: Teddie Aggeles, M. K. Buhler, and Rebecca Gall. An extra nod to Rebecca for the fabulous web design.

Hugs to Richard Pahl, who has encouraged my writing since my very first play.

Affection, always, to friends Kate Argow, Bonnie Brandburg, and Diana West.

Special thanks to B. P. Winzeler, who has grace at all times, in all places. WWSD.

A big shout out to Danita Hiley for introducing me to the original Roscoe and for many happy walks in West Virginia.

Appreciation to Pamela Asire for her menagerie and her willingness to read my drafts.

Gratitude to realtor Nancy Potter and real estate attorney Rita Thomas for their expertise. (Readers, please note that all errors are my own; I'm in the business of making things up.)

Kudos to Linda Jo Bugbee of Beloved Afghan Hounds for her generous support and her gorgeous dogs. Abra sends regards to Elivia.

A deep bow to my editor Barbara Moore, and pats on the head for Whiskey and Norman, who live at her house.

Apologies to Flannery, my own dear Devon rex.

And thanks to Scooter . . . for the midnight inspiration.

ONE

"THIS ISN'T A TONIC. It's toxic," I rasped, setting the glass down so hard that its contents splashed onto Mother Tucker's bar.

"Tonics aren't supposed to be tasty," Odette intoned. "They're supposed to cure what ails you."

"Who said anything ails me?"

My top salesperson gave me a look that could freeze lava. Then she took a sip of her *chocotini* and waved toward the bar crowd.

"Shall we take a poll? Ask whether anyone here thinks Whiskey Mattimoe needs a tonic?"

Talk about a setup. Odette's mellifluous voice can compel complete strangers to do her bidding. I've decided that her velvety Tonga accent is the reason she sells more real estate than anyone else in west Michigan. That plus the fact that she pretends not to understand the word *no*.

"No," I said emphatically. "We don't need a poll."

"True. Your misery is obvious." Odette shoved the vile cocktail toward me. "It's a traditional African tonic. Drink up."

I eyed the sparkling contents suspiciously. "Your people drink this?"

"No. Your people drink this," she said.

"I don't have people in Africa."

Odette narrowed her eyes. "Of course you do. How else did so many of my people end up here?"

Embarrassed, I held up the glass and peered deep into it. "Okay. Why do 'my people' drink this in Africa?"

"For the malaria."

I put the glass down. "There's no malaria in Magnet Springs."

Odette sighed heavily. "Then what is your problem?"

Good question. It was officially spring. The days were getting longer, warmer, and sweeter smelling. Daffodils and crocuses were blooming. People were starting to smile again. Some were even falling in love. Or at least in lust. Not with me, though. And therein lay my problem: I wasn't getting laid.

"Uh-oh," Odette murmured. "Are you wearing the camisole?"

Following her gaze, I immediately understood the question. Handsome Nash Grant, the lust of my life, was entering the bar. For my birthday, two weeks earlier, Odette had tried to boost my bland beige wardrobe by giving me a black silk and lace camisole. With it she had included these written instructions:

Wear at all times. Be prepared to peel off whatever you put on over it.
Remember: You can't go wrong in a black camisole.
Well, you can, but you'll thank me later.

In case I missed the point, she had added a simple equation:

Black Camisole = Sex Appeal
You need it.

Now, reflexively, I yanked my camel-colored mock-turtleneck over my head. I had it almost all the way off before I remembered that my sexy black camisole was in the laundry hamper at home … and I was wearing one of my oldest yellowish-white bras. In public. In front of Nash Grant.

Odette gasped in horror at the same instant I realized my gaffe. Fortunately, my head was inside my shirt. Even though the whole room could see me, I couldn't see anybody. Whiskey the Ostrich. Who says denial is a bad thing? When my exposed torso felt a chill, I began fumbling for my sleeves. I seemed to have lost one. The sweater rolled back down, but only my left arm slid into its rightful place. Still groping under the fabric with my right hand, I reluctantly opened one eye.

"Hot flash?" teased Nash Grant in his soft Mississippi accent.

"Not yet!" I replied indignantly. "I'm only thirty-four!"

He laughed. "That makes you officially the youngest grandma I know."

"*Step*-grandma," I corrected him gravely. "I'm young enough to be Avery's sister."

"Of course you are." Nash made a mock bow, the bar lights glinting off his thick, walnut-colored hair. If I hadn't been tangled in the straightjacket of my shirt, I might have swooned.

"Do you need a hand there, Whiskey?" he asked. "You seem to be missing one."

Before I could answer, Nash deftly reached under my sweater to connect my right arm with my right sleeve. He guided the entire limb safely home. A delicious tingle shot through me; I knew my face was flushed.

"Thanks," I mumbled.

"My pleasure. Any time." Our gazes locked just long enough for his coppery eyes to penetrate mine. I was sure he saw clear through to my brain waves, which were screaming, "I want you bad!"

Nash said a few things to Odette. Then he was gone, moving along the bar to shake hands and trade pleasantries with other patrons. He didn't help anyone else put on a shirt, however.

If only Nash weren't the father of my late husband's grandchildren. Bottom line: if only he weren't determined to make up with my late husband's daughter. Nash and Avery had produced twins as the result of a one-night stand. She expected me, Leo's widow, to finance her new family since her kids were Leo's heirs. But Nash was determined to do the right thing. On sabbatical from the University of Florida, where they'd met, he tracked Avery down. She and the twins were living with me; now Nash was courting her. Under my roof.

"Where's the camisole?" Odette hissed.

"Waiting to be washed. You should have bought me *two*."

"You can afford a second. I suggest you buy it tomorrow. And start wearing it in public! You need to replace the image of that hideous brassiere now burned into our retinas …"

Walter St. Mary appeared on the other side of the bar. He glanced from my beverage to me. "You've hardly touched it! I thought the Leprechaun made you do it."

"The what?"

"The Leprechaun. Where I come from, that's what we call Irish whiskey and tonic. It's been known to make a few lasses take off their shirts." Walter winked.

"It didn't—I didn't—" I gave up.

Mother Tucker's proprietor checked his watch. "They're crowning Miss Blossom at two-thirty. Isn't your office intern one of the contestants?"

"Faye Raffle," confirmed Odette. "She's going to win. I've got fifty dollars riding on it."

I turned to Odette in disgust. "You bet on a beauty pageant?"

"I bet on our office intern. If Faye wins, I'll donate the money to her college tuition fund. So will everyone else in the office."

"There was a pool? Why didn't I know about it?"

"Try reading your office bulletin board."

"Jonny's one of the judges," Walter said, referring to his partner in both business and real life. "Rico Anuncio was supposed to be on the panel, but he didn't return from his cruise in time. Jonny's nervous about making the right choice. He's never had mainstream taste in female beauty."

"I'm sure he'll do fine," I said as I handed Walter my credit card. "I'd trust his taste over Rico's any day."

Odette snorted in agreement. She and I disliked the flamboyant owner of the West Shore Gallery. The previous fall Rico had threatened us with a frivolous lawsuit, for which we weren't yet ready to forgive him. We'd enjoyed every day he was gone on his round-the-world cruise. My secret hope was that he'd fall in love with an exotic person or place and forget all about returning to our town. Odette would be more than happy to get him an astonishing price for his Magnet Springs home. Rumor had it that he was due back soon, however.

While Walter processed my plastic, I asked Odette, "Do you really think Faye can win? I hear Tammi LePadanni's daughter is drop-dead gorgeous."

Tammi LePadanni was a part-time agent in our office. In other words, a hobbyist. I kept her on staff for one reason only: she was a doctor's wife—ergo, she knew rich people.

Odette made a rude raspberry noise. "You're forgetting the Q-and-A portion of the competition. Tammi LePadanni's daughter couldn't speak a declarative statement at gunpoint."

"Really?"

"Really. You've got to hear her to believe it. Everything from her Angelina Jolie lips sounds like a question." Odette glanced at her diamond-studded wristwatch. "The fun starts in five minutes. Let's go!"

I hastily completed my credit card receipt to include the usual 25 percent tip for Walter. Since he never charged me full price for anything, I was always trying to say thanks.

"What's Tammi LePadanni's daughter's name?" I asked Odette. "Don't tell me it rhymes, too."

"Brandi LePadanni. Feel a kinship to the girl?"

"I don't drink my name, and I hope she doesn't drink hers," I quipped. "Especially since she's under age."

"And is Whiskey your real name?" Odette asked innocently.

"You know it isn't. Are you saying Brandi is a nickname, too?"

"Short for Brandolina. Awful, isn't it? Tammi's parents loved Marlon Brando."

"Then why not name her Marla? By the way, I've met Dr. Le-Padanni. He looks like late-stage Brando. Wonder where the daughter got her good looks? Mom's no beauty queen, and Dad's a real barker."

"Speaking of canines," Odette said, "what's the latest on yours?"

I cringed as I always did at the mention of Abra. The Afghan hound was my late husband's legacy and, second only to my real-estate business, my biggest headache. Aside from her penchant for stealing purses and other forbidden treats, Abra was high maintenance in the extreme. Just grooming her long blonde tresses required more time and patience than I was born with. Add to that her propensity for escape. And for consorting with criminals.

"Last I checked, Deely was installing a mesh cover over the kennel," I said. "And laying concrete along the fence line. Hopefully that will contain the bitch."

"Which one?"

I grinned. I'd hired Deely Smarr, fondly known as the Coast Guard nanny, to assist my shrewish stepdaughter and her infant twins, but the capable woman was also babysitting Abracadabra. She had the perfect background for the job: Military Damage Control. An expert at fixing boats, guns, and assorted life forms, Deely had only one flaw that I could see. She was a founding member of Fleggers—a.k.a. Four Legs Good—a radical animal rights advocacy based in Ann Arbor. Deely believed that animals, including Abra, were our equals. A terrifying premise. Nonetheless, she understood that the general public needed protection from my dog.

Odette and I were crossing Main Street toward Town Square where Miss Blossom was about to be crowned when we spotted my office manager Tina Breen. She was easy to spot because she was jumping up and down and waving her arms.

"Whiskey! Oh my God, Whiskey!" Tina shrieked in her dentist's drill voice. "Abra is loose again! She stole Miss Blossom's tiara!"

That was a big deal. In fact, it was a felony.

Magnet Springs has been a tourist town since before the Civil War. As a result, our long and convoluted history has spawned many an insane tradition, one of which is this: Miss Blossom is annually crowned with a tiara made of solid gold and emeralds, a bequest from the obscenely rich, widowed mother of the first Miss Blossom. Legend has it that back in 1847, Mrs. Slocum Schuyler was so proud of her beauty queen daughter that she commissioned a tiara. Upon her death, Mrs. Schuyler bequeathed the tiara to the village of Magnet Springs expressly for the coronation of all subsequent Miss Blossoms. We've been obsessed with safeguarding the damn thing ever since.

"Look!" screeched Tina Breen, pointing across Town Square. Sure enough, there went my big amber dog, a glistening green crown gripped in her pearly whites.

TWO

"Call the Coast Guard!" I told Odette. "I'm going after Abra!"

"Oh, please." My star salesperson rolled her eyes. "I'll call Deely, but who are you kidding? That's an Afghan hound. She's already out of sight."

Odette was right. The golden blur of Abra had vanished behind a row of Main Street shops. I held my breath, but she failed to reappear. Odette handed me her cell phone.

"I'm sorry, ma'am," Deely Smarr began. "I take full responsibility for the cadet's escape."

"What cadet?" I asked. "I'm calling about Abra."

Deely explained that in her dog-training program, The System, a learner at Abra's level was called a cadet. I assumed that was the equivalent of a freshman. Or maybe a dropout.

"Just tell me how she got out this time," I sighed.

"As you know, ma'am, I've been moonlighting as Avery's personal trainer. We run together three times a week."

"What does that have to do with my dog?"

"Abra's been running with us," Deely explained. "Like Avery, she's still trying to lose that last pregnancy fat. Today I let her off leash, and she bolted."

"Why?"

"I can't say for sure, ma'am, but she may be incorrigible."

"No, I mean why did you let her off leash?"

"In The System, each student is given more responsibility than we think she can easily handle. It's called the Learning Challenge."

"It's called a big, fat mistake! Abra went and stole Miss Blossom's tiara! I'll be back in court before you can say Judge Wells Verbelow!"

"Whiskey," Odette interrupted. "The judge wants to talk with you."

I wheeled to face the jurist. "Wells! How the hell are you?"

"I'm good, Whiskey. Which way did she go?"

Odette, Tina, and I pointed. Wells inserted two fingers in his mouth and whistled shrilly. From the crowd behind us burst a huge and grotesque hound. He bounded past us, copious jowls flapping, saliva spraying everywhere.

"Mooney to the rescue!" Tina exclaimed.

Wells said, "Technically, this is a retrieval rather than a rescue."

We followed Mooney with our eyes until he disappeared behind the same shops where we'd last seen Abra. The Rott Hound, as my eight-year-old neighbor dubbed the judge's Rottweiler-bloodhound mix, was renowned for his track-and-attack skills. But, man, did he leave a trail of drool.

"He won't hurt her, will he?" I heard myself say. Sometimes I sound like I actually care about Abra.

"No, he'll take her down and then use his Paw Maneuver to immobilize her," Wells said.

I'd seen the results of Mooney's Paw Maneuver once before. It was the canine equivalent of a stun gun.

"He presses his massive front paws into his quarry's solar plexus —like this." Using his own body, Wells demonstrated the move for the benefit of Tina and Odette. Tina looked horrified. Odette yawned.

"Are they going to proceed with the coronation or not?" she said.

"That will be up to Acting Mayor Goh," Wells replied.

We heard the distinct sound of someone tapping on a microphone. Then the crowd shifted just enough to clear our view of the stage, where Peg Goh stood flanked by four lovely teenaged girls, all of them dressed in formal gowns and all of them frowning.

"Uh—may I have your attention," Peg said as the microphone in her hand squealed. "Due to circumstances beyond our control, we have temporarily lost possession of Magnet Springs' historic Miss Blossom tiara. However, the judges and contestants have agreed to continue with the coronation, following a short recess. Please bear with us."

The microphone hummed ominously. Peg added, "Will Whiskey Mattimoe kindly report to the judges' stand? *Now.*"

"Uh boy," I muttered. "Here we go again."

Less than a year ago I was hauled into court because of Abra's thievery. In fact, that was how I met Judge Verbelow, who later asked me out. Wells is a nice man, a fair man, but not the kind of guy who rings my chimes.

"Would you like me to go with you?" he asked.

It couldn't hurt, I thought. As we threaded our way through the crowd, I felt hot eyes on me and overheard more than a few hostile comments.

"Ignore them, Whiskey," Wells whispered. "Remember, you're innocent until proven guilty."

Guilty? That's when it hit me: this looked like a jewel heist. The biggest jewel heist in Lanagan County history.

I stopped. "You don't think I planned this, do you?"

Wells laid his hand on my forearm. "Of course not. This has all the earmarks of a professional job."

I stared. "You mean—"

"I mean, it's not Abra's first theft, Whiskey. She has some remarkable skills, illegal though they may be. It's also possible that she's been corrupted. Further corrupted." He lowered his voice. "Have you seen anyone hanging around Vestige lately?"

The judge was referring to my home three miles outside of town. I was blessed to have had enough time with my late husband Leo to transform a few lakefront acres into an idyllic rural abode. Leo wasn't blessed to enjoy it for long; he had died suddenly almost a year ago. No wonder I was depressed. I had been trying not to remember the coming anniversary of his death. Could I have been trying so hard that I failed to notice Abra conspiring with jewel thieves? If so, where was the Coast Guard nanny, and why didn't she control the damage?

"Whiskey Mattimoe to the judges' stand," Peg Goh repeated into her microphone.

At least I've got a judge on my side, I thought. To Wells I said, "If this gets sticky, could you—uh—represent me in court?"

"Sorry, Whiskey. I'm a jurist, not a practicing attorney. But I could recommend someone."

We arrived at the judges' stand, where five familiar faces awaited me, all of them stern. Peg spoke first, "Whiskey, what's going on?"

"I wish I knew. Thank God Mooney's on the case. If anyone can bring her back alive, he can."

"We don't want Abra back," whined a tall man in spandex. "We want the tiara!"

"Welcome home, Rico," I said, trying to keep the acid out of my voice. "We didn't think you'd arrive in time to judge Miss Blossom."

He tucked a strand of sun-streaked hair behind one ear. I tried to ignore the four new piercings in his earlobe, each hole bearing an oversized diamond stud.

"I wouldn't have missed it for the world," he crooned. "I live to evaluate beauty."

Rico looked me up and down.

"Speaking of which, you don't look half as bad as you did the last time I saw you. Now, if you could just get laid …"

Wells boomed, "That's enough." He turned to our acting mayor. "Peg, have you notified the police?"

"Jenx is off duty today, but Brady's on his way over," she said.

Henrietta Roca, local innkeeper and life partner of Police Chief Judy "Jenx" Jenkins, held up her cell phone.

"I called Jenx. She's painting our dormers. As soon as she can climb down the ladder and close up the cans, she'll get her butt over here."

"We need a moment of meditation," announced the soothing voice of Noonan Starr, New Age guru and massage therapist. She had already assumed the lotus posture.

"I would if I could, but I have bad knees," said shy Jonny St. Mary, the chef half of the Mother Tucker team. "And now that Rico's here, you don't need me."

"Yes, we do," Hen said quickly. "Martha never showed up for judging duty. So we're still one short."

"Halloooo!" We all looked toward the querulous call. Octogenarian shopkeeper Martha Glenn appeared to be feeling her way through the crowd—probably because she was wearing a large straw hat, backwards. I knew it was on backwards because the immense pink bow would have looked better in the rear. Also, the fat satin ribbons trailing over Martha's wizened face were obviously impeding her view. She stumbled into part-time Officer Brady Swancott and nearly tripped over his canine sidekick, Officer Roscoe. Ever the young gentleman, Brady steadied Martha on her spindly legs.

"Allow me," I said, removing Martha's hat expressly in order to rotate it.

"Thief!" Martha shrieked. "Officer, make her give that back!"

"Give it back, Whiskey," Brady said.

Without a word I set it on Martha's head, right way around.

She glared at me. "You again." The way she spoke, you'd think I was her personal tormentor.

"Yes, it's me, Martha. Whiskey Mattimoe." I flashed my warmest smile. We all knew that Martha was slipping into senility; sad to say, she was no longer fit to run Town and Gown, the upscale women's clothing store where most of Magnet Springs shopped.

"Why aren't you wearing that camisole?" she demanded. "You look like a fool!"

I heard Odette's musical laugh, followed by Rico's raucous one. For the second time in fifteen minutes, my face flushed.

"And there's that dog of yours …" Martha said.

"Yes, well, we're looking for her," I mumbled.

"I said, *there's that dog of yours*! Right over there!" Martha pointed a trembling finger past my shoulder.

The crowd parted itself like the Red Sea. Abra the Affie had returned, the historic Miss Blossom tiara still in her teeth. She arrived with the dignity of visiting royalty when in fact she was an out-and-out thief. Trotting along behind her was Mooney the Rott Hound, beaming like a paid escort.

The way people cheered, you'd think my dog was some kind of hero. I decided to pretend that none of this was really happening. Then my eyes met Wells Verbelow's, and I knew I had penance to pay. He looked grim.

"What's the matter?" I shouted over the roar of the crowd. "She brought it back!"

Wells nodded. "That part's good. What I don't understand is how Mooney got her to do it. His criminal-control repertoire clearly exceeds my understanding."

"He didn't do the Paw Thing?"

"He couldn't have. She'd still be immobilized."

Wishful thinking.

Wells went off to tend his dog. Abra pranced over to the sniffling young woman I recognized as last year's Miss Blossom. The girl screamed and shrank back in terror. I surmised that Abra had stolen the crown right off her head. That would explain why my dog had the power to reduce the reigning queen to a quaking mess. Acting Mayor Peg Goh soothed Miss Blossom until she could summon the courage to gingerly remove the tiara from Abra's grinning mouth. Another cheer went up.

"Put it on! Put it on!" the crowd chanted. Again, the beauty queen looked stricken. No doubt the antique tiara was thoroughly slimed. Henrietta Roca produced a bright red bandana, which the reigning queen gratefully used to wipe down her crown and then her hands. Keeping a wary eye on Abra, she then placed the tiara on her own head. The applause was deafening. Abra twirled around once and took a bow, whereupon Officer Swancott seized her by her rhinestone collar and yanked her from the stage.

"How'd she get away from you this time?" The voice belonged to Jenx, who was not only our Chief of Police but also the only full-time law enforcement agent in Magnet Springs. She wore painter's overalls and a painter's cap instead of her usual navy-blue uniform. She also wore lots of paint. Completely lacking vanity, Jenx wouldn't care that there was more maroon pigment smeared on her face, hands, shoes and clothes than she'd applied to the dormers of Red Hen's House. The effect was comical. I laughed for the first time all day.

"You find jewel theft funny?" Jenx asked, inflating to her maximum five-foot-five-inch height.

"Not remotely," I said. "And I never find Abra funny." I guffawed again.

"How nice for you," Jenx said. "I hope you'll still be laughing when the Schuyler Trust attorney takes you to court."

"What?" That got my attention. Legal threats generally do.

"Of course, it's always possible that he'll waive the action. But I doubt it."

"Back up," I said.

Jenx explained that a trust established by Mrs. Slocum Schuyler stipulated to the ongoing maintenance and security of the Miss Blossom tiara. In perpetuity. An attorney had complete oversight of the crown. Basically, his job was to prosecute anyone who messed with it.

"Abra brought it right back!" I said.

"That won't matter. According to the Trust, anybody who 'mishandles' the thing is in deep doo-doo. Why do you think the contestants always look nervous?"

THREE

"ALL BEAUTY QUEEN CONTESTANTS are nervous," I argued.

"Not like that," Jenx said, indicating the trembling troupe on the Town Square stage.

I was about to protest that they were agitated because of Abra, but that wouldn't help my case. Besides, Jenx had a point. I'd often wondered why girls competing for the Miss Blossom title seemed completely stressed out.

"I shouldn't be telling you this, but the Trust requires them to sign a contract," Jenx whispered.

"What kind of contract?"

Jenx scanned the crowd to make sure no one was observing our tête-à-tête.

"They have to provide a detailed financial disclosure: their family's assets, debts, and credit history."

"What for?"

"The Trust wants to make sure they're not running for the title just to get access to the tiara."

I squinted at the crown atop Miss Blossom's red-blonde head.

"Why would anyone do that? It's the ugliest crown I've ever seen. Old-fashioned and clunky. Plus, it's green. I thought tiaras were supposed to shimmer."

"Like rhinestones, you mean?"

I nodded.

"Here's the thing," Jenx confided. "Those emeralds are top quality. They were mined in Brazil more than a hundred and sixty years ago."

"Big deal. They ain't diamonds."

"No, they're worth a hell of a lot more."

Before I could comment, a short man in a dark suit sidled up to me.

"Whitney Mattimoe?" he inquired.

"Whiskey," I corrected him. "I don't use my legal name."

"You will in court," he replied and handed me his business card. I didn't have to read it, thanks to Jenx.

"Well, if it isn't Attorney Kevin Sweeney," she said.

"You handle the Schuyler Trust?" I gulped.

He looked startled. "As a matter of fact I do."

"So … you're planning to sue my ass?"

"Actually, I was going to refer some business your way."

I glanced at Jenx in total confusion. Was I in trouble for Abra's antics or not?

"Kevin," I said, "did you witness the fracas with the tiara?"

To my astonishment, the stiff little man laughed.

"That was your dog, wasn't it? I've heard about her. A canine criminal."

"Not this time! She brought it right back. She's rehabilitated, mostly. Ask Jenx." When I saw the dubious expression on the chief's face, I hoped he wouldn't. "Am I in trouble?"

Attorney Sweeney waved a small, well-manicured hand. "I don't think so. In fact, this little 'incident' may have done us some good."

"How so?" Jenx interjected.

"Well, first of all, the crowd saw how quickly law enforcement responded. Including the Chief of Police—on her day off. Or so I assume …" He eyed Jenx's attire distastefully. "Second, the civilian response was awesome. Judge Verbelow and his dog deserve a public commendation. The message of the day is *you can't mess with the Miss Blossom tiara and get away with it*."

"Here, here!" I affirmed. "Now, about this business you're sending my way—?"

"Ah, yes," said Kevin Sweeney. "Perhaps you and I could discuss that another time."

"Don't mind me," Jenx said. "I'm going back to my paintbrush."

"Don't you want to stick around and see who wins?" I asked.

"I'm not into skinny girls. Give me a broad with muscles any day." And she was gone.

I studied Kevin Sweeney. Barely thirty, he seemed young to be attorney of record for a historic trust. But what did I know? If he could help me make money, I'd forgive him for being a lawyer.

"Are you familiar with Winimar?" he asked.

The name didn't resonate. "Is that a town?" I said.

"It's big enough to be. But, no, it's a country estate. A few miles from here."

I frowned. Having lived here all my life and worked six years in local real estate, I knew the territory. Yet I'd never heard of Winimar. Sweeney seemed relieved that I hadn't.

"The family has kept it private—since the mid-1800s," he said.

"How is that possible?"

"It's very secluded. Trust me, you have to work to find it. All eighty acres. And therein lies the problem. Well, part of it."

I waited. Attorney Sweeney cleared his throat. "It's the old Schuyler estate. And, well, legend has it that the place is … cursed."

"*Cursed*? As in jinxed?"

He nodded uneasily.

I didn't know whether to make a joke or make a break for it. So I asked a question. "Why would you think it's cursed?"

"Personally, I don't have an opinion," he said quickly. "I'm just the administrator. But it's only fair to tell you that some people believe it is. Some people have written about it."

"Who? When?"

Sweeney lowered his voice. "The first book about Winimar appeared around the turn of the twentieth century. The second was written in the 1970s. Both authors were what you might call 'spiritualists.'"

"Are the books still in print?" I asked.

"Fortunately, no. But copies do exist. And rumor has it that another book is in the works."

"What are the books about?"

Attorney Sweeney's Adam's apple bobbed up and down.

"Things that happened there. Or *allegedly* happened there."

"Well, which is it?" I demanded.

"History provides proof of some events, but only anecdotal evidence of others."

I waited.

"What we do know, Whiskey, is that no one has lived at Winimar for over a hundred and thirty years."

"Why not?"

He looked toward the stage, where Peg Goh was preparing to restart the competition.

"Do you know the story of the first Miss Blossom?"

"Besides the fact that her mom made her wear that ugly crown?"

"Winimar is named for her. Her real name was Winifred, but her mother called her Mar. For her middle name, Margaret."

"Mar is much better."

Sweeney wasn't interested in my opinion. "Mrs. Schuyler was widowed when Mar was young. From 1840 through 1845, she used most of her inheritance to build Winimar, a utopian estate dedicated to her beautiful daughter. All went well until July 1848, when Mar Schuyler was found dead in her bedroom, her throat slit. That was three months after she ended her reign as the first Miss Blossom."

"Did they arrest somebody?"

"Yes. One of the men who built the place. He was convicted and hanged in 1849. One year later, Mrs. Slocum Schuyler died exactly the same way."

"Her throat was slit?"

"Yes."

"And then the house was abandoned," I surmised.

"Temporarily. It remained unoccupied until Mrs. Schuyler's grandnephew took up residence there in 1872."

"What happened to him?" The question filled me with dread.

"Nothing happened to him."

I let out a small sigh.

"But in 1875, his wife's throat was slit. No one has lived there since."

"Understandably."

Sweeney said, "There have been squatters, however."

"Don't tell me—"

"We can't authenticate those stories. But both books about Winimar include accounts of trespassing hunters finding unidentified skeletons or corpses on the property. Male *and* female. Some with their skulls crushed. Frankly, the place is a boneyard."

"A *jinxed* boneyard. You want me to sell it, don't you?"

Sweeney nodded. "The Trust is willing to pay triple the standard commission. And I'm authorized to insure your life for up to one million dollars through the duration of our contract."

"I don't need more life insurance," I said, sounding bold beyond belief. "Make it *quadruple* the commission and you've got yourself a deal."

"Done," said Sweeney, extending his right hand.

What the hell. I was feeling lucky today. Abra and I had drawn a get-out-of-jail-free card.

FOUR

Attorney Kevin Sweeney said he'd fax me the paperwork from his office in Grand Rapids on Monday. Peg Goh was tapping her microphone, about to restart the Miss Blossom competition.

I had one more question for Sweeney before the fun began: "If there have been at least three murders there, how come nobody in Magnet Springs knows about Winimar?"

My newest client blinked. "Who said nobody knows about it?"

"I didn't know about it. And I've lived here all my life."

"Then you understand what makes a resort community run," Sweeney said.

"The scenery?" I guessed.

"The secrecy," he replied.

"You're right. Nobody who runs a business in this town would want to talk about a thing like that."

"Nobody can talk about it. Sign here."

From his breast pocket, Sweeney withdrew a pen and a folded contract. With my name on it.

"What the hell is this?" I said.

"Gag order. Standard stuff." He held out the pen, which I couldn't help noticing was a Montblanc. I looked again at his charcoal gray suit. European cut. Sweeney seemed extremely successful for such a young lawyer. From my standpoint that could be either good or … very, very bad.

"I don't sign anything my attorney hasn't seen first," I said. That was a lie. I signed contracts every day without calling my lawyer. But most were boilerplates. This would be my first-ever gag order. And my first cursed property. I could probably use a little legal backup. Bluffing, I said, "Maybe Judge Verbelow should look this over."

Attorney Sweeney said, "Whatever makes you feel comfortable."

Hmm. If he was so sure the local jurist would approve, I was probably safe. I scanned the short document. Basically it banned me, the undersigned, from divulging anything I knew or thought I knew related to the history of Winimar.

"What about the full disclosure required by law when selling real estate?" I asked Sweeney.

"Of course, we'll fully disclose the known condition of the property," he said. "This is to prevent fear-mongering and negative publicity. It's in our mutual interest to get the best price possible, isn't it, Whitney?"

I penned my signature with his Montblanc as Peg Goh introduced the three Miss Blossom finalists. All were eighteen years old, which was part of the tradition. One, Faye Raffle, worked for me. Another, Brandi LePadanni, had a mother who worked for me. The third was no one I knew or cared about. She wasn't especially good-looking, either. Sure to be second runner-up.

But I couldn't predict the winner. Faye had classic girl-next-door beauty: sleek brown hair sweetly styled to frame her face, luminous skin, big green eyes, and a thousand-watt smile. In a straight-off-the-rack pink satin gown, she looked like the prettiest of bridesmaids. Brandi, on the other hand, was gorgeous verging on exotic. Voluptuous without being fleshy, her curvy figure filled out every fiber of her strapless snow-white gown. The contrast against her olive skin was stunning. Brandi wore her mane of blue-black hair in a daring upsweep. She smiled alluringly at the assembled crowd, her lush ruby lips gleaming. My eyes moved back to Faye: Prom Queen versus Miss Universe. If this were only about beauty, Brandi would win. But if Odette was right and Brandi couldn't talk, then Faye had an excellent shot. Captain of the Magnet Springs High School Debate Team, my office intern was a whiz with words.

Reading from index cards, Peg Goh addressed the girls on the stage:

"Contestants, as acting mayor of Magnet Springs, Michigan, I am proud to recognize your achievements today. Even though only one of you will be chosen to wear the Miss Blossom crown, all of you are winners in the eyes of your fellow citizens."

"What a crock! Two of them will be branded as losers forever."

Odette had joined me. Lest I missed her point, she made an L with the thumb and index finger of her right hand and pressed it to her forehead.

Peg Goh kept reading from her cards. "Whether or not you win, this experience will leave you with greater maturity, compassion, poise, and pride—and probably a new hairstyle. Thus, you are a winner regardless of whether or not we crown you Miss Blossom."

Assuming she had finished, the crowd automatically applauded. But Peg had more cards to read. "Remember that life is a continuous competition. Learn to accept defeat with grace and success with humility. And always, always bear in mind that your greatest competitor is yourself. Wearing the crown is not nearly as important as how you make it shine. Being a gracious winner can be more difficult than being a gracious loser—or, as we prefer to say, *non-winner*. And now, let the judging begin."

Again, there was applause, but it died as soon as Peg flipped to the next card. She read, "I have already introduced our judges, who have prepared one question for each contestant. Ladies, when I call your name, please step forward, listen closely, and prepare to give your answer. After I hand you the microphone, you will have thirty seconds to reply."

Peg cleared her throat.

"Emma Kish—here is your question."

The girl I had pegged to finish third moved to the edge of the stage. A bony, sharp-featured blonde in blue taffeta, she listened intently as Peg spoke: "If you were to become the next Miss Blossom, how would you make sure that your friends did not feel inferior?"

Emma's dress rustled as she reached for the microphone. In a shockingly flat voice, she said, "First of all, my friends have a lot more money and stuff than I do, so there's no way they would care if I won Miss Blossom. I mean, they're not even here, so I think that proves they wouldn't care if I won or not. There's just not that much cash involved. It's not like winning is really going to change my life or anything. So I'm sure it's not going to change my friends."

Polite applause as the blonde handed the microphone back to Peg.

"Thank you, Emma. And now, Brandolina LePadanni, here is your question."

The vision in white tossed her head and swept to the lip of the stage as the Town Square crowd roared. Brandi might as well have been Catherine Zeta-Jones for her effect on the audience. She waved and nodded, more intent on building her fan base than attending to Peg's question:

"The marks of Miss Blossom are good manners, good taste, good sportsmanship, and good hair. Please name four other qualities that you would bring to the role."

Brandi was still waving to her audience when the question ended, so there was a moment of dead air as Peg held out the mike. When Brandi finally took it, she cradled the microphone like a spray of roses.

"Four other qualities?" she asked.

Peg nodded.

"That I would bring? To the role? Of Miss Blossom?"

Next to me, Odette stifled a snicker. Brandi's dark eyes searched the blue sky above. Her fans held their collective breath. Finally, in a clear voice, Brandi queried, "Good shoes? Good dancer? Good manicures? And … good teeth?"

No one applauded immediately, possibly because they thought someone might answer Brandi. When Peg thanked her, the crowd took that as their cue to clap.

"And now, Faye Raffle, here is your question."

Our office intern stepped confidently downstage, beaming her bright smile out over the audience.

Peg said, "Sometimes it's difficult to distinguish in others the difference between tears of laughter and tears of sorrow. How do *you* tell the difference, and what do you do about it?"

Faye took the microphone with the grace and confidence of a TV anchorperson. In a well-modulated voice, she replied, "Both are contagious, but tears of joy are more so. Tears of sorrow make me want to offer tissues rather than cry along. When someone is in emotional distress, they need something to cry into more than they need someone to cry along with. I try to be there for both kinds of criers, offering whatever they need. That's why I always carry extra Kleenex."

Applause filled Town Square and reverberated from the surrounding buildings. At six-foot-one, I could easily scan the crowd. Our girl was the people's choice. Now we'd find out if she was also the judges'.

FIVE

The Miss Blossom contest judges adjourned to deliberate.

Odette said, "Uh-oh. Here comes Tammi, and she's not happy."

I looked where Odette was looking until I spied our part-time agent, mother of the world's most inarticulate beauty. Tammi was striding straight toward us, her eyes fixed on me.

"Whiskey!" she called out. "What's this I hear about Mattimoe Realty betting against my daughter?"

"I'm the wrong person to ask about that," I replied truthfully. "I never read the office bulletin board."

Tammi glared at Odette. "*You*. I heard *you* started it."

Odette offered her trademark shrug, the lightning quick rise and fall of her narrow shoulders that meant "*Who gives a shit?*"

"Is that all you can say for yourself?" Tammi demanded.

"Better prepare your daughter to be a *non-winner*," Odette advised. "My money's on Faye, and I'm phenomenally lucky at games of chance."

Tammi clenched her fists, sputtering so incoherently that I understood the source of Brandi's disability. Then she stalked off, no doubt in search of other traitorous Mattimoe Realty employees.

"For Faye's sake, you should hope she *doesn't* win."

I spun around to face Attorney Sweeney, who was apparently small enough to slip under my radar.

"Who are you?" Odette said.

Introducing them, I found myself itching to say the word *Winimar*. But I resisted, identifying Kevin Sweeney only as administrator of the Schuyler Trust.

"You're here to oversee the Miss Blossom competition?" asked Odette.

"Yes, mainly," Sweeney said. "That's why I made that remark about hoping your young friend Faye's a non-winner."

Then he blushed clear down to the roots of his curly hair, and I concluded that he had come perilously close to violating his own gag order.

Odette was staring at Sweeney in that crazed-stalker way of hers. "Faye will win. How can we protect her?"

His eyes shifted to the retreating form of Tammi LePadanni. "Whatever you do, keep that one away from her."

"Tammi?" I echoed. "Oh, she's a bitch, but she'll get over it."

Sweeney shook his head ominously. "This much I can tell you: If there's one element we don't need in this competition, it's an overzealous mother. Now if you'll excuse me—"

"You're not going to watch the coronation?" I asked.

"Not from here. Looking forward to our meeting on Monday, Whitney."

He shook my hand. I couldn't help noticing that his palm was sweaty.

Odette and I watched the stiff little overdressed lawyer fade into the crowd. She said, "You let him call you Whitney?"

"From his mouth, it sounds like money."

She snorted. "It sounds like trouble. What did you agree to that you need to see a lawyer on Monday?"

Choosing my words cautiously, I said, "I'm going to sell a property that he administers."

"Not Winimar, I hope!"

I gaped. "You know about Winimar?"

"Everyone who sells real estate in west Michigan knows about Winimar."

"I didn't! I'd never heard of it!"

"That's because Leo didn't want you to know about it."

"Why not?"

Odette raised a pencil-thin eyebrow. "Why do you think? He tried to spare you every unpleasantness so that you could focus on doing what you do best."

"Which is what?" I genuinely wanted to know.

"Getting deals done. You're a closer, Whiskey."

As opposed to an opener. Or a schmoozer. Odette didn't have to say it because I knew it. Leo was the charming half of our duo. I was the "sign on the bottom line" half. Now that he was gone, I was trying to do it all. And not doing much of it well. Fortunately, I had Odette in the field and Tina in the office. Between the two of them, many of Leo's responsibilities were covered.

"There will never be another Leo," Odette sighed, as if reading my mind. She probably was reading my mind. Sometimes Odette manifested an alarming clairvoyance, particularly when screening prospects on the phone. I called it her telephone telepathy. I also called it creepy.

Peg Goh tapped on her microphone again. Instantly, the Town Square crowd hushed. We were about to witness a coronation. Peg read from a new index card.

"It is traditional, at this point in the ceremony, to pay tribute to the first Miss Blossom, Winifred Margaret Schuyler, and her mother, Mrs. Slocum Schuyler, without whom this pageant would not be what it is today."

Peg signaled the reigning Miss Blossom to step forward. Warily, the young woman scanned the crowd. Satisfied that Abra was no longer in the vicinity, she moved downstage.

"Without the generosity of the Schuylers," Peg read from her card, "today's Miss Blossom would not have the honor of wearing the historic Miss Blossom crown."

Like a QVC spokesmodel, the current Miss Blossom pointed to her oversized green tiara. The crowd clapped because they were supposed to. Louder than the applause were numerous sarcastic comments about how ugly the thing was. Pretending not to hear them, Peg moved on to her next card.

"Before I announce the judges' decision, let us take a moment to offer a silent tribute to all the Miss Blossoms who have gone before. May they rest in peace."

Peg lowered her head as if in prayer, and everyone followed suit.

To Odette I whispered, "*Rest in peace*? She makes it sound like they all die!"

"Not all. The ones who move away often live to be quite old. That's why we'll have to get Faye out of here."

Before I could comment, Peg said, "It gives me great pleasure to announce the judges' decision for this, the one hundred and sixtieth Miss Blossom Contest." She cleared her throat. "The second runner-up is … Emma Kish."

Since her friends weren't here, and the winner's pot was small, Emma obviously didn't care how the pageant turned out. Yawning, she crossed to Peg and accepted her small bouquet of red roses. Then she retreated to the far edge of the stage, where she took out her cell phone.

Peg resumed speaking. "May I remind contestants and audience alike that first runner-up is a vital position. Should Miss Blossom, for whatever reason, be unable to fulfill her duties, the first runner-up will stand in for her. And now … the first runner-up is … "

I noticed Tammi LePadanni standing in the first row of the audience, arms held high, all her fingers crossed.

"Brandolina LePadanni," Peg announced.

The crowd went crazy—whistling, clapping and hooting. I assumed that most of that noise was a tribute to the as-yet-unannounced winner rather than the first runner-up. Faye must have had a lot of school friends present. Plus, Mattimoe Realty employees know how to make noise. The sway of the masses momentarily blocked my view of the stage. When people settled, and my sightline cleared, Tammi was no longer in position. I couldn't see her anywhere.

The sneer on Brandi LePadanni's face suggested that she was not a gracious *non-winner*. The slant of her head and the swish of her walk confirmed it. Crossing the stage, Brandi managed to collide with stationary Faye. The bump, which knocked Faye off base by six inches, looked suspiciously like a ram. Brandi did not apologize. She haughtily accepted a mid-sized rose bouquet from our acting mayor and then curtsied deeply to the audience. Given the tightness of her gown, I was amazed that the seams held.

"Bravo, *bravissimo*, Brandolina!" Tammi cheered.

Yes, the stage mother from hell had reappeared. Now standing next to Peg on the platform, she was operating a camcorder at close range. Peg whispered for Tammi to *please leave*, her request unintentionally broadcast via microphone to the entire assembly. Ignoring Peg, the mother of the first runner-up circled her daughter and then slowly crossed the stage, camera running. Waving her bouquet, Brandi curtsied two more times for the videographer's benefit. "You're the real winner, baby!" Tammi shouted as she finally exited.

Though completely justified, Peg's vexed expression startled those of us who knew her best as proprietor of the Goh Cup, Main Street's humming coffee and lunch shop. In her late fifties, Peg was a naturally genial, maternal type. Nothing ruffled her. Yet Tammi LePadanni just had.

"Uh, if we could move on now … to—um—the reason we're all here today, to—uh—the crowning of Miss Blossom," Peg sputtered, shuffling her cards in search of just the right one. We waited breathlessly for the inevitable. Apparently, Peg couldn't find the card she needed. After a long moment, she blurted, "Oh, heck. You all know who the winner is. Let's give Faye Raffle a real big hand!"

And so we did. Our office intern glowed as last year's Miss Blossom placed the Schuyler heirloom on her head. Faye staggered slightly as if the crown's heft surprised her. *It must be as heavy as it is gaudy*, I thought. The former Miss Blossom looked mighty relieved to be rid of it. Maybe the thing induced headaches as well as Abra attacks. Speaking of which … I wondered what Officer Swancott had done with my dog. With *Leo's* dog, I revised quickly. A full year after my husband's death I still couldn't claim ownership of his legacy. Abra wouldn't let me. I surveyed the crowd. No cops or dogs in view.

Wearing the emerald crown and holding an oversized bouquet of red roses, Faye gave token hugs to the members of her Court. Though in the middle of a cell phone call, Emma Kish managed to return Faye's embrace. Brandi LePadanni didn't hug Faye back, however. She simply whispered something in her ear. Something that made Faye blanch and shrink back.

Then the five judges stepped forward to congratulate the girls. Rico, Noonan, and Hen went directly to Faye. Jonny started with third-place Emma. Martha Glenn, who had managed to reverse her hat again, mistakenly congratulated "Queen Peg" and then loudly demanded to know what she'd done with her crown. "The damn thing's worth a fortune! You won't get away with it!"

Brandi had separated herself from the court, and was enthusiastically posing for Fast Eddie Fresniak, the photographer from our weekly newspaper, the Magnet Springs *Magnet*. He seemed magnetized by Brandi's opulent beauty, all right. I wondered if he'd have any film left for the actual winner.

Moments later, Peg cued up some recorded music and signaled those on stage to begin their recessional. To improve visibility and reduce liability, Hen and Noonan made sure that Martha's hat was on right, the huge pink bow in the back; then they guided her down the steps. Next came Rico and Jonny, followed by last year's Miss Blossom, who looked five years younger than she had when the event began. Still on her cell phone, Emma exited next. Then came Brandi, accompanied by Fast Eddie, who was snapping her every move. Finally, to another round of cheers, Faye waved and stepped off the platform. As she did, the wooden stairs beneath her collapsed. With a painful scream, the new beauty queen toppled sideways, landing in a crumpled mass amid the broken boards.

"Stand back!" A male voice rose above the gasps and shrieks. Attorney Kevin Sweeney darted out of the crowd toward our fallen Faye. Fast on his feet, he was the first to reach her side. He flung off his expensive suit jacket, hastily removed his gold cufflinks, and rapidly rolled up his sleeves. As he bent over her, I assumed that he was assessing her wounds. But when he straightened, I realized his true intent: to save the Miss Blossom tiara. Sweeney raised it in the air like a hockey trophy. Some people actually cheered.

"Is there a doctor in the house—I mean, in the square?" Peg shouted. It occurred to me then that the first runner-up's father was a physician. But I'd seen only the first runner-up's mom. Dr. LePadanni was a large man, impossible to miss even in a mob. He must not have come. I turned to Odette. "Is Reginald here?"

"Please!" She made a face in response to her husband's name. "Reginald's a shrink. He can't *help* anyone."

Another cheer went up. The Coast Guard nanny was bending over Miss Blossom. Deely Smarr to the rescue! She may have let Abra get away, but she would more than make up for it now. That girl could fix anything.

SIX

"I can't fix this," Deely Smarr told the crowd. "Faye's unconscious and needs an ambulance. Somebody call 9-1-1!"

Somebody with a cell phone already had, probably Emma Kish. Sirens wailed in the background.

Officer Brady Swancott and Canine Officer Roscoe were managing crowd control and maintaining a space around Faye. I wondered where her proud parents were. And also where Abra was.

My second question was answered when a familiar blonde Afghan hound bounded out of the throng, heading straight for Attorney Sweeney. He was still holding the Miss Blossom tiara over his head, but not mindfully. And not for long. Distracted by the commotion surrounding Faye, Sweeney never saw Abra coming. Since he wasn't nearly as tall as last year's Miss Blossom, snatching the tiara from him was a cinch. Abra barely had to clear the ground. Then she was gone.

Deely saw the crime go down. Well, we all did, but Deely is Abra's official trainer, so I looked to her to do something, and she did. She watched Abra tear down Main Street. Then she pulled out a collapsible pair of binoculars and watched some more. I assumed she could still see the dog even after Abra's trajectory had surpassed the scope of the human eye.

Surely Deely's underwhelming response was appropriate to The System, the esoteric dog-training program invented by her late father and endorsed by Fleggers everywhere. I'd heard The System described as the Zen of Dog Training. That might have been accurate. And I might have lacked the necessary enlightenment to appreciate it.

But I can tell you this: I wasn't the only person shrieking for Deely to "go catch that damn dog!"

"Do you have any idea what that tiara is worth, Whitney?"

I didn't need to look down in order to know who was speaking.

"No, Kevin, I don't. But something tells me I'm about to find out."

The curly-haired lawyer was snapping his gold cufflinks back in place. I noticed that Abra had left a pawprint on his white Versace shirt.

"For insurance purposes, we value the Schuyler heirloom at half a million dollars," he said, still focused on his cuffs.

"Half a mil for that ugly thing?!"

The attorney shot me a look that screamed "redneck."

I backpedaled. "If it's worth that kind of money, why not lend it to a museum?"

"Because Mrs. Slocum Schuyler stipulated in her trust that the tiara was to be part of the annual Miss Blossom competition. In perpetuity."

I could tell by his monotone that he'd spoken that line at least a thousand times.

"Okay," I conceded, "but did she stipulate that stylish girls in the twenty-first century would have to *wear* it? Couldn't we just put it in a display case on stage?"

When he didn't bother to reply, I whined, "Why can't the winner wear a rhinestone tiara like Miss America?"

Sweeney shrugged his arms into the sleeves of his Versace jacket.

"Whitney, why don't you go sell real estate and leave the practice of law to lawyers? Or better yet, go retrieve your felon-hound and her booty before you both end up in court."

I straightened so that I was officially towering over him. "Are you threatening me?" Pushing back hard seemed the best defense … despite my desire to earn a whopping commission from Winimar.

Sweeney peered up at me. "Attorneys never threaten. We litigate."

I swallowed. "Do we still have an appointment Monday morning?"

"Of course. Though you might want to bring your lawyer."

"Last year's Miss Blossom wants to talk to you, Whiskey." Odette was at my side, pretending that Sweeney wasn't. I profoundly admired her ability to shun others.

Most folks were intently watching two paramedics work on Faye. But the willowy strawberry blonde who had just given up her crown was watching me.

"I'm Crystal Crossman," she said, extending a slender hand.

"Sorry about that trauma with my dog," I began. "She's in rehab—"

"This isn't about your dog," Crystal hissed, her eyes tracking Sweeney as he moved off. "This is about the Schuyler curse."

"You know about it?" I gasped. Was I the last person on earth to learn the word Winimar?

"Know about it? I'm trying to outrun it! Former Miss Blossoms need to get the hell out of Lanagan County. I'm flying to Vegas tonight."

"To take a vacation?" I asked.

"To save my life! Don't tell me you've never heard the stories?!"

Okay, I wouldn't tell her. I remade my face into an indulgent mask that said, "Of course I know everything, but you can blather on if you want."

"That's why we need to talk, Mrs. Mattimoe. Faye's my friend, and I know she works for you." Tears gleamed in Crystal's long-lashed blue eyes. "Since her parents aren't around to help her, I hoped maybe you could."

"Faye's parents are dead?"

Crystal recoiled. "Who said they were dead? They're on assignment in Venezuela! Faye's parents are foreign correspondents. Don't tell me you didn't know that, either?!"

I definitely wouldn't admit I didn't know that. But it explained the dearth of blood relatives at the scene. I glanced anxiously at the paramedics, who were strapping the new Miss Blossom, *sans* tiara, to a back board. She was still unconscious.

"What did you want me to help her with?" I asked Crystal.

"How about riding in the ambulance with her? The poor girl's all alone with a curse on her head! I'd go, but my plane leaves Grand Rapids at six, and it's after 3:30 already. I've got to get out of this dog-bait dress and hit the road!"

Sure, I was willing to accompany Faye to the hospital. But first I needed an answer from Crystal: "If winning Miss Blossom brings such bad karma, how come there's always somebody who wants the title?"

She blinked at me as if I'd just asked why girls wear mascara. "Duh! For the glamour!"

"What 'glamour'? This is Magnet Springs!"

Crystal Crossman shook her head as if unable to believe that a woman fifteen years her senior could be so dense. "When Faye regains consciousness, ask her about the contract." She pointed toward the paramedics. "You'd better go!"

Contract? Did she mean the financial disclosure that Jenx had mentioned? Was there more to it? If so, how much more?

I jogged after the paramedics and their precious cargo. To my extreme annoyance, Fast Eddie had decided to snap pictures of the winner after all … now that she was unconscious.

"Eddie!" I barked, inserting myself between him and his subject. "I thought you used up all your film on the first runner-up! How come you didn't shoot Miss Blossom while she was still standing?"

Fast Eddie Fresniak pulled his pock-marked face from behind his Canon camera and glowered at me. "Move, Whiskey! I've got a job to do, and you're blocking my shot."

We were all moving, but I made sure to stay between Fast Eddie and Faye, even when Fast Eddie did his best to dodge around me. Sixteen years after leading my high school volleyball team, I was still swift on my feet.

"You're interfering with my reporting of the news!" he panted.

"Does the 'news' include a dozen shots of Brandi LePadanni's cleavage?"

We had reached the ambulance, and the paramedics were gently sliding Faye into the back. Fast Eddie tried to get a shot over my left shoulder. I blocked him in a maneuver sweetly reminiscent of my old Court Zone 3 defense. He swore at me.

"I'm her boss, and I'm riding with her," I told the paramedics as I clambered in. Fast Eddie managed to snap one just before the rear doors slid shut. I couldn't wait to see myself in Monday's paper, giving Magnet Springs the finger.

Siren wailing, we pulled away from Town Square. The paramedic was checking Faye's pulse.

"What's wrong with her?" I asked anxiously. "Does she have a concussion, or what? You don't think she injured her neck, do you?" Images from the movie *Million Dollar Baby* flashed before me. "Oh, God. Tell me she's not paralyzed!"

The paramedic said, "Even if I knew, I couldn't tell you. HIPPA law."

"Hip, hip, hooray for you! I'm freaking out over here! Her parents are on another continent, and this pageant thing is cursed!"

"Hey, at least she's breathing. Why don't you hold her hand? Let her know you're here for her."

I gripped Faye's small dry hand in my large sweaty one. Then my cell phone bleated.

"You need to turn that off," the paramedic said.

"Just let me get this. I'm in real estate."

"Whiskey, are you in that ambulance?" It was Jenx.

"Yes, but this time I'm not on the gurney. Faye is."

"I know. Hen called. I just passed you on my way back to Town Square. I'll make sure Brady's doing all right there and then get my butt over to CMC."

That was shorthand for Coastal Medical Center, our destination.

"Turn it off!" the paramedic commanded.

I told him I needed just a few more seconds.

Jenx said, "So Abra's on the lam again? With the tiara?"

"Afraid so. Listen, I was talking to Crystal Crossman. She said something about a Miss Blossom curse?"

"That's what I was trying to tell you—*without* telling you. Damn lawyers make everything so complica—"

The paramedic snatched my phone from my fingers and slipped it into his pocket.

"Hey!" I said.

"You'll get it back. Until then, hold her hand and enjoy the ride. Like you said, *you're* not on the gurney."

SEVEN

Faye Raffle moaned.

"Did you hear that?" I asked the paramedic. He was checking her vital signs.

"*Ughhh*." The moan again. But Faye didn't stir. And the paramedic didn't reply.

Anxiety seized me, making it hard to breathe and harder yet to talk.

"That wasn't like a … death rattle, was it?" I rasped.

Faye's eyelids fluttered. The hand that I wasn't holding with both of mine flopped around like a fish on a dock. The restraints kept her from moving much. But she could move, thank God.

"Where is it?" she cried.

"Where is what?" asked the paramedic.

"Forget about that stupid crown, Faye! You are going to be fine!" I over-articulated as if English wasn't her first language. Or as if she was profoundly brain-damaged.

"My head," Faye gasped.

"Does it hurt?" asked the paramedic.

"No! It's bare! Where's my tiara? I'm responsible for that thing!"

"RELAX!" I shouted, using volume to transcend her potential head injuries. "MY DOG'S GOT IT!"

Faye's already pale face turned as white as a hospital sheet. "Abra took it again?"

"YES, BUT DEELY'S ON THE CASE. ALTHOUGH SO FAR SHE HASN'T DONE MUCH."

"Are you hearing-impaired? Or just nuts?" said the paramedic.

"Neither," I replied with a great deal of dignity.

"Then kindly shut the hell up."

I managed to reassure Faye just by holding her hand and smiling. She seemed much calmer by the time we reached CMC.

In the ER waiting room, I was sifting through the world's oldest and most tattered magazines when Jenx hobbled in, still in her painter's overalls, still a red-splattered mess. She was limping because she had twisted her ankle stepping off the ladder at Red Hen's House. But she didn't get a chance to explain that before the overly alert ER receptionist recognized Jenx and jumped to conclusions. Between the limp and the splatters, she assumed that our brave chief had been shot. It took two medical professionals to verify that Jenx was not wounded, just sticky. From wet paint.

By the time they left her alone, Jenx's eyes bulged with fury.

"Uh-oh," I said. "You're not going to have one of those 'fits,' are you?"

"I don't have 'fits,'" she fumed. "I have a gift for geomagnetic conduction."

Not a joke. Jenx was the latest in a long line of Jenkinses whose volatile tempers could alter the local magnetic fields. Any minute now I expected every piece of life-support equipment at CMC to flatline. Or explode. Fortunately, the chief got a grip on herself. The worst that happened was all the phones rang, and the fluorescent lights flared.

"I thought you were sending Officer Brady over," I said, frankly wishing she had. He's docile for a cop because he's an art historian. Or maybe he's just docile. Brady's a part-time police officer, a part-time graduate student, and a part-time stay-at-home dad.

"Thanks to that dog of yours, I had to leave Brady at the scene," Jenx snapped.

My heart clutched. "*Now* what did she do?"

"Besides steal the Miss Blossom tiara for the second time today? As she was fleeing Town Square, she knocked over an old man."

I groaned. "Is he—all right?"

"Don't you mean, 'Is he going to sue me?'" Jenx said. She still sounded pissed.

"Well, is he?"

"Lucky for you, he likes dogs. Luckier yet, Abra didn't break his hip."

"Who is he? I'll follow up with an apology."

"Vito Botafogo."

"The sausage vendor?" I asked.

"The one and only."

"Good grief! How old is that guy?" I recalled Vito Botafogo from my childhood. As far back as I could remember, he'd been an old man running a sausage stand, at every local event—from high school football games to the county fair to the Miss Blossom competition.

"Too old to get out of Abra's way," Jenx said. "He's gotta be over eighty."

"I don't remember seeing him this afternoon," I mused. "Or smelling his sausage."

Vito's spicy links were redolent and guaranteed to trigger instant salivation. How could I have missed them?

"Maybe you were distracted," Jenx said, "by your delinquent dog. If Vito doesn't sue you, Wee Sweeney will."

"*Wee* Sweeney?" I repeated.

"He's almost as short as I am," Jenx explained. "And I'm a girl. I can't stand that prick!"

"Is he really a prick or just a lawyer?"

"Both." Jenx surveyed the waiting room. Except for the receptionist who'd tried too hard to help, we were alone. "Let's go someplace we can talk."

"What's wrong with here?" I said. "I'm waiting for news about Faye."

Jenx squinted up at the fluorescent lights. "I don't trust the force field."

So we headed for the cafeteria, where we huddled over cups of hot but stale coffee.

"Once upon a time, the Schuyler family did a lot of good in Magnet Springs," Jenx began.

I said, "Something tells me this isn't a fairy tale."

"Nope. The Schuylers made a lot of money building railroads. Then their luck went bad. Real bad. Everything they touched turned to shit. And the crap's still coming down even though nobody named Schuyler lives in Magnet Springs anymore."

"Is there still a Schuyler somewhere?"

Jenx looked uneasy. "I've signed so many damn gag orders for Wee Sweeney I can't remember what I'm allowed to say."

"He made *you* sign gag orders, too?"

"Anybody involved with either the tiara or the estate has to. I'm up to my eyeballs in both."

"How?"

I understood that the local police force had to keep order during the Miss Blossom contest. But I couldn't imagine their role at Winimar. Based on what Sweeney had told me, plus the fact that I'd never heard of it, I assumed the estate lay outside Jenx's jurisdiction.

"It's in our jurisdiction," Jenx said.

"Sweeney said it was a few miles outside of town."

"So's Vestige, and we come when you call."

Indeed they did.

"You're saying there's a curse on the estate *and* on the crown?" I asked.

"I didn't say that!" Jenx held up her hands. "I can't say anything."

"Okay … Can we play Twenty Questions?"

"You can try."

I sipped my bitter coffee and thought about what had happened today, including what Crystal Crossman had told me. I also recalled the tragic fate of Mar Schuyler, the first Miss Blossom. And the first *former* Miss Blossom.

"Is it true that former Miss Blossoms are cursed?" I said.

Jenx stirred her coffee for a long minute. Finally, she said, "Maybe."

"What kind of answer is that?"

"Keep going."

I rephrased the question. "Do bad things happen to former Miss Blossoms?"

"Sometimes," Jenx mumbled, still stirring her coffee.

"Have a lot of them died? Wait!" I reconsidered my approach. Since the contest dated back to 1847, *most* former Miss Blossoms would have died by now. Presumably of old age. Or not. I tried again: "Have most former Miss Blossoms died prematurely?"

Jenx nodded emphatically. I remembered Odette saying that we'd need to get Faye out of town if she won. Did she mean during or after her reign?

"So … Miss Blossom is in danger *after* she gives up her crown?" I asked.

Jenx nodded again. I thought about Crystal's comment that Faye had a curse on her head.

"Is she in danger while she's still wearing it?"

The Police Chief shot me a look overloaded with emotion. During the few seconds when our eyes locked, I read fury, sorrow, and worry there. She resumed stirring her coffee with so much energy that it sloshed onto the table. I grabbed a napkin and blotted the spill.

"Is Faye in danger?" I whispered.

"She's in the hospital, isn't she?" Jenx whispered back.

"Is this connected to the curse on Winimar? Or are there two separate curses?"

Jenx nodded. I wasn't sure what that meant, but it couldn't be good. My head throbbed. I'd never had to deal with a curse before, and now there were probably two. I'd agreed to try to sell one. My dog had stolen the other.

A cell phone bleated. When I reached for mine, I realized that the paramedic had failed to return it. *Damn.*

"Chief Jenkins." Jenx's paint-spotted face darkened. "I'll be right there."

Grimly she announced, "There's been a car accident. A girl is dead."

"Oh, no," I said. "Anyone we know?"

Jenx's eyes were bulging again. "The former Miss Blossom, Crystal Crossman."

EIGHT

"ARE YOU SURE IT was an accident?" I asked Jenx. "Or was it the Schuyler curse?"

"Either way, the state police are at the scene, and we're going to join them."

"We are? Last time I checked, I sell real estate. Nice clean work with very few corpses."

Jenx raised her eyebrows. "Not the way *you* sell real estate."

She was referring to my unfortunate tendency to attract clients who are criminals. I'd like to claim it's a professional hazard, but I'm the only realtor I know with that problem.

"You don't want my help," I said. "I have a weak stomach …"

"You're all I got," Jenx said. "I can't release Brady and Roscoe from Abra duty. So try not to barf or faint—and, whatever you do, don't talk about the curse."

"What about Faye? I want to be here for her."

Jenx reminded me that CMC has the slowest ER in Lanagan County. We could survey the crash site and get back in plenty of time to assist Faye.

"Let me tell her we have an emergency," I insisted. "So she doesn't think we abandoned her."

"Okay, but you're not naming names. It won't do Faye any good to hear that her friend just got killed!"

I agreed and went to look for my office intern in the maze of the ER. I didn't get far before a nurse in scrubs stopped me and asked if I was Faye's next of kin. When I explained that her parents were in Venezuela, and I was her boss, the nurse hesitated. So I added, "You know there's a curse on her head."

Big mistake. The nurse called security, and I was about to be escorted out, or trundled off to the psych ward, when Jenx intervened with her trusty badge and ID. So we were allowed to leave without an escort. Also without seeing Faye, who was having her insides scanned.

I had some good luck: I got my cell phone back. Turned out the paramedic had left it and a note with the ER receptionist: "Caution: Owner may be deranged."

After all that, the prospect of visiting a fatal crash site seemed less daunting. I climbed into Jenx's personal vehicle, a badly dented Ford pickup.

"Doesn't it send a mixed message when the chief of police drives a smashed-up truck?"

"Why?"

"It looks like you're an unsafe driver!"

"Hey, it's not my fault people hit me," Jenx said. "It's my magnetic field. I attract oncoming vehicles."

With that, I cinched my seatbelt tighter and kept my eyes peeled for suspiciously swerving cars. The new fear only briefly distracted me from thoughts of Crystal Crossman. She said she was going to Vegas to beat the curse. But she hadn't made it.

One advantage to arriving as late as we did: the dead body had already been removed. The scene of the accident was a narrow gravel road about eight miles from Interstate 196, which leads to Grand Rapids. I couldn't tell what kind of car Crystal had been driving since its front half was now an accordion attached to a big tree. There was no other vehicle.

When Jenx jumped out to join the state boys, I stayed in the pickup. She made me. That was okay, since I desperately wanted to avoid getting a closer look. One glimpse of Crystal's shattered windshield told me I'd seen enough. I took out my cell phone and checked for missed calls. There weren't any. Then my phone rang; I recognized the caller ID.

"Please tell me you're tracking that diva dog," I told Deely Smarr.

"Brady and Roscoe are following one set of tracks. Judge Verbelow, Mooney, and I are on another."

"Why are there *two* sets of tracks?" I asked.

"Because Abra stole the crown twice today, ma'am. We're not sure which trail is hotter, so we're following them both."

"Have you found anything interesting?"

Deely paused. "I'm not at liberty to say, ma'am. But I've informed Avery that I'll be late starting tonight's shift with the twins. She said it doesn't matter because they're all going over to Mr. Grant's house. To spend the night."

I felt sick. Absolutely overcome with the urge to hurl. My hostile, ungrateful, unattractive stepdaughter was blatantly courting the man I wanted. Never mind that he was the father of her children. She didn't deserve him. Hell, she didn't deserve me. Moreover, Nash had told me months ago that they were never in love. He had worked hard to find her and the babies when she didn't want to be found. His reason? The man had a burning need to acknowledge and support his children. Apparently, he was a moral icon. I was still mystified as to why he'd ever tangled Avery's sheets in the first place. And I certainly didn't want to believe it could happen again. But if Deely was right—it *was* happening. I couldn't stand it.

"Are you there, ma'am?" she asked.

I choked out some kind of reply and hung up. Then I slammed my head four times, hard, against Jenx's padded dashboard. It hurt like hell, but it helped the way a broken foot distracts you from a toothache. I nearly jumped out of my skin when someone rapped on the window.

Jenx was motioning for me to roll it down. I was surprised that the window was manual; I'd almost forgotten how to operate that type.

She said, "Having a seizure? Or just bored?"

"Why?"

"Looked like you were trying to knock yourself out. My truck was rocking!"

"It didn't work," I sighed. Then I told her what Deely had said. All of it.

"So what if Abra left two trails?" Jenx said. "We got two good tracking teams."

"That's not the problem! Avery is sleeping with Nash!"

"You just figured that out?"

Speechless, I cranked up the window and laid my aching forehead on the dash. I must have dozed off because I dreamed briefly about my first husband Jeb Halloran and woke up feeling better. Jeb often had that effect on me. Even so, I'd refused to have sex with him since Leo died. It just didn't seem right. After all, Jeb and I had gotten a divorce; we must have had a good reason. Jeb was currently on tour promoting either his Celtic CD or his rockabilly CD, I couldn't remember which. He was versatile but penniless.

"That was no accident," Jenx announced, slamming her door. "Somebody ran Crystal off the road."

"Do you have a witness?"

"Not yet. And not likely."

"Then how do you know she didn't just lose control of her car? She was in a big hurry to get out of here."

"Tire tracks," Jenx said. "The gravel doesn't register specifics, but it gives us a picture. Looks like a big, heavy vehicle came up behind her real fast. And stayed behind her, till she got out of the way."

"Too bad you don't know more than that," I yawned.

"We do. We know what color it was, and pretty soon, we'll know what kind."

"How?"

"The other guy nudged Crystal's bumper a few times. Looks like she sped up and then started fishtailing. She must have been all over the road just before she sailed off it. The other car got a little too close. Crystal's swung into him." Jenx smiled with satisfaction. "We got some of his paint!"

"How do you know it's a *him*?" I said.

"When the law gets broken, it's usually by a *him*. Especially if there are fast cars involved."

"Okay. What color is 'his' fast car?"

"Black."

"Oh yeah, that narrows the field."

Jenx seemed on the verge of dissing me, but she refrained and added a line to her notebook instead. Then she turned the ignition key and stared at something just above my eyes.

"Nice bump on the ol' noggin, Whiskey."

I felt my forehead and groaned. Not just from the pain but also from the realization that I was sporting a lump the approximate size and shape of a sparrow's egg. Lucky for me, the only mirror in Jenx's truck cab was the rear view, and she wouldn't let me move it.

"You really don't want to see that," Jenx said. She was trying hard not to laugh.

I suggested Jenx wash her face and change her clothes before we made a second pass at CMC. She agreed, which meant we had to swing by the Magnet Springs police station downtown. Brady and Roscoe were there; they appeared to be on break.

"I thought you guys were trailing Abra!" I exclaimed, more upset with the German shepherd than his human counterpart. The dog works full-time and gets good benefits.

"We lost her," Brady said. He didn't bother to look up from his computer screen.

"Were you on the hot or the not-so-hot trail?" I asked.

"Hard to say. They merged."

I waited for him to offer encouragement or at least say something more than a few syllables long. When he didn't, I did what my next-door neighbor Chester recommends: I asked the dog what was new. And I asked him nicely. But here's the difference between Chester and me: he can talk to dogs, and frankly I don't know how. I smiled. I made eye contact. I even got down to Roscoe-eye-level. I stopped just short of sniffing his ass. Or letting him sniff mine. Then I made a few gurgling, whimpering sounds that should have translated. I was asking for help, one dog to another.

Roscoe licked the lump on my forehead and yawned. Then he circled a few times, lay down on the linoleum at Brady's feet, and started snoring.

"Damn," I muttered, still on my knees.

"He thought you were telling him to take a break!"

I didn't wonder for one second who was talking. What I wondered was how he'd gotten here.

"Hey, Chester," Brady said. "Are you here to join the posse?"

"Yup. Deely called to say they could use another tracker, so I got a cab and came right over."

"Any idea where Abra went this time?" I said.

"Not yet, but we'll find her. Hey, do either of you guys have change for a fifty? I need to pay the cabbie."

That wasn't as unusual as you might think. Though only eight, Chester inhabited a superstar world and lived in a castle. The Castle was the actual name his mother had given their home. She was Cassina, the internationally renowned harpist-singer-diva. Fabulously rich, she'd built a twenty-thousand-square-foot palace next door to me. In it, she employed an ever-changing army of cooks, maids, drivers, and gardeners, none of whom kept tabs on Chester. He regularly showed up at my place, claiming to be locked out of his. I didn't doubt it. Cassina changed staffs so fast that many hirees probably never met Chester. And she was too engrossed in her career to remember that she was also a mother.

"Why didn't you use one of Cassina's drivers?" I asked, rifling through my wallet.

"Because she's using one, and Rupert's using the other."

Rupert was Chester's biological father and brand new to his life. Following a near-death experience, Rupert had decided it was time to get to know his son. So he made up with Cassina, and was now functioning as her producer and presumably her lover. Chester hadn't said much about it.

I traded him four tens and two fives for his fifty. When he slipped out to pay the cabbie, Brady said, "He's a good kid even though he's rich and his home life's a mess. Is Cassina going to let him keep Prince Harry?"

I shrugged. Chester loved Abra and her illegitimate son, Prince Harry the Pee Master, a Golden-Affie mix, or so we guessed. Cassina didn't want animals in her house, excepting her band members, so she was opposed to letting Chester adopt Prince Harry, but she allowed the five-month-old pup to live with him part-time. We all hoped that Cassina would eventually consent to adoption. The key was housebreaking Prince Harry. Deely and Chester were tackling that issue.

"What are you looking at?" I indicated Brady's computer.

"A little background." After clicking a few more keys, Officer Swancott gave me his full attention. "The missing tiara is part of the Schuyler trust, along with Winimar. You knew that, right?"

Since about four o'clock, I thought resentfully. "You can talk about it? You didn't sign a gag order?"

"Oh, everybody signs a gag order." Brady made a face. "But we're conducting a criminal investigation. I just ordered copies of the two books written about Winimar and the Schuyler curse. For the Department."

"Online? I thought they were out of print."

"You've heard of used booksellers? If it was ever in print, you can probably find it somewhere. *If* you know where to look."

"And you know where to look," I echoed.

"Any graduate student worth his salt would."

"Hey, Grad School Boy! What did those two books set us back?" his boss inquired. Jenx had just emerged in uniform from her office. Her hair was wet from her quick shower, but I could still detect flakes of red paint on her fresh-scrubbed face.

"Nothing petty cash couldn't handle," Brady replied. "I ordered them delivered overnight. We should have both books by Monday."

"Which is when *you* can read them," Jenx said, toweling her hair. To me she added, "If it's longer than a memo, I assign it to Brady. I hate to read. Always have."

"If you hate to read, how'd you get to be Chief of Police?" I asked.

"Big Jim got sent to detox and never reported for duty again. I thought you knew that."

Of course I knew that. But it felt so good to mess with her. Chester bounded back in, Prince Harry yapping at his heels.

"What's he doing here?" I asked. "He's no tracker. He can't even pee where he's supposed to."

"Deely said Prince Harry knows his mom in ways nobody else does," Chester replied. "So he might be able to detect something Roscoe or Mooney would miss."

"I seriously doubt it." We were all watching Prince Harry lift his left rear leg against Brady's desk.

"At least he's peeing like a man dog now," Brady observed. "Instead of squatting like a little girl."

Chester chortled as if that was the funniest comment he'd ever heard. Then again, it might have been. Life with Cassina and Rupert probably wasn't a laugh-a-rama. More like a drama-rama. From what I'd seen, they craved daily theatrics.

"Where's Deely?" I asked, wiping up Abra's son's mess.

"Still out in the field with Mooney and the Judge," Brady answered.

"How come the paid help punched out early?"

"Like I said, our trail went cold. And I had business here."

I turned my attention to Chester and Prince Harry.

"Uh—shouldn't you rush your dog outside when he does that so he learns the proper place to pee?"

"Too late now," Chester sighed.

NINE

I CONFRONTED JENX AND Brady. "Level with me. What the hell is happening with Abra?"

"What happened to your forehead, Whiskey?" Chester interrupted. "Did you faint when Abra stole the crown?"

"No. I've given up fainting."

"Now she beats herself up," Jenx said.

"Just give me the scoop on Abra," I barked. "Do I—or do I not—need to hire a criminal defense attorney?"

"You might want to read those books I ordered," Brady said.

"Why? Is my dog cursed, too?"

My dog? I grimaced and reminded myself to stop pairing that particular possessive pronoun with Abra. Especially when talking to the police. It sounded self-incriminating.

"Frankly, it's too soon to say," Brady hedged.

"What does that mean?"

"Well, we don't know how the curse works with dogs. With humans, it only seems to manifest *after* the person returns the tiara."

"The former Miss Blossom trap," Jenx interjected. "The curse starts when they give up the crown. Then they gotta run like hell before the local bad vibes take them down."

"Dating all the way back to the first Miss Blossom," Brady added.

"You mean, we won't know if Abra's cursed till she turns in her bounty?" I said.

Brady and Jenx nodded.

"Oh, she's cursed, all right," I mumbled. "Or I am."

Then a logic problem dawned. "But if what you say is true, why did Crystal Crossman tell me that Faye has a curse on her head? She was just crowned today!"

Jenx and Brady exchanged furtive looks. Something stinky was going on, for sure.

"Spill it!" I demanded. "Gag order or no gag order."

Brady said, "You'll need to talk to Faye."

"If they'll let us back in to see her." I assessed Jenx's uniformed appearance. "You still have paint on your face."

"Yeah? Well, you still have lousy luck," she retorted. "It's a wonder I let you tag along. Just don't mention that curse again in front of the medicos."

Something tickled my ankle. I glanced down in time to see Prince Harry sniffing my shoe. He looked innocent enough. Cute even. Then he lifted his leg.

"Noooooo!" I shrieked, scooping up the peeing pup and fairly tossing him to Chester. "Outside *now*! Don't you know you'll never get anywhere if you can't learn?!"

Chester cast me such a hurt look that I assumed he'd misunderstood my rant.

"Not you, Chester! *You* learn all the time."

"I'm going to have to insist that you stop the negativity, Whiskey. You're spooking my pup."

Clutching Prince Harry, he left. Jenx cleared her throat.

"What?" I said defensively.

"Did you ever think you might be jinxing things with your anxiety?"

"What things?"

She looked to Brady for help, him being the grad student. He cleared his throat.

"I think Jenx means … that you're too intense, Whiskey. You need to lighten up."

"Lighten up?! About what? My dog stealing a priceless tiara that's cursed? Or me agreeing to sell a historic property that's cursed? Or the fact that I never knew anything about either of those things when the whole town has always known everything about them?!"

"Well, not everything—"

"I'm not finished! Or do you mean I should lighten up about my dog's bastard son being unadoptable because he leaks like a stinky sieve? Or my no-good stepdaughter losing weight and starting to look good enough to screw the man of my dreams?! *Which of those things am I supposed to lighten up about*?!!!"

"Any or all would be an improvement." Brady, the pacifist. Before I could blow him over with my next tsunami of rage, Jenx stepped in. Literally. She got right in my face, her arms crossed over her uniformed chest.

"Hey! Show the officer some respect. He's trying to help."

I took a slow, steadying breath. And then I took three more. "Okay," I said finally. "Sorry, Brady. I guess I'm a little uptight."

"A little?" Jenx said.

"That's okay, Whiskey," said Brady. He was stroking Officer Roscoe, who had risen in his defense.

I took in the trained attack dog's bared teeth and stepped back a few paces.

"We know what you're really upset about," Brady added.

"You do?" This I wanted to hear.

"Sure," said Jenx. "The whole town knows."

Brady nodded. "You're upset about next Wednesday."

I didn't react, at least not out loud.

"The first anniversary of Leo's death," Jenx said. "It's gotta be hard on you."

Brady added, "I've downloaded some material on how to get through it. Advice on taking stock of your life. Making peace with your losses. Moving on."

"You need to move on," Jenx advised.

Brady handed me a fat manila folder. The label read: **HELP FOR WHISKEY**.

He said, "I know it's tough, but the upside is you're still relatively young."

"Relatively?" I repeated.

"What Brady means is you've got the rest of your life in front of you," Jenx said. "We hope you'll spend it in Magnet Springs, but we'd understand if you had to leave. Some of these articles say a fresh start in a new town can work wonders."

"What new town? Where on earth would I go?! I own a business here. A good one!"

Did my friends want me to leave?

As if reading my mind, Brady said, "Nobody wants you to leave Magnet Springs! You have a lot of friends here."

"How about taking a vacation?" Jenx suggested. "You could use a break."

"I can't take a break now! My dog is a wanted felon! And I've got a once-in-a-lifetime chance to earn a fabulous commission … if I don't die doing it."

"Whiskey, nobody has ever been able to sell Winimar," Jenx said.

"Have they died trying?" I wasn't sure I wanted to know.

"I don't think so," Brady replied cautiously. "But I haven't read the books yet."

Jenx said, "Who's gonna buy a piece of property where everybody dies?"

"Not *everybody*," Brady corrected her. To me he added, "The books arrive Monday. I'll give you an approximate body count Tuesday morning."

"But I'm supposed to sign the sales contract Monday," I whined.

"You'll figure it out," Jenx said, checking her Timex. "Let's head back to CMC."

The front door opened a crack. Chester peered in, still holding a squirming Prince Harry. He looked at Brady and stage-whispered, "Is Whiskey rational again?"

"I'm always rational—" I began, then stopped myself. "Except when I'm not. Sorry, Chester, for screaming at your dog."

"That's okay. You're still wrestling with the grieving process, and we understand that." He grinned, exposing his missing front teeth. The gap gave him a childish charm that belied his grown-up vocabulary. "I called Deely on her cell phone. They're tracking back toward town. Prince Harry and I are going to meet them. Wish us luck!"

———

Back at Coastal Medical Center, we found a different receptionist on duty in the ER. Lucky us. She explained that Faye had been admitted for observation.

The attending physician was reviewing Faye's history when we arrived in her room.

"I'm finished here," he said.

When Faye introduced us, the physician rechecked his chart and suppressed a sly smile.

"You'll be pleased to know, Ms. Mattimoe, that the CAT scan of Faye's brain revealed no curse."

"I said it was on her head, not in it," I replied with dignity. The doctor winked at Faye and departed.

"Does everyone think I'm nuts?" I asked my office intern.

"I don't know," she answered earnestly. Looking at Jenx, she said, "I suppose you're here to question me about the theft of the tiara."

"No. We like Whiskey's dog for that crime since we've got at least two hundred witnesses. I'm here to discuss your fall. Can you tell me what happened?"

Faye said she couldn't remember much past starting down the stairs. "I was waving and holding my bouquet, plus the check Peg gave me, and the next thing I knew, I was falling. It was like the earth opened up and I was suspended in the air. That's all I recall till I woke up in the ambulance, and Whiskey was shouting at me."

Jenx glared in my direction. "Why the hell would you shout at somebody in an ambulance?" She turned her attention back to Faye. "You say you were holding your bouquet and the prize check. Do you know what happened to them when you fell?"

"No. I just remember them flying out of my hands."

The missing check intrigued me. Who could have scooped it up during the ensuing chaos?

"Did anything unusual happen on stage?" Jenx asked Faye.

"Aside from Brandi ramming into me and threatening me, you mean?"

I replayed my memory of voluptuous, arrogant Brandi swinging her hip into Faye, hard, as she crossed the stage and later saying something that turned my office intern ghostly white.

"How did she threaten you?" Jenx demanded.

Faye shifted position gingerly, as if everything hurt, especially what she didn't want to tell us.

"I … don't think I can repeat what Brandi said."

"Why? Was it obscene?" I asked.

"No. But she said I couldn't repeat it."

"Tell us," Jenx pressed.

"Okay … She said her mom would destroy me."

"Oh, get real. Tammi's only in the office one day a week," I said. "She can't bother you that much."

Jenx said, "Did Brandi say how her mom would 'destroy' you?"

"Totally," Faye replied. "She said I'd regret being chosen Miss Blossom for the rest of my days. And there weren't many days left."

"Brandi said all that?" I wondered aloud. "She can hardly talk!"

"She talked to me," said Faye, shuddering. I pulled the thin cotton blanket up to her chin in a lame attempt to comfort her. I'm not good in that department. Too bad her parents were as far away as Venezuela.

"Is there anyone local we can call to come sit with you?" I asked. "I'll stay as long as you want me, but you won't want me long. I get antsy in hospitals."

"Correction: she gets in big trouble in hospitals," Jenx said. "Do your parents know what happened?"

Faye explained that the hospital had reached her mom and dad; they would be on the next available flight home. I felt almost as relieved as she did.

"Good, good! So, you don't need anything else then?" I rose to leave.

"You came with me, Whiskey, and I'm not going yet," Jenx said. I sat back down. "Faye, do you think Brandi or her mother made the steps collapse while you were on them?"

"I don't know how they could have. All I know is Brandi threatened me. She's beyond scary. And so's her mom."

Tell me about it, I thought, recalling the way Tammi LePadanni tried to screw my full-time agents out of hard-won listings. They did all the work wooing clients who happened to belong to the country club Tammi frequented. Then when she saw her fellow members at the pool, on the golf course, or in the lounge, she strong-armed them into signing with her instead of the person they'd consulted. Oh yes, Tammi had enemies. Now she had one more. But why threaten Faye Raffle?

"After you fell, Crystal told me to ask you about the 'contract,'" I said, hoping that Faye wouldn't ask me about Crystal. "She said that's why girls are willing to put up with all the hassles involved in becoming Miss Blossom. What's the 'contract'?"

Faye looked at Jenx before she continued. The Chief nodded ever so slightly.

"It's for services rendered—for being beautiful enough to be Miss Blossom." She looked away, fighting back tears. "I really can't say more about it right now."

Faye sniffed, so I handed her a tissue. After blowing her nose, she asked, "Do you know if Crystal got out of town? She needed to leave."

When I faltered, Jenx said, "Crystal's problems are over."

Faye's pale face brightened. "Good. She's such a cool person. I hope she has a great life wherever she ends up."

Jenx cleared her throat. "Back to you, Faye. Did Brandi say she'd take your prize check? Or anything else?"

"Like the tiara, you mean? No. She just said I would regret winning because her mom was going to destroy me. Oh—and she said that *she* was going to end up being Miss Blossom."

"Idle threats!" I waved my hand dismissively.

Faye added, "She said I'd be dead by Wednesday."

TEN

"How's that for a coincidence?" Jenx said as we climbed into her bashed-in pickup. "Faye's going to die on the first anniversary of Leo's death."

"No, she's not!" That came out sounding angrier than I'd intended. I was still having trouble accepting that Leo was permanently gone. I couldn't bear to think that something awful was about to befall young Faye Raffle. "Tammi LePadanni put a curse on her—with a little help from her sore-loser daughter. You can bust 'em for that, right?"

"For Brandi telling Miss Blossom that Tammi's gonna destroy her? Oh, yeah. That's a felony." Jenx snort-laughed.

"Can't the law protect people against threats?"

"Nope. The best Faye can do is file for a personal protection order. I told her how, and I'm prepared to walk her and her parents through the process."

"Will they go before Judge Verbelow?" I said.

"Yup. That part shouldn't be too bad."

"What part of getting protection is bad?"

"Facing your harasser in court. Tammi and Brandi will have an opportunity to rebut the charges."

"How can they? Tammi made a spectacle of herself in front of everybody, going on about how her daughter deserved to win and Faye didn't. And we saw Brandi ram Faye. Then we saw the steps collapse!"

"All circumstantial," Jenx said. "It's Faye's word against Tammi's *and* Brandi's. And you know Tammi will hire a good lawyer. She can afford to."

"What did Faye mean about a contract for 'services rendered'? Miss Blossom isn't expected to perform sexual favors for anyone, is she?"

"No," Jenx said firmly. "That couldn't happen. Gag order or not."

I was unusually quiet as we drove back to town. Jenx rambled on about local gossip, but for once I wasn't interested. After a few miles, I asked, "Is there any way we can connect what happened to Faye to what happened to Crystal?"

"You mean, you don't think the Schuyler curse killed Crystal, after all?"

"Not without a lot of human help. That's the question, isn't it? Whose interest does the 'curse' protect? And how?"

Now we were both silent. Then I had a new thought.

"Did you say the paint scrape on Crystal's car was black?"

"Yup."

"Tammi LePadanni drives a black Lincoln Navigator."

"I know," Jenx said. "Wee Sweeney drives a black car, too. A Hummer."

"Big car for a little guy. Probably gives him the illusion of omnipotence."

"That's why he likes being a lawyer," Jenx agreed, and we laughed. After a beat, she added, "Rico Anuncio drives a black car, too. A Lexus RX 330, like yours."

I knew that. "Any other suspects?" I was half kidding.

"Odette's car is black," Jenx said.

Before I could retort, she added, "Odette hates Tammi. I'm not sure why."

"Tammi's a slacker who steals other people's commissions when she can get away with it. Odette, on the other hand, is a real estate superstar. Nobody works harder, and nobody messes with her turf. But Odette would never hurt a civilian."

When Jenx didn't reply, I added, "You can't seriously wonder if her car killed Crystal!"

"Not with Odette behind the wheel," Jenx agreed.

"Guess who else drives a black vehicle?" I teased. "Our very own chief of police. This thing's so banged up, one more accident wouldn't even show."

"Not true, Whiskey. The vehicle that hit Crystal is wearing some of her car's blue paint. The key is to find that vehicle before it gets fixed."

"Can we go snoop around a few garages?"

"You can. I'd need a warrant, and I don't have enough evidence to get one. Yet."

"Did Crystal have any enemies?" I was having a hard time imagining a nineteen-year-old who looked like that pissing off someone so bad they'd want to kill her. "An ex-boyfriend, maybe?"

"Brady's looking into that," Jenx replied.

When we returned to the station, he had the answer: Until recently, Crystal had dated a thirty-three-year-old boat repairman named Dock Paladino.

"'Dock'? Like where you put your boat?" I said incredulously. "What kind of name is that?"

"Better than Dick," replied Brady. "This is interesting: Dock Paladino is currently dating Brandi LePadanni. She met him a few weeks ago when he was working on Dr. LePadanni's boat. Rumor has it she threw herself at him, and he dumped Crystal."

"Then Crystal should have killed *him*. Or Brandi. Or both. Does he drive a black car?"

"No. He drives a black truck. A brand-new Dodge Ram."

I rummaged through my purse for the notebook I kept handy in case I had a chance to list real estate. But I wasn't carrying my usual voluminous bag. Today was Saturday, and even though realtors are always on the clock, I had awarded myself a well-deserved day off. Who knew I'd get invited to sell a jinxed property and help solve a murder? I grabbed Brady's pad and pen.

"Give me Paladino's address. And Tammi's and Wee Sweeney's, too. I know where Rico lives. That's four garages I'm going to check out."

"Not a good idea, Whiskey."

"Not for you, maybe. You need a warrant. I don't."

"True," Brady said, "but you could still get shot for trespassing."

I put the pen down. "Somebody could shoot me for snooping and get away with it?"

"Maybe not, but you'd be dead."

"You might as well give her the addresses cuz she's going to get them and go snoop anyhow," Jenx said. So Brady did. Actually, he let me see the addresses in his file while his back was turned. Giving them to me would have been a breach of protocol.

"Brandi's dating a guy my age?" I cringed as I copied Dock's address.

"Not quite," Jenx said. "You just had a birthday. You're a year older now."

"He's fifteen years older than she is," I pointed out.

"And Leo was fifteen years older than you."

"But when we met, we were all grown up and divorced already! Brandi's only eighteen."

"Legally an adult," Jenx said. To Brady she announced, "I'm going to interview Vito Botafogo about what he saw when Abra knocked him down."

I'd forgotten about the sausage vendor. "He's not in the hospital, is he? I really don't want to make another trip out there today."

"He's recuperating at home, and I'm sure he doesn't want to see you, either. But flowers would be nice."

I intended to send some.

"Is his address in this file, too?" I flipped pages until I found what I needed. Jenx wished me good luck, unofficially, and left. From the kitchenette Brady asked if it was safe for him to come back to his desk.

"Do you think Vito would prefer roses or carnations?" I said.

"Roses, definitely. But they have to be red."

"Of course!" Since my cell phone battery was running low, I borrowed Brady's phone to place the order through our local florist. I debated about how to word the card. By now I'd issued enough apologies that I ought to be good at it, but saying you're sorry without encouraging a lawsuit is always tricky. I did the best I could and hung up.

"When do you expect an update on Abra?" I asked Brady.

"If there was good news, Deely would have called." He glanced out the window at the darkening sky. "They'll have to come in soon."

All the more reason for me to get out of there and embark on my own quest. If I couldn't recover my dog or, more important, the loot she'd stolen, then I could at least do my part to nail a killer. We all serve in our own ways.

"Just don't get caught," Brady advised. Unofficially.

ELEVEN

It was almost eight-thirty when I headed for the evening's first destination. I had decided to make discreet visits to two black vehicles: Tammi LePadanni's and Dock Paladino's. Attorney Kevin Sweeney lived all the way over in Grand Rapids, too far for a house call—or rather, garage call—that night. Plus, I was due at his office Monday morning. I could check out his car in the parking lot before I went in. How hard would it be to spot a Hummer? As for Rico Anuncio, I didn't have sufficient motive to consider him a suspect. True, I intensely disliked the man and would have dearly loved to prove him guilty of murder. But he'd been out of town for months, returning just in time to judge the Miss Blossom contest. I couldn't for the life of me connect him to Crystal Crossman's death. Nonetheless, I reserved the right to remain suspicious.

Tammi LePadanni's lavish home was my first stop. Her husband was an orthopedic surgeon in a region that attracted both sports enthusiasts and retirees. No wonder they were rolling in it. Unlike most orthopods I had known, however, Dr. LePadanni didn't look like a former jock. He looked like an overstuffed wild boar. Like the kind of guy who ate whatever he wanted whenever he wanted, and never exercised. In other words, like a hypocrite. I wasn't sure how he could motivate his patients to diet and work out when he obviously did neither. Maybe he'd already had his joints replaced with mechanical ones, and his sales pitch was "Live large, lazy, and bionic."

Before consulting Brady's file, I knew Tammi's neighborhood but not her exact address. The LePadannis lived at Pasco Point, arguably the best four-digit zip-code suffix in Magnet Springs. Perched high on a bluff overlooking Lake Michigan, the subdivision boasted a baker's dozen multimillion-dollar estates, each with its own ostentatious name and brigade of servants. The LePadannis' mansion was called Providence, no doubt an allusion to the surgeon's self-image. As I approached, the setting sun's last rays were staining the estate blood red.

I braked at a sufficient distance to appreciate the architect's Mediterranean-inspired design; it featured a tile roof, stucco exterior, arched doorways, leaded windows, two walled courtyards, and an elaborate spewing fountain that reminded me it had been too long since I'd had sex. From my vantage point, I could glimpse part of the large garage, a separate Mediterranean-style structure tucked behind the house. Luckily, there was no security gate, but I wasn't likely to find the garage unlocked. And breaking a window, even if I could do it quietly, would surely set off an alarm.

I turned around on Scarletta Road, heading east. In about a quarter-mile, I came to a dirt lane curving into a pear orchard. I pulled in far enough to conceal my car from the main road, grabbed a flashlight and work gloves from my realtor kit, and hiked back to Pasco Point. The sun's fleeting afterglow was all that illuminated the sky. I inhaled deeply. Even Lake Michigan smelled like spring, its humid freshness invigorating. I arrived at Providence just as darkness settled over the subdivision.

Keeping my head down, I traced the perimeter of the house. It seemed to go on forever. Of course there was the obligatory exterior lighting. Oddly, though, it was ornamental only; nothing functional in terms of security. And nothing I couldn't stay clear of. I was almost appalled by how easy it was to approach the LePadannis' four-car garage.

As I'd expected, the overhead doors were closed, and the side door was locked. But the side door had a window, and someone had left a light on inside. I peered in, careful not to touch the glass in case it was wired. The two bays closest to me were empty. In the third bay sat a small, sleek sports car. The fourth bay held a large van. Neither vehicle was Tammi's Lincoln Navigator, but both were black. It must have been the family color.

A muffled cry shattered my concentration. I looked toward the back of the house. An enormous room was lit as if for surgery, its whiteness spilling out through floor-to-ceiling windows onto the lawn. Inside that room stood an apparently hysterical Brandi LePadanni. She was still wearing the form-fitting strapless gown in which she had earned the title of First Runner-up. But her blue-black hair had come loose and now streamed over her shoulders and into her face. She gestured wildly, her scarlet mouth shaping words I couldn't read, although I was quite sure they were questions. Furious questions. Watching her, I thought of Sophia Loren fuming at Marcello Mastroianni in some old movie with subtitles. Brandi was fuming at her father, who sat very still in an oversized leather chair. To prove how upset she was, she picked up her Miss Blossom First Runner-up bouquet in both hands and smashed it repeatedly against the library table. The roses exploded like spattering blood. Still Dr. LePadanni didn't react. Then I heard an approaching vehicle and, before I could think, twin headlight beams swept the back yard. I dropped low and bolted for the rear of the garage, desperately hoping I hadn't been spotted.

Ducking around the corner, I stumbled over something I couldn't see. There wasn't even any feeble ornamental lighting back here. As I went down, I knew by its rattling roughness that the obstacle I had tripped over was a pile of firewood, remnants of a long winter. I lay very still on the musty earth, straining to hear anything besides my own amplified heartbeat. The newly arrived vehicle rumbled. But no overhead garage door activated; no horn honked. The driver was waiting.

I heard what happened next: the finality of a heavy wood door closing hard followed by heels clicking rapidly across pavement. A car door opened and shut; an engine gunned; tires squealed. Whoever had come was now in a big hurry to go. And they had a passenger. I didn't need Odette's quasi-clairvoyance to guess who.

How hard was it to gracefully climb in and out of a vehicle while wearing a skintight formal gown? Not a question I could answer, but I was willing to bet that Brandi LePadanni could.

Who had come to take her away? Her boyfriend? Her mother? A friend? And what were they driving? It didn't sound like a small car. But I couldn't aurally differentiate between a pickup and an SUV.

Just in case the good doctor decided to follow his daughter, I waited a full three minutes, which felt like thirty. The early spring evening at Pasco Point was strangely silent. No other cars, no voices. Birds twittered faintly as they settled in their nests. A light breeze stirred new leaves. Somewhere a dog barked aggressively; a second joined in the chorus. As I listened, I realized they were close by, just muffled. Their deep barks grew increasingly frenzied. I hoped they were secured behind very strong doors.

Then I remembered something I should never have forgotten: the LePadannis kept pit bulls. In a kennel inside their house. Tammi had mentioned it several times. She enjoyed horrifying others with her canine preference.

"They're the best protection money can buy," she bragged. "Better than the best electronic alarm system. One look at them and the would-be burglar runs for his life!"

I wanted to run for mine. The mental image of two unleashed pit bulls was all it took for me to break out in a fresh dew of sweat.

Cautiously I started along the side of the garage, keeping as low a profile as a person my height can. The dogs sounded more and more agitated. What was happening inside Providence?

When I stepped out into the driveway, I wavered. The mansion stood in total blackness, not a single window illuminated. I had the eerie sense that someone had pulled the plug. Even the ornamental exterior lighting was out. Had Dr. LePadanni forgotten to pay the electric bill? Or was he so cheap that he turned everything off by—

I checked my illuminated watch dial—9:18? The pit bulls sounded crazed. Apparently they didn't like the dark any better than I did. I shivered. Something about Providence just wasn't right.

TWELVE

I sprinted most of the way down Scarletta Road, slowing only when I could no longer hear the pit bulls.

The LePadanni dogs brought to mind my own missing canine. Where was she? How was she? Leo would wonder at my complete inability to handle her. With Odette and Tina's help, I could manage the real estate business he'd started. But even with Chester and Deely on my side, I couldn't contain Abra.

"I'm trying, darling," I panted. Yes, I still spoke out loud to my dearly departed. Probably more often than I should. "Forgive me, Leo. And don't ask what I'm up to next."

My car was so well hidden in the darkened pear orchard that I couldn't easily find it. Now that the sky was black, the dirt road seemed longer, curvier, and spookier than I remembered. Disoriented, I swung my flashlight beam in ever widening arcs. Since the orchard backed up to Pasco Point, I worried that some rich resident might glance out a third-floor bedroom window, spot the bouncing light, and call the cops.

But I found my car before that happened. I was almost too tired and hungry to think about Dock Paladino's Dodge Ram … until I remembered the peanut-butter crackers I kept in my realtor kit. Intended to get me through the Open House from Hell, they would work just fine in this emergency, especially when paired with my reserve can of Red Bull. Yessir, I soon felt focused enough to go hunt dents.

Driving toward Dock's place, I thought about Brandi's temper tantrum and wished I could have heard the soundtrack. Why would she rant at her father, and why would he take it? More important, where was the non-winner's mother and her black Lincoln Navigator? And what was up with the dogs in the dark? Had the doctor gone to bed without feeding them?

Dock Paladino lived near his work, in an apartment overlooking the Magnet Springs Marina. That sounded like an attractive address, but Dock's flat was above the bait shop. I smelled fish at a hundred and fifty paces—which was the distance at which I parked so he wouldn't see or hear me coming. The expansive marina lot was well-lighted but empty, save for my SUV and Dock's black truck, which he had conveniently stationed under a security lamp. Fleetingly, I wondered if he'd just come from Providence with the First Runner-up. If so, and if Dock was in a mood to celebrate, I doubted she'd still be wearing her formal gown.

Staying out of the light at this location was impossible. I skirted the lot, taking an indirect approach to Dock's truck as I kept an eye on the wide lighted window above it. Ruffled pink curtains fluttered there, revealing a missing screen. Dock must have inherited someone else's decorating choices. Music floated down—and not the romantic kind. I recognized Hole's "Celebrity Skin" cranked way too loud to make Dock a good neighbor. But then he had no neighbors, only a bait shop that was closed for the night, some empty boats, and an intruder (me), who was grateful for the cover of sound. Even though I hated singer Courtney Love.

I laid a gloved hand on the hood of Dock's truck. Warm. He'd just arrived. The security lighting revealed a hood that wouldn't latch because it was slightly askew; also, a broken right headlight and a dent in the undercarriage just below the truck's elevated bumper. I leaned down and clicked on my flashlight. My heart jumped. Blue paint.

Before I could straighten, a prolonged shriek cut the night. It came again. And again—from Dock's apartment. I needed a moment, but then I was sure. Not a cry of terror. Oh no. This was the scream of a woman in ecstasy. Presumably Brandi LePadanni. According to Officer Brady Swancott, she was Dock's current squeeze; the boat repairman had dumped Crystal for her. As the shrieks continued, I wondered if Dock could really be *that* good. Or was she just *that* loud? It made sense that a girl who couldn't utter declarative sentences would register extreme pleasure by screaming.

I'd seen what I needed to see and heard way more than I cared to, so I dashed across the lot toward my car. Then I slowed, laughing. Given what was going on upstairs, there was no chance in hell anyone would see me leave.

———

Mid-afternoon the next day, Sunday, I was at the Goh Cup, reviewing my notes and enjoying a steaming double-mocha-super-latte. In a few minutes, I planned to cross the street to the police station. Jenx was about to be very impressed by my unofficial sleuthing.

"Here." Odette dropped a brown paper package on the table in front of me. "You can repay me later. On second thought, you can repay me by opening this and using it now."

"Did I … place an order?" I asked warily. Last I knew, Odette was one of the few women in Magnet Springs not involved in multi-level marketing.

"You issued a public cry for help."

She sat down across from me and signaled owner Peg Goh to bring her her usual. "I don't suppose you've had time to get yourself a backup."

"A backup?" I was genuinely mystified.

My top sales agent leaned across the table, her ebony face a mask of patience for the impaired. "A backup black camisole."

"Uh—no. See, after we—"

Odette kept talking. "I was so appalled by what I saw yesterday I couldn't possibly wait till Monday to handle this."

"But Martha's Town and Gown is closed on Sunday—"

"You're telling me? I drove all the way to Pioneer Mall in Grand Rapids for this. It had better fit." She snarled the last part.

"Thanks," I lied. Then a new thought struck. "Don't you have an Open House this afternoon?"

With a flick of her scarlet manicure, Odette waved my question away.

"I brought the sellers an outstanding offer last night, which I expect they'll accept."

She tapped the paper bag with the long oval nail of her index finger. "*This* was a priority, so I instructed Tina to find another agent to baby-sit the Open House. Just in case a backup offer comes in. My work there—and here—is done."

When I didn't comment, Odette said, "Well?"

I figured she was fishing for a compliment in addition to her commission.

"Well what?" I snapped.

"*Go put it on!*"

I regarded the bag in my hand. "Now? I want to drink my coffee while it's hot—"

Odette sank her nails into my wrist. "Whiskey, I gave up half my Sunday and drove eighty miles to save Mattimoe Realty's public image. Good God, woman, do you have any idea how many people in this town are talking about your tatty brassiere?!"

I didn't. And I didn't want to.

"Put the bad press to bed by wearing this *now*."

"But I've got jeans on—"

Odette sighed like a mother pressed beyond endurance by a recalcitrant child. "How many times do I have to tell you? A black camisole works with anything and on anyone. That's the beauty of it! That's why *you* can do this!"

She dangled the paper bag in front of me like a bone before a dog. It reminded me of Deely luring Abra into the house. I blinked away the image and snatched back the bag.

"Fine," I said. "But I'm taking my coffee with me."

Odette didn't object. Peg arrived at that moment with her espresso.

"What's in the bag?" asked our acting mayor.

"Uh—Nothing. I just—um—have to go to the bathroom…"

"Oh! Okay then. You get right in there!"

The way Peg looked at me I could tell she thought I needed an adult diaper.

"It's not about *that*!" I said loudly.

Peg frowned. "Okey-dokey. I thought maybe Odette had bought you an emergency camisole. I'll get you one tomorrow."

Without further comment, I bolted for the john.

It turned out to be a very nice camisole. Even silkier than the first one and a perfect fit. Just for the hell of it, I struck a sexy pose in the restroom mirror. Nobody else was using the john. Hmm. I didn't look half bad for a tomboy all grown up. My dark curls were forever out of control, but I had a good body—if you liked women tall, lean, and strong with modest-sized perky breasts.

The restroom door flew open and I dove for the paper towel dispenser. The last thing I needed was a rumor that Whiskey Mattimoe vamped in public lavatories.

"Hey! Nice top!" Jenx boomed. "Shows off your tits. Small but sweet."

"My tits aren't small! I wear a C-cup!"

"Ooh. She wears a C-cup!" Jenx mimicked from inside her stall. "I don't even flirt with women who wear less than a double D!"

"You don't flirt, period. You and Hen are practically married."

"Not in this state."

"I was on my way over to see you," I said. "I hit the jackpot last night—!" Jenx flushed, then flung open her stall door.

"Whatever you did last night, you did on your own! I don't know or want to know what you're talking about!"

I waited a beat before saying, "Jenx, there's nobody else in here."

She adjusted her holster. "Okay then. Just come on over to the station when you're ready. I'm picking up a couple of Peg's spinach pies to keep me going till supper."

After she'd washed her hands and left, I tried out a few more sexy poses in my new camisole. Tossing my head and pursing my lips enhanced the overall effect. I thought the camisole even made the bump on my forehead look smaller. How could Professor Nash Grant possibly resist?

The door opened again, and my stepdaughter lumbered in. Avery Mattimoe took one look at me and exploded in laughter. To appreciate that, you need to know this: Avery has no sense of humor. Plus, she hates me.

"Is Jeb due back in town, or are you just horny?" she said.

I opted not to reply. Instead, I concentrated on pulling a whole bunch of paper towels out of the dispenser, which wasn't easy since the damn thing was motion-activated. That meant I had to wave my hands frantically to avoid answering.

"You look like a spaz," she said finally. "And FYI: black is not your color."

That got me going. "For your information, Avery, black looks good on everybody."

"Except you." She stomped into her stall, slammed the door, and proceeded to pee like a horse.

I stormed out, leaving my latte by the sink.

"Nice," Peg said, acknowledging my camisole. But then she was always polite. I wanted the truth.

"Is black my color?" I demanded.

"Black is the absence of color," said New Age guru Noonan Starr, who had taken a seat at the juice bar. "Or, if you will, the negation of purity."

"Hear, hear!" Odette said.

Noonan added, "Whiskey, you have enough light on the inside to wear black on the outside. Don't let self-doubt stifle your life force."

"How about Avery? Can she stifle it?"

"Only if you give her that power. And why would you?"

I was troubled. Avery was gaining self-confidence. I hated to admit it, but she was verging on … looking good. Granted, she was still overweight and prone to galumph like a water buffalo, but she'd lost twenty pounds. Almost as tall as I am, Avery was wider through the hips and shoulders and thus able to carry more weight.

She wasn't likely to turn into a real-life Cinderella, however. Avery spoke shrilly and cried snottily. Just not as often anymore. And she retained her annoying nervous tic: when stressed, she stuck her tongue out, a reflex her late father had found charming but which made me want to hurt her.

We all studied Avery as she emerged, smiling, from the bathroom.

In recent weeks, her skin had cleared up, and her nearly color-less blonde hair had taken on a new luster and bounce. Running three times a week with the Coast Guard nanny was making an amazing difference. I silently vowed to start running, too.

Peg murmured, "Doesn't Avery look wonderful now that she's having sex?"

THIRTEEN

JUST WHEN I THOUGHT the situation couldn't get more painful, a new customer entered the Goh Cup: Nash Grant. At least I was wearing my black camisole.

Too little, too late. The professor only had eyes for Avery. Right in front of everybody, she rushed into his arms, and he gave her a big wet kiss. I wished I hadn't left my coffee mug in the john; it would have made a handy barf bag.

I was tempted to loudly ask the happy couple who was watching their twins—just to shake the romantic moment—but I knew the answer. Deely had left a message at Vestige saying she was with little Leah and Leo at Nash's. I tried to be grateful that Avery and Nash weren't sticking their tongues down each other's throats at my house.

Peg gave them the best table in the house—the one in her front window—so that passersby on Main Street would see how blissful they were. After serving them, she returned to our table, where I sat in numbed silence.

"Whiskey, dear," Peg said kindly. "Could I interest you in a cup of my Spring Tonic? On the house, of course."

"You should try it," Noonan advised, sliding into the seat next to me. "It's 100 percent herbal."

"Does it taste good?" I asked.

"Didn't you hear her? It's herbal!" Odette said.

"It's based on a traditional Native American cure," Noonan offered, "used for centuries to make women more confident and attractive."

"Bring it on," I said.

Odette regarded me doubtfully. "If that camisole isn't working, you may be beyond help."

Changing the subject—sort of—I asked the three women if they knew Dock Paladino.

"Personally, or by reputation?" Odette said.

"Either."

"Let me warn you, Whiskey: he's way out of your league."

"That good, huh? Well, it would explain the screaming."

I smiled and refused to elaborate. After all, I had promised the police I'd keep my undercover activities under wraps.

Peg seemed stunned. Odette eyed me suspiciously. Noonan studied the floor. There was a moment of strained silence.

Then Noonan gushed, "He's talking about me, isn't he? And he swore on his mother's grave that he never would! What we did together was confidential: two consenting adults in a mood to experiment. It was never meant to be shared with another human being!"

I was speechless. So were Odette and Peg. As embarrassed as I was for Noonan, I was relieved not to be the most pathetic person in the room. For a change. Peg brought two Spring Tonics. Noonan chugged hers and left.

I turned to Peg and Odette. "Noonan with Dock Paladino? I thought he only did girls under twenty!"

Odette said, "He does anybody he wants. But don't get your hopes up ..."

To me, Peg said, "Lately he's been with Tammi LePadanni."

"You mean Brandi," I corrected her.

Peg and Odette shook their heads.

"Dock and Tammi came in here twice last week," Peg said. "Both times, they stuck two straws in a jumbo iced cappuccino and sucked it down like some kind of foreplay." A wishful expression transformed her lined face. "It was ... erotic."

I felt sick. And not just because everyone but me appeared to be having amazing sex. Was it possible that Tammi and not Brandi had been at Dock's apartment last night? That threw my whole theory, such as it was, in the dumpster. Could it have been Tammi, not Brandi, who dashed out of Providence, turning the lights out behind her? Maybe Mom's little dalliance was why Brandi threw a tantrum. But why didn't Dr. LePadanni seem to care?

In my head I replayed the orgasmic screams. Hardly the voice of a forty-something-year-old. Then again, maybe Tammi shrieked like a little girl. Maybe, in the throes of passion, I didn't sound like myself either. I couldn't remember back that far. Tammi did have a fairly high voice, though, now that I thought about it.

I stirred my Spring Tonic, wishing it was a different color. Purplish brown beverages don't inspire confidence. Plus, this one smelled like rotten mushrooms.

"What's in this?"

Peg shrugged. "I bought it online from a natural foods whole-saler."

"Without reading the ingredients?"

"Whiskey, this is a tourist town. People will drink anything that *sounds* good."

Cautiously, I tasted it. Not half as awful as it smelled. Oddly, Peg's Spring Tonic tasted like Scotch Whiskey Lite with a twist of lime and … something else.

"I bet Jeb would like this," I remarked, thinking of my first husband's fondness for the finest single malts. "It has that 'cool burn' he enjoys but can rarely afford."

"Jeb doesn't need a tonic," Peg observed. "He's content all the time."

True enough. My ex required very little, which was a good thing since he could afford almost nothing. Just an old Nissan van wagon, a few musical instruments, and some grunge clothes. The sexy smile was his birthright. Jeb looked like James Taylor used to.

My eyes slid across the room to Nash Grant. He was holding Avery's hand and peering at her lovingly.

"Let it go," Odette hissed. "Your best hope—besides Jeb—is that you meet someone new and either the tonic or the camisole kicks in soon!"

———

Across the street, a few minutes later, Jenx made a face at me. "Have you been drinking?"

"Just an herbal Spring Tonic," I said. "Smells like Scotch, doesn't it?"

"No. Smells like lots of Scotch. I wouldn't piss off any cops if I was you."

"I'll try not to." When I sat down across from Jenx's desk, she motioned for me to move back. Way back.

"Woo! What's that stuff supposed to do for you?" she asked, waving the fumes of my breath away.

"Make me more confident and attractive."

"To who? Winos?" Jenx left her desk to adjust the building's ventilation system. I reminded myself that the chief was a woman, so her reaction didn't count. Then I remembered that she was a lesbian wired to like women, and I got worried. Especially when she returned with a surgical mask.

"Do me a favor and put that on," she said, tossing it to me. "You're making my eyes water."

"Odette and Peg didn't complain," I muttered.

"Peg sold you the drink, and Odette was glad to get rid of you."

The mask in place, I recounted what I'd seen last night when visiting Providence and the Magnet Springs Marina. By now, I'd learned enough about police work to save my theories until after I'd laid out all the facts.

To my disappointment, Jenx didn't bother to write down any of the fascinating details. She didn't bother to comment, either. Finally, I said, "Would you like me to write up a report?"

"And have an official written record of your illicit activities?!"

I took that as a no.

"Well, what *do* you want from me?" Even though my voice was heavily muffled, the petulance came through.

"I want you to forget about this case," Jenx said. "What you've seen so far means nothing."

"Nothing?! Dock Paladino ran Crystal off the road, and either Brandi or Tammi put him up to it! They're all screwing, you know!"

"I thought Brandi and Dock were screwing."

"Tammi, too. Peg has proof!"

"Peg's seen Tammi in bed with Dock?"

"No. But Peg's seen Tammi and Dock making out at the Goh Cup. They got erotic with cappuccino. And something's not right at Providence. Since when can't an orthopod pay his electric bill? Plus, we know Tammi put a curse on Faye! By the way, are Faye's parents back?"

Jenx cleared her throat. I assumed she was trying to tell me that I still stank—until she said, "That's something I need to talk to you about. Faye's parents couldn't get a flight home, after all. Major labor strike in Venezuela. No planes in or out of the country. We don't know for how long."

I couldn't imagine what that had to do with me. And then I got it.

"Oh no … I am not a child-care provider! We've been through this!"

Indeed we had. Despite my protestations, I seemed to attract other people's children the way Jenx's truck attracted oncoming vehicles. In addition to Avery and her twins and Abra and her pups, I'd ended up watching Chester while Cassina was on her World Tour. No sooner had I offloaded those responsibilities than I was about to be saddled with a cursed teenager.

"Faye's supposed to die on Wednesday!" I reminded Jenx. "I really don't have time for that."

FOURTEEN

Jenx didn't give a damn how busy I was.

"You'll take care of Faye Raffle," she said simply and changed the subject. "Did Deely tell you what they brought in last night?"

"My dog? Or is that too much to hope for?"

"Way too much. But Mooney and Prince Harry retrieved some … souvenirs."

"Yeah?" I knew enough about trackers to be wary. "You mean like scat?"

"Not *like* scat. Real scat. Abra's for sure. Dr. David verified it."

"Nice. And Prince Harry helped find it?"

"Carried it home in his own little mouth. Deely was right. That pup's tuned in to things about his mama no one else can appreciate."

"Least of all me. So where was her scat last seen?"

"On the north side of town. Her trail crisscrossed itself. Like she was trying to confuse us."

"Trying?"

If Jenx had made any progress solving Crystal Crossman's murder or removing the curse on Faye's head, she wouldn't talk about it. Five minutes later, I was en route to Coastal Medical Center for the third time in two days. My mission: to pick up Magnet Springs' very own Miss Blossom, and bring her back to Vestige. Hopefully *not* to die.

I wouldn't have admitted as much to Faye, but her prospects looked dim now that I was assigned to protect her. Not only did I have zero defensive training, but black magic scared me sleepless. Whenever I watched a Harry Potter movie, I had nightmares for a week. Deely might have been able to help us, but she was spending more and more time at Nash Grant's. I wasn't sure how often we could count on her for anti-curse duty.

When I walked into Faye's hospital room, she was dressed and ready to go. She was also ghost-white and trembling.

"Did they show you the bill?" I asked.

"No. They delivered this." She held out a white cardboard box about five inches by six and maybe three inches high—the kind some florists use for boutonnieres. I was very sure I didn't want to see what was inside. Faye's haunted eyes told me I had no choice.

"One question," I said. "Will it make me faint?"

"Maybe. I don't know how weak you are."

I steeled myself and cautiously lifted the lid.

Miraculously, I didn't faint. The contents of the box were gross but not overwhelming. On a bed of crumpled tissue paper lay a finely woven antique bracelet and matching earrings. Each featured dangling acorns with gold caps. Gaudy and out of fashion.

But that wasn't the problem. It was what the loops and acorns were made of that made them revolting.

"Human hair," Faye said in case I hadn't got it.

"Anyone's we know?"

"The first Miss Blossom. Here." Her hand shaking, she passed me a folded note written on aged ivory-colored vellum. The creases of the page were worn almost to the point of tearing.

In the spidery handwriting of a distant era, I read the following:

> *Here lies the hair of my beloved daughter, Winifred Margaret Schuyler, who was tragically slain as she lay in her bed on the night of July 30, 1848. I washed away the blood with my own loving hands and trimmed her tresses for this memento mori. Beauty ends. Vengeance is never satisfied.*

Below Mrs. Schuyler's message, someone with a red Sharpie had added:

ALL FORMER MISS BLOSSOMS MUST DIE.

Forcing a smile, I handed the note back to Faye. "Now, now. You've got a whole year before you need to worry about that."

She said, "I've got until Wednesday."

It was going to be a long drive back to Vestige.

"Who sent this to you?"

Faye had no idea. Obviously it was someone with access, legal or otherwise, to the Schuylers' heirloom jewelry, which was probably valuable though hideous. A nurse's aide had brought Faye the box after it was left at the unit desk with an envelope addressed to Miss Blossom.

"That note was in the envelope. Along with this." Faye produced a thick strand of blonde hair about an inch wide and three inches long.

My heart skipped a beat. I would have known that hair anywhere. I should; it covered most of my furniture.

"Abra," I gasped.

"Could Abra send a package?" Faye asked.

"Maybe, but that's not what I mean. Whoever sent this has Abra! Or did have her. She's very hard to contain."

"Why would they send this to me?"

"To creep you out, obviously! It worked, didn't it?"

If anything, Faye looked paler now than she had in the ambulance yesterday. Somebody had upped the curse just as I became temporary guardian. My rotten luck.

"Please call Jenx," Faye said.

I intended to as soon as we got outside. Fear of phone confiscation was the only reason I wasn't already dialing. I hustled Faye out of CMC as fast as her jittery limbs would carry her, the box of spooky jewelry tucked under my arm. Once we were in my car, I got Jenx on the line and brought her up to date.

"You're sure the stuff's authentic?" she asked.

"It's human hair, all right. There's nothing quite like it."

"But you can't tell if it's Mar Schuyler's hair. Or if the note's really from Mrs. Schuyler."

"Look!" Faye had reopened the box and was holding the bracelet as if it were a small but deadly sleeping snake. "There's engraving on the back of the clasp!"

"Hold on," I told Jenx.

Leaning close but not touching, I read aloud the words finely etched in the darkened gold:

In loving memory of Winifred Margaret Schuyler
1829–1848

Then Faye found the initials WMS inscribed on one acorn cap in each earring.

"The jewelry's got to be what we think it is!" I exclaimed into the phone. "You'll need an expert to analyze the note. Maybe he can figure out who added the postscript."

"And all the fingerprints. How many are *yours*?" Jenx sounded weary. "I don't suppose you thought about putting on surgical gloves before you and Faye groped everything? Even though you were in a hospital …"

"Sorry," I said, wincing. "If Chester had been here, he would have stopped me."

"That's because Chester's a good volunteer deputy," Jenx said.

She instructed me to drop the package off at the station before driving to Vestige. "I want to reassess the threat to Faye. This is an alarming development."

Sparing Miss Blossom that verdict, I said instead that Jenx collected Victorian jewelry and couldn't wait to see Faye's. I don't think she bought it.

Faye stayed in the car while I dashed into the police station. Brady was on duty. Or at least on the computer.

"Where's Jenx?" I said.

"In a meeting. She told me to help you."

I surveyed the area around Brady's desk. "Where's Officer Roscoc?"

"Taking a mental health day. Abra's recidivism depressed him."

I was sorry to hear that. Peering over Brady's shoulder at his monitor, I asked what he was doing.

"More online research into Winimar. Trying to find out who's writing the book in progress. If there is a book in progress. Noonan gave me website addresses for a couple New Age bulletin boards devoted to legendary cursed properties."

He tore himself away from the screen long enough to don plastic gloves and scrutinize what I had brought. First I showed him the note from Mrs. Schuyler and the Sharpie person.

"You're in grad school," I said, pointing to a phrase on the page. "What does that mean?"

"*Memento mori*? Literally it means 'remember to die'—or 'remember that you must die.' During the Victorian era, it was the name given to personal ornaments worn as reminders that death was ever near."

"*Remember-to-Die Jewelry*." I shuddered. "As if weaving a murdered girl's curls into acorns wasn't ghoulish enough."

I showed Brady the hair jewelry. Followed by Abra's hair.

"There's a connection," he mused.

"Sure. Whoever sent this has Abra."

Brady frowned. "There's more to it. Faye can expect a second package."

"Officer, step back from the New Age research! It's making you think you're psychic."

"I know I'm not psychic. Just good at discerning patterns." He raised his left hand, which held the bracelet and earrings. "Hair jewelry." Then his right hand, which contained Abra's strand. "Hair of the missing dog that stole jewelry." He gazed at me gravely. "Think about it."

"Do I have to?"

"Somebody's playing major head games, Whiskey. Are you sure you want to get involved with Winimar? Living with one curse at a time isn't enough for you?"

"Ask me again on Wednesday." I considered the hideous antique ornaments. "Doesn't Rico Anuncio feature heirloom jewelry in one section of his gallery?"

"Sometimes. Why?"

"You think it was just a coincidence that he returned from his around-the-world cruise in time to judge Miss Blossom—and suddenly the tiara goes missing? And then this stuff shows up?"

"Be logical, Whiskey. How could Rico have trained Abra to steal the crown? He's been away!"

"He could have hired someone!"

"But what's in it for Rico?" Brady insisted.

"Money. He has contacts in the antique jewelry business. He could find a buyer for the tiara."

Brady was not impressed. "You need to focus on protecting Faye. Where is she?"

"In the car."

"Alone?!" Officer Swancott gave me a look usually reserved for negligent parents.

"Uh—"

Before I could form a single word, a car horn roared as if someone were leaning against it. Make that *my* car horn. Brady crossed to the front door in two strides; I was right behind him.

For some reason, Faye Raffle had moved into the driver's seat. She was now slumped against my steering wheel, apparently unconscious. It looked bad, especially since whatever had gone wrong happened on my watch.

But I knew she couldn't be dead. It was only Sunday—Miss Blossom had three more days to live.

FIFTEEN

BRADY REACHED FAYE FIRST. I was almost as fast, but since he was the life-saving professional, I let him win. The car windows were down, this being an unseasonably warm April day. So Brady was able to reach right in and check Faye's pulse. I held my breath. Okay, I'll be honest: I closed my eyes, too. And I didn't reopen them until I heard Faye sobbing.

"She's okay! She's okay!" I cheered, ignoring the clash of my extreme relief against her tearful unhappiness. Bawling had to be better than dying. Much better.

Brady asked her to tell him what had happened, but she couldn't stop crying long enough to talk. Finally, Faye wailed, "It's the curse!"

"Which curse?" I asked. "The one on Winimar, former Miss Blossoms, or you?"

"Me!" Faye indicated the side of her head just above and behind her left ear. Her symmetrical hairstyle was history. A wide swath of hair was … missing. Cut off at a jagged angle.

"How did that happen?"

"I don't know! I moved to the driver's seat so I could lay my head on the steering wheel. I think I dozed off. One minute I was waiting for you, and the next I felt a painful yank on my hair. When I opened my eyes, somebody spritzed me in the face."

"With what?" I said. "Mace? Pepper spray?"

"Aqua Net. Can't you smell it?"

She was right. The pungent scent of Aqua Net Extra Superhold lingered in the air.

"Did you see anyone?" said Brady.

"No," Faye said, rubbing her eyes. "Thanks to the Aqua Net."

"How about a voice? Or footsteps? Did you hear anyone?"

Faye shook her head.

"Do you think it was a man or a woman? Or more than one person?"

Faye hesitated. "At first, I thought it was a guy because the whole thing was so fast and rough. But now I'm not sure …"

"Why not?"

"How many guys know the power of Aqua Net?"

"I do," Brady volunteered.

"You went to art school," I pointed out. "You did découpage."

He conceded that Faye's assailant was most likely either a female or a gay male with hair issues.

"It was probably Tammi LePadanni," Faye said darkly. "Or her evil daughter."

Just then the station door opened to reveal Jenx and Dr. Emmanuel Crouch, Lanagan County coroner. Either they'd heard the horn blast and come to investigate, or they were on their way out.

Brady asked Faye if her eyes were still burning. When she said yes and added that she could hardly see, he called out to Crouch: "Doctor, could you give us a hand here?"

The coroner said, "Is the patient alive?"

"Yessir. Very much so."

"Then I'm afraid I can't help."

"But sir—she has an eye injury!"

Crouch peered distastefully at Faye from the safety of the station's top step. "If she stops breathing, give me a call."

He extended his right hand to Jenx, pumped hers once, and then used an alcohol wipe to clean his affected palm. As he turned away, Jenx spat at his bald pate. Crouch swabbed that, also, and checked the clear sky above for signs of rain.

I waited until he had lowered his ample gray-suited self into his white Cadillac and driven sedately away. Then I shouted to Jenx, "What was he doing here?"

She glanced meaningfully at Faye, who was still rubbing her eyes. "We had a little business to conclude …"

Then I remembered that Faye didn't yet know Crystal had died. Clearly Jenx wanted a better way to tell her.

Brady said, "Chief, do we have an eye irrigation kit?"

Jenx said she'd go look as Brady and I led a vision-impaired Miss Blossom into the station. When the chief failed to reappear, I went off to find her. She was in the kitchen, throwing teabags against the wall. Boxes of teabags. When she started hurling coffee cans, I intervened.

"That's enough! You're going to rattle the magnetic fields!"

With a considerable effort, Jenx stopped herself. Panting hard, she said, "Ghoul Man makes me crazy."

"I know, I know. Crouch can't stand lesbians."

"It's not that he can't stand us. It's that he has to pray for us!"

I murmured something I hoped sounded comforting and started picking up her mess.

"What's even worse is Crouch won't cooperate on the investigation into Crystal's death," Jenx added.

"But he has to, doesn't he? I mean, he's the coroner."

"There's a wrinkle. She died on the county line. Neither coroner wants the case. So the state police are sorting things out."

"I don't see how that's your problem," I said.

"It means I'm out of the loop! And I can't be out of the loop when I'm in on the curse! I need access to facts! Hell, I need access to Abra and that blasted butt-ugly crown! How else am I going to save Faye?"

"Are you sure they're connected?"

Jenx sighed heavily. "A curse is a curse, and it spawns more curses."

"Who said so?"

"Noonan. And she knows weird shit."

We never found the eye irrigation kit. Brady and Faye made do with a Dixie cup and some warm tap water. Ten minutes later, though still red-eyed, Miss Blossom was able to see.

Then came the hard part. As gently as possible, Jenx broke the awful news about Crystal. Faye wept quietly. She asked a few questions, most of which Jenx couldn't answer. Finally, Faye blotted her eyes, blew her nose, and thanked the chief for her time and her tact.

To me, she announced, "I'm ready for Vestige."

No doubt about it: our reigning beauty queen had exceptional poise. I told her so once we were in my car.

"Thank you," she said. "But I like to think I have gravity. It keeps me grounded."

I doubted that she had ever been grounded—in the punitive sense. What was it like to parent a kid as fine as Faye? She was almost too good. The kind of girl teachers adore and other students resent: pretty, smart, responsible, graceful, polite.

Then it hit me: Faye was the Anti-Avery.

Curse or no curse, that couldn't be a bad thing. Having Faye around Vestige just might be my lucky charm.

———

An ambulance stood in my driveway. That was slightly less alarming than it sounds. The flasher wasn't churning, and I knew the owner, David Newquist, DVM.

Painted white with bright yellow stripes, the reconditioned ambulance proclaimed:

ANIMALS ARE PEOPLE TOO.
WE SAVE ANIMALS.

Along with his girlfriend, the Coast Guard nanny, the vet believed that animals deserved as many individual rights as humans. I didn't like that theory even though I was pretty sure Abra already had a higher standard of living than I did.

But why was Dr. David here now? To deliver Abra? If so, where had he found her? And, flasher or no flasher, why did she need the Animal Ambulance?

In a single continuous motion, I turned off my car and leapt out of it.

"Hewwoh, Whiskey!"

I couldn't see where the voice came from, but I recognized it.

Dr. David emerged from the rear of his vehicle, a large squirming cat under each arm. Meows and howls filled the air.

"Deewee and I want to thank you foe the new wescue," he announced. Translation: Deely and I want to thank you for the new rescue. At least I thought that was what he said. Dr. David, though an expert at animal talk, had major pronunciation problems.

"What new rescue?" I said, hoping my translation was bad. The vet jerked his head toward the inside of the ambulance, where the yowling intensified.

"Gwab a cuppa cats and fowow me!" When he noticed Faye, he added, "You, too."

SIXTEEN

"Uh, David—where are we going with all these cats?"

I was hoping against hope that this wasn't remotely what it looked like.

The more I listened to Dr. David, the clearer he sounded even though I didn't want to believe what he said: "To the temporary shelter. Around the back. Grab some cats. These guys are hard to hold!"

"But—I don't even like cats," I began. "And you're telling me there's a cat shelter behind my house?"

"Not behind it. Inside it. We're taking them in through the back door."

"Wait! I never said you could do this!"

"You must have. Deely brought the paperwork to our last Fleggers meeting, and we approved the motion."

While I argued, Miss Blossom was following the vet's orders. Faye had climbed into the Animal Ambulance and was confidently extracting two black-and-white cats from the large cage.

"Here, Whiskey," she said, folding my arms around the writhing creatures.

"I can't hold on to them!" I cried in dismay, as one clawed his way toward my shoulder.

"Act like their boss, and everything will be fine," Faye said. After expertly detaching the cat from my flesh, she replaced him in the crook of my arm.

"She's right," Dr. David declared. "Follow me."

If herding cats is impossible, holding them isn't much easier. As I followed Dr. David around the side of my house, I had to stop every few yards to renew my grip on the squealing felines, one of whom decided to anchor his needle-sharp talons in my armpit. I could feel my own blood staining my camisole.

To my further surprise, my back door stood wide open, propped in place by Prince Harry's crate.

I shouted angrily to Dr. David, who was yards ahead of me. "You have a key to my house and the code to my alarm system?" The last part was pure bluster. Everyone in town knew I rarely used my alarm system.

"Deely let me in," he called back. "You gave your permission in the document you signed."

"What document?" Never in my right mind would I invite a single cat into my already dog-infested home, let alone an ambulance full of them.

"Right this way," Dr. David directed me. He had already crossed my kitchen and was headed toward the stairway leading to the second floor.

"Oh, no!" I bellowed. "I sleep up there! And I don't sleep with animals, least of all cats!"

"They won't be in your room, Whiskey. Deely has secured the area."

Incredulous, I pounded up the stairs after him, my head aching with anger. Or maybe the pain came from the second cat, who had sunk his claws into my scalp. In any case, I was spitting mad by the time I reached the second floor and took in Deely's Grand Plan.

Dr. David deftly dropped his two cats over a chest-high barrier installed in the doorway to the twins' room. Then he detached mine and deposited them in the same location.

I wanted to shout that he couldn't do this because the twins slept here. But I had already grasped a key fact: Sometime between my leaving the house that morning and my returning to it now, in late afternoon, Avery had removed all the twins' furniture and other possessions. Probably with a little help from Nash Grant and the Coast Guard nanny. The room was bare, except for several multi-level carpet-covered cat climbing installations, about a dozen litter boxes, and as many food and water dispensers. Plus a few dozen mewing cats.

"Here," Dr. David said, unfolding an ominously familiar piece of paper with my signature at the bottom.

The fateful document was one that Deely had asked me to sign a few months earlier, when I was feeling very grateful. I'm a sucker for charities, particularly those that don't seem to ask me for much. I assumed Deely knew I wasn't an animal person. So what could she expect from me?

The paper in question was a Statement of Intention to Assist, prepared by Four Legs Good (a.k.a. Fleggers), or—to be specific— by their lawyers. Basically, it said that the undersigned would, when space became available, be willing to house, on a short-term basis, a limited number of homeless animals. Unfortunately for me, the phrases "short-term," "limited number," and "animals" were undefined. I returned the paper to the vet.

"Now that Avery has moved the twins to Nash Grant's house, Deely decided that the necessary space had become available," Dr. David explained. "Spring is a good time to round up homeless cats for spaying and neutering. We're making Vestige our Sterilization Center."

"You can't perform surgeries here!" I cried.

Dr. David looked offended. "Of course not! Your home is hardly a sterile environment. The cats will be here before surgery and during recovery. Then we'll do our best to place them in foster homes." His bright turquoise eyes darted around my second-floor hallway.

"Don't even go there," I said quickly. "This room is the absolute limit. No expansion. No fostering. Just bring them in, snip off whatever you have to, and ship them out again. Fast."

He nodded distractedly; I could tell that he was still sizing up my upstairs.

"Wait a minute," I said as a new horror dawned. "Until they're 'fixed,' how do I keep the males and females from ... uh ... *commingling*?"

"You'll cage the males," Dr. David said. "In fact, you'll want to do that immediately."

"Are they marked?"

"What do you mean?"

"Don't tell me I have to grab each cat and check between its legs for the gender!"

"Deely will help with that part. I'll get her over here ASAP."

"You bet you will! And here's another thing: my 'short-term basis' will be very short indeed! One week. At most," I added, growing more confident. Faye had been wise to remind me to act like the boss. "This crop of cats only, and then I'm out of the sterilization business. Finished. Chop-chop!"

"Okay, fine," Dr. David said, but he didn't appear to be listening.

Faye appeared then with no fewer than five spotted kittens. Rather than dropping them into the room, Faye opened the barrier slightly and slipped them inside.

Dr. David nodded approvingly. "Too far to drop when they're that young. Glad one of you knows what you're doing."

"Aren't they too young to sterilize?" I asked, eyeing the fuzzy kittens. Although I didn't know much about cats, I figured they had to have a couple things in common with dogs.

"Yes, they're still nursing and need to be with their mother. We'll foster them soon."

Faye interjected, "Aren't they adorable, Whiskey? There's nothing cuter or more fun than kittens!"

I could think of a million things cuter than kittens and a hell of a lot more fun. A good bottle of Pinot Grigio, for starters.

"I'll go get the next load," Faye said and skipped away.

"How many cats are there?" I said with dread.

"In all? No more than forty," Dr. David replied. "This room's smaller than we like for that number, but it should do, provided you change their litter boxes twice a day."

"Provided *I* change their boxes?" I snatched back the Statement of Intention to Assist. "Show me where it says I'm taking care of forty cats by myself!"

Dr. David pointed to yet another vaguely worded statement: "Using supplies and medical care provided by Fleggers, the undersigned hereby assumes full responsibility for the maintenance of said homeless animals during the period for which he/she supplies the premises."

Furious with myself, I balled up the paper and tossed it into the Cat Room. Two felines pounced on it and batted it around like a toy.

"Good!" Dr. David said. "You'll want to engage them in play like that morning and night. It helps release their built-up stress."

"What about my built-up stress? I don't have time to play with forty cats! I run a real estate business! And I'm trying to restart my social life. Can't you see I'm wearing a camisole?!"

"Very nice," the vet said. "I'll have to get Deely one of those."

"David, the point is *I can't do this*. Even for a few weeks. If Deely were still here, we might be able to pull it off. But she's watching the twins at Nash Grant's house now! Avery practically lives there!"

"Calm down, Whiskey." He laid his hairy hand on my shoulder, which involved a slight upward reach since he was under six feet tall. "Fleggers provides more than just supplies. Deely will come by every day to assist you."

"Tell her she's on poop patrol. I can barely keep up with Abra and Prince Harry's output, let alone forty felines'!"

"Abra's not around right now," Dr. David reminded me.

"I'll be here to help," Faye announced, moving past us to deposit a large tuxedo cat and a medium-sized ginger-colored tabby. She looked at the vet. "I'm staying here until my parents get back—or the curse gets me. Whichever comes first."

"I heard about that," Dr. David said. "Congratulations on the crown. Condolences on the curse."

"Thanks."

A jolt of excruciating pain struck the back of my neck. I screamed.

Dr. David moved fast to remove the source of my agony. He presented a small, repulsive creature I hadn't noticed before: it had short, scruffy gray fur and a heart-shaped head with enormous eyes and ears.

"What is it?" I asked, stepping back in horror.

"That's a Devon rex!" Faye exclaimed. "My aunt has one."

"On purpose?"

Faye nodded. "Such an interesting breed. They can practically fly. I wonder what an expensive cat like that is doing with these unwanted strays?"

"Given his good looks and amazing talents," I muttered.

Dr. David said, "Many purebreds have a microchip or tattooed ID. But not this guy."

After returning my attacker to the Cat Room and handing me an alcohol swab for my bleeding neck, the vet added, "As long as Yoda's here, we're going to need a bigger barrier."

SEVENTEEN

FAYE WENT OFF IN search of something that could augment the cat blockade. Through the mesh gate, I shot Yoda, the Devon rex, my surliest look. In response, he licked his entire body. With passion. In fact, he noisily enjoyed the process beyond all bounds of decency. Which led me to the following conclusion: dogs may be gross and stinky, but cats feel no shame. About anything. Ergo, cats are the sociopaths of the animal world. What other reasonably intelligent creature is never troubled by guilt? Besides Abra.

Against the background noise of Yoda's grunts, slurps, and sighs, Dr. David and I discussed the latest misadventures of my Afghan hound. To my chagrin, he suggested I roam Lanagan County looking for her.

"And when would I have time to do that? Between running my real estate business and caring for forty horny cats!"

"They won't be horny for long; we start the surgeries Wednesday," Dr. David said. "Why not use Abra as an excuse to get some fresh air? It's spring, the weather's nice, and your dog is on the loose. Get on that bike you used as a murder weapon. Apply your powers for *good* this time!"

That stung. Dr. David wasn't even living in Lanagan County back when I committed my infamous crime of self-defense. I pointed that out.

He shrugged. "Local lore." Only he pronounced it "wocaw waw." The vet added, "You need the exercise, and you just might see Abra. You know you love that dog."

"I don't even like that dog! But I would like to redeem myself as a dog owner and citizen by returning the tiara. Faye wants her picture taken just once in that hideous thing. Fast Eddie didn't point his camera at her till she was wounded and crownless."

"So get your bike out and go!"

"But why do I have to ride my bike?" I whined. "Why can't I drive my car, like everybody else in America?"

"First of all, you can get up close to places and see things on a bike that you can't in a car. Second, everybody in town says you *love* to ride!"

Dr. David may have been wrong when he said I loved Abra, but he was right that I loved to bicycle. Or used to. I had profoundly conflicting feelings about Blitzen, however. That was the name of my top-of-the-line touring bicycle, the last gift my late husband gave me before he died. Not only was Blitzen tainted with a heavy residue of grief and longing because of the link to Leo; she was also, alas, a killing machine. No question that Blitzen had saved my life and the life of at least one other person. Still, I couldn't mentally get past the fact that, in my hands, a touring bike had turned into a lethal weapon.

"You haven't ridden since … the *incident*, have you?" said Dr. David.

Mutely, I shook my head.

"Then I'm giving you the same advice my father gave me every single time I fell off a horse: get back in the saddle!"

I wanted to know how many times the vet had fallen on his head. But just then Faye arrived, dragging a dusty old screen door.

"Will this work?" she panted.

I recognized the door from the stock of miscellany in my basement. It had belonged, once upon a time, to one of our rental properties. When Leo replaced it, he insisted on saving the original despite my protestations that we'd never reuse it. Who knew it would become a Yoda-proof barricade for the temporary Cat Sterilization Center? All I knew was that I never wanted that bizarre little creature attached to my neck again. And I certainly didn't want it to breed.

Dr. David examined the door. He thought he could modify it to fit, provided I had the appropriate power tools. No problem. Leo had left behind a well-stocked free-standing workshop next to our garage.

"What are you waiting for?" The vet was staring at me. "Change out of that camisole and go for a bike ride!"

Faye said, "I'll help Dr. David with the door. I learned how to use power tools in Shop Class. And I don't mind working up a sweat."

The Anti-Avery, indeed.

With a rare sense of peace in my heart, I wolfed down a power bar, changed into cycling clothes, and grabbed my phone, a couple water bottles, and a well-worn map of Lanagan County. I even took the time to correctly inflate Blitzen's tires using the high-tech pump and digital pressure gauge that Leo had bought me. Then I was on the road, reveling in the fact that you never do forget how to ride a bicycle. Of course, there's no guarantee your butt won't hurt … unless you have what I had: a gel-padded, anatomically correct seat. *Thank you, Leo!*

Lanagan County is known as the Fruit Basket, a.k.a. West Michigan farm country. Although some orchards and vineyards run right up to our Great Lake, more and more of that rich shoreline is being turned into homesteads—expensive homesteads, like Pasco Point. Would a jewel thief and dognapper live among Lanagan County's most affluent? More likely, the culprit—if he or she were still in the area—would be lurking in one of our remote regions. Or at least in a cheaper zip code. Thus, I decided to focus on the inland countryside, where there was plenty of room for hiding. And plenty of space for Abra to cavort in on the off chance she'd stolen the crown just for sport. I doubted she'd voluntarily stay out of sight for long, given how much she craved gourmet dog chow and Chester's slavish attention. Abra was a thrill-seeker and a diva, not a masochist.

Since samples of her scat had been found on the north side of town, I decided to start there, then work my way into the country. The north side of Magnet Springs was the proverbial wrong side of the tracks. Every town has one, even a tourist town. Three years earlier, Leo and I had bought four rundown homes there and renovated them into decent low-cost rentals. Slum landlords we were not.

Now I cruised past those homes. Three were on the same block of Karney Street; the fourth was around the corner on Amity Avenue. With the help of my property manager Luís Regalo and his part-time assistant Roy Vickers, all my rentals looked good, even the ones in this neighborhood. I slowed, wondering exactly where Mooney and Prince Harry had found Abra's scat. Could she have paused to do her business near one of my properties? What were the odds? Abra often accompanied me when I checked on my units. She even knew some of the tenants' names and voices: the ones who gave her treats or otherwise fussed over her when she deigned to visit.

I mentally ran through my tenant files, reviewing who lived where. No obvious potential felons leapt to mind. The best lesson Leo had ever given me in this biz was to thoroughly screen applicants.

As he put it, "Better to weed them out before you rent than try to evict them after they've trashed the place or failed to pay you."

Because I followed his advice, I had top-flight tenants. Their rent money arrived on time, and they protected their homes. They also called me at the first sign of trouble.

My cell phone rang. I extracted it from my fanny pack, wobbling only a little on my two narrow wheels.

"Ma'am? I just got off duty with the twins, and I'm at your house helping David and Faye organize the cats. They said you're upset about the shelter."

"Deely, I don't even like cats! When I signed that form, did you think I actually wanted to be helpful?"

"That's what you said, ma'am."

"Well, here's a better idea: how about I write Fleggers a big fat check and be done with my good deed?"

"Money's not the issue," the Coast Guard nanny explained. "It's helping hands we lack. I'm sorry I couldn't give you a heads-up, but David had to move those cats today."

"How long will they be there?"

"As short a time as possible, I promise. And we're installing a bigger barrier to contain the airborne cats."

"Airborne *cats*? As in *plural*? Don't tell me Yoda's breeding already!"

"No, ma'am. There's only one Yoda. So far …"

Suddenly I recalled Faye's wise advice to talk like I'm the boss. "Deely, I need you to sort out the genders and put all the boy cats in boxes. Or wherever it is you can stash them so they don't make more babies."

She said that she and Faye were already on it.

"I'm on my bike on the north side of town, looking around for Abra," I added. "Can you remember where Prince Harry found her scat?"

"Yes, ma'am. Second block of Amity, third house from the corner on the left-hand side. He found it by the front porch steps."

Involuntarily, I jerked the handlebars hard to the right and uttered an expletive.

"Are you okay?" Deely asked quickly.

"That's one of my properties! I'm going back for a look-see."

"We checked the neighborhood. There was no other sign of Abra."

"Maybe. But Mrs. Brewster lives there, and she doesn't miss much. Did you interview her?"

"No, ma'am. I was too busy trying to get the scat out of Prince Harry's mouth before he could swallow it. We ended up chasing him back to the station."

I turned Blitzen around. Sixty-six-year-old Yolanda Brewster was the self-appointed Boss of the North Side. During the warm months, she and her portable TV spent most days and evenings on her porch. During the rest of the year, she parked her wheelchair in the living room next to the picture window. Although she loved her "stories"—the soap operas, sitcoms, and cop shows she avidly followed—the dramas on the street interested her more. If Yolanda didn't know about it, it hadn't happened.

EIGHTEEN

"Miz Mattimoe, what you doing here? Didn't you get my rent check? I sent it on time just like I always do."

In response to my knock, a large, silver-haired black woman had rolled her chair to the front door and was peering at me through the screen.

"I got it, Mrs. Brewster. That's not why I'm here. I've got a little problem with Abra I'd like to talk to you about."

"That blonde dog o' yours got you down again? She a pretty thing but not right in the head. Uh-uh. That dog got a screw loose."

Leave it to Yolanda to say it like it is. She pulled the door open for me.

"You wanna come in and talk about her? Or you in a hurry like you always is?"

"I got all the time it takes," I said, wishing I could bring Blitzen inside with me. This was not the neighborhood in which to leave an unlocked bicycle worth a thousand bucks.

Mrs. Brewster read my mind.

"Bring that bike on in here with yourself. If you don't, you gonna make me crazy watching you stew."

Gratefully, I did as I was told.

"You want something to drink?" Mrs. Brewster asked. "I got sweet tea and sodas for when my grandbabies come visit. You can help yourself."

I declined and silently admired how neat my tenant kept her sunny living room. Not a speck of dust had landed on a single surface, which was more than I could say for any space I occupied.

"Mrs. Brewster, are you aware of what Abra did yesterday?"

"You mean stealing Miss Blossom's crown and running away with it? Everybody in Magnet Springs heard about that. What else you want to know?"

If God existed—and most days I was pretty sure He did—Yolanda Brewster was probably His drill sergeant. There was no bluffing that woman. I cleared my throat.

"The posse tracking Abra found her ... *you know*. . . her waste products. By your porch."

"They found her shit, you mean?"

I nodded.

Mrs. Brewster frowned. "Woman your age can't say 'shit'? You need to grow up, girl! Get yourself a big life."

"Shit, yes," I agreed. "So—do you know anything about that?"

"About Abra crapping by my front steps? She do that all the time!"

"What do you mean, 'all the time'?"

"That dog o' yours come around here once in a while. Without you. I figure you don't know what she up to. Something about my front yard attract her. Or maybe she just dig my vibe."

Mrs. Brewster laughed warmly at her own wit. But the word "dig" sent a tremor through me. I wondered if Deely or the Judge had looked for signs that Abra was digging in Mrs. Brewster's yard, an old bad habit of my felonious hound.

Once again, my tenant guessed my thoughts. "Now don't you be worrying about that dog digging up my yard. If she was up to that, don't you think I be calling you?"

"I know you would. What I'm wondering is whether she dug one hole. Yesterday."

Mrs. Brewster's large ochre eyes narrowed, and her brow furrowed.

"Did Abra bury that crown here? That what you're asking, hmm?"

"Yes."

Mrs. Brewster said, "Oh, she had it, all right. But she didn't bury it. She didn't bury nothing here."

A wave of relief surged through me although I wasn't sure why. My tenant's response moved me no closer to finding either my wayward dog or the Miss Blossom tiara. It suggested, though, that Abra had outgrown her tendency to bury stolen merchandise in other people's yards. A habit that made recovery both difficult and messy.

"Well, that's good to know," I said.

"Not here, uh-uh. She did her business by my porch steps, like she always do. Then she jump into that truck and away they go."

My mouth dropped open. I felt the air rushing in and my tongue drying up, but I couldn't speak.

Mrs. Brewster said, "Look at you! That dog got the power to shake you up good! Why you give her all that power?"

"I don't give it to her! She claims it as her birthright! She's an Afghan hound, you know."

"I don't care if she the Queen o' Sheba! Don't nobody bow down if they don't want to. You want to, Miz Mattimoe. You let that dog run your life!"

With that, she rolled her chair out of the room. I felt like I'd been slapped, but in a good way. Mrs. Brewster was right. Only it was complicated …

I put up with Abra because Abra was the only living part of Leo that I had left. Except for Avery, who was never mine, and her twins, who never would be mine. And Prince Harry, who with any luck would become Chester's. Leo had bought Abra to please me. He died before realizing that was a complete misjudgment. Nonetheless, his wish had been to delight me. So I felt a profound and enduring obligation to protect that dog. But I was failing miserably.

"Drink this."

Mrs. Brewster had rolled back into the room bearing a tall glass of iced tea. It was not only restorative but also flavorful, ranking higher on both counts than the so-called Spring Tonic Peg had served me.

"What's in this?" I said.

"Besides tea? A little mint, a little honey, a teeny-tiny bit of ginger."

"It's delicious! Somebody should bottle this."

"What for? It's only good cuz I make it fresh. Now what you gonna do about that dog?"

"I'm going to find out about the truck she jumped into and track it down!"

Mrs. Brewster shook her head emphatically.

Confused, I asked, "I'm *not* going to find out about the truck and track it down?"

"Oh, you'll find out about that truck, all right. But that's not my question. What you gonna do to keep that dog from running your life?"

"I don't know. I hired a damage-control specialist. Nothing seems to work."

"Maybe that's cuz you like living crazy."

"Not me! I crave control. I just can't get any."

She gave me a leveling stare. "Miz Mattimoe, you buy, sell, and rent real estate. You can get whatever you want. You just need to think about what that is."

Besides Nash Grant? I was completely bollixing that quest.

"Mrs. Brewster, please tell me what you know about the truck that Abra jumped into."

"Well, now … it was big and black, and it parked out there across the street a few minutes before Abra come 'round."

"What time was that?"

"Five o'clock. 'Sanford and Son' was just starting. And then Abra got in, and it burned rubber taking off that away."

She pointed north up Amity Avenue.

"Did you get the license plate? Or the make and model of the truck?"

"Uh-uh."

"That's too bad." I didn't try to conceal my disappointment. "Did you tell Jenx or Brady what you saw?"

"No. You the first to ask."

"If only you had more information …"

"How much more you need? I know the driver."

NINETEEN

I stared at Mrs. Brewster. "You know the driver of the truck Abra jumped into?"

"Uh-huh. You do, too."

Recalling my conversation with Brady, I took a guess: "Rico Anuncio!"

My tenant frowned. "Who's that?"

I started to explain but quickly realized that she didn't know the flamboyant gallery owner.

Mrs. Brewster said, "The person I saw, she work for you."

Now my head was spinning. "Who?"

"That doctor's wife—the li'l woman with the big hair and big mouth. She make me nervous."

"Tammi LePadanni?" I gasped. "How do you know her?"

I couldn't imagine what would bring a resident of Pasco Point to this side of town.

"She do a little business with one of my nephews. He in jail now."

"You mean … drugs?"

"My boys don't do drugs!" Mrs. Brewster was offended. "Du-Mayne cut a man for cheating him in a poker game. That's why he in jail. Nothing to do with drugs. Or Tammi LePadanni. DuMayne used to raise pit bulls. Last year she come over here and buy two of his dogs."

So that's where the LePadannis got their pit bulls.

"How come DuMayne didn't give *you* a couple dogs?" I asked. "Didn't you want protection?"

She scowled. "Do I look like I need protection?!"

"No, ma'am," I replied. "Please help me get this straight: Just before five o'clock yesterday, Tammi LePadanni pulled up in a truck. Then Abra arrived with the crown, did her business by your porch, jumped into Tammi's truck, and they drove north out of town. Is that right?"

"That's how I saw it," Mrs. Brewster confirmed. "Maybe she was driving a SUV, but it was big as a truck."

"You're sure it was Tammi? It couldn't have been someone else?"

"It was Tammi, all right. When she open the driver's door, I got a good look. Abra jump in right on top o' her. Made her scream. Made me laugh." The memory made Mrs. Brewster laugh again. "She wearing sunglasses, but I know that woman. She real small, and she got that wavy hair and that pointy chin. She think she hot stuff cuz she a doctor's wife. Can buy whatever she want. Well, la-dee-da. She can frost my cake!"

"My feelings, exactly!"

"Then how come she work for you? She good at selling houses?"

"No, but she's good at bringing in prospects who have lots of cash."

Mrs. Brewster shook her head in a way that suggested I was going straight to hell. I shifted the subject. "You're sure Abra had the crown in her mouth when she went off with Tammi?"

"Uh-huh. I know what it look like. Used to go to the Miss Blossom Fest back when I could walk. Big ugly green and gold thing only a white woman could love."

I thanked Mrs. Brewster for her time and her iced tea and asked her to please call me if she saw either Abra or Tammi on her street again. She assured me that she had an army of neighborhood "deputies" who did whatever she asked. They were all on notice to watch for the big blonde dog and the nasty doctor's wife.

I wheeled Blitzen back out onto Amity Avenue and peered north. Two more blocks and the town ran out of houses, fading into open countryside. Where could Tammi have taken Abra? At Providence, I'd seen no trace of the woman, her car, or my Affie. And I'd heard only pit bulls. My mission *du jour* had been to find a black vehicle with dents. Could I have missed key evidence simply because I was looking for something else?

One thing was clear: I had to tell Jenx what I knew. The chief answered on the first ring and wasn't happy to hear from me.

"I'm waiting for an important call," she snapped.

"This is an important call!" I proceeded to tell her what Mrs. Brewster had told me.

"So you think Tammi LePadanni stole Miss Blossom's crown?" Jenx asked.

"Mrs. Brewster saw her do it!" I exclaimed.

"No. Mrs. Brewster thinks she saw Abra with the crown in her mouth jump into Tammi's SUV."

"It's the same thing!"

"Not in my business, it's not. But thanks for sharing. I'll put your call in the log."

"This is huge!" I insisted. "It could break our case wide open!"

"*Our* case? Last time I checked, you were in denial that Abra was your dog."

"So who's your 'important call' coming from?"

"Vito Botafogo. When I interviewed him last night, he was trying to remember something that happened just before Abra knocked him down. He said he'd call me back today if he did."

I groaned. "Oh, yeah, that's a lot more important than, say, an eyewitness account of Abra and Tammi taking off with the crown!"

"It could be. You want to do something with Mrs. Brewster's lead, don't you?" Jenx said.

"No, I want *you* to do something with it! *You* catch criminals. I'm a civilian. I sell real estate."

Jenx reminded me that the entire Magnet Springs police force consisted of herself, her canine officer, and her part-time human officer.

"How are you doing in the search for Crystal Crossman's killer?" I said. "Are Brady and Roscoe following up on the blue paint I saw on Dock Paladino's truck?"

"It's on the list. We appreciate any civilian help we can get. Provided it's help and not complications. You wanna pursue Mrs. Brewster's lead? That's cool. Just keep it on the lowdown and don't jam yourself up. I don't have the manpower to come save you."

While she was talking, I unfolded the frayed Lanagan County map I'd grabbed from my garage. I wondered if anything interesting lay north of town and, if so, how far I'd have to ride to get there. I must have stared at that map for a long moment.

"Are you there?" Jenx said.

"I'm … here." I blinked at marks made in red ink and a too-familiar handwriting. Something near the intersection of County Road H and an unnamed, unpaved road about five miles northeast of where I now stood had interested my late husband. On the map Leo had circled an area the size of a nickel and written: **NO!!!!**

I described for Jenx what I was looking at.

"That's Winimar," she said. "Leo tried to sell it the year before he died."

That couldn't be right. If he had, I would have known about it. I told Jenx so.

"I didn't say he listed it," she pointed out. "He had a client in the market for a large piece of land. Leo showed the place. That's all."

I demanded to know how she knew about it when I didn't. Her sigh filled my ear.

"Whiskey, don't ask. Leo made me promise never to discuss this."

"Leo's dead!" I blurted.

"And his secrets should be buried with him," Jenx said.

"But you know one I don't know! And I'm his wife!"

"You're his widow. Let him and his wishes rest in peace."

"Jenx, you already told me he tried to sell Winimar. Why can't I know the rest of the story?"

When she replied, I could tell that she was choosing her words with care.

"Something happened to Leo while he was at Winimar. Something he believed might endanger you … if you ever found out about it."

"Then why do you know about it?" I demanded.

"Leo thought a law was being broken. He wanted Big Jim to investigate. But Big Jim was on a bender. So I went out."

"Was Leo right?"

Jenx didn't reply.

"Well?" I prompted. The line clicked, and Jenx said, "I got a call coming in. Might be Vito."

"Oh yeah," I said sourly. "You better talk to the senile sausage vendor. That might be important."

And I closed my phone.

TWENTY

Anger. Resentment. Confusion.

Those emotions churned in me as I pedaled Blitzen, hard, away from Magnet Springs and out into the greening country. My agitation was so complete that I tuned out most of the surrounding signs of spring. And after a bitter west Michigan winter, we Wolverines worship that sweet season.

While feelings charged my heart, questions flooded my brain: What did Leo see at Winimar? Why would he hide what he knew from me? What possible risk did he think I would face?

Did Leo see something that could explain the "curse" of Winimar? Was it going on even now? Did it have anything to do with Abra's theft of the tiara and whatever Tammi LePadanni was up to?

If, in fact, Leo had shown Winimar to a prospect, then the property was probably listed for sale. Two years ago. Was Sweeney administering the trust at that time? I couldn't remember ever hearing Leo mention the attorney. If Sweeney was on the job back then, he would have tightly controlled access to Winimar. So he would have known which agents visited. Did he know what Leo had seen? Did he threaten Leo?

He might have tried, but Leo didn't cow easily, especially when lawyers came at him. I smiled, imagining my man defending his honor and my safety as he saw fit. While I didn't always agree with Leo, I did respect his choices.

A quick check of my watch revealed that it was almost eight o'clock. I had less than an hour of decent light left. Not enough time to reach Winimar, explore the place—especially if it was wooded—and then bicycle home. That was assuming I could find an entrance to the abandoned estate.

Leo's blood-red circle with the exclamation **NO!!!!** was etched as indelibly in my brain as on the map. Gauging the pace of the sinking orange sun, I decided that I had just enough time to reach the vicinity of Winimar, search for possible ways in, make a few notes, and then pedal fast back to Vestige. The next morning, en route to Sweeney's office in Grand Rapids, I could return by car and explore as much or as little as time and my nerves allowed.

Lanagan County's rural roads are paved only if they're state or county highways or arteries leading into Ritchie, the county seat. In other words, most long-distance cyclists end up on unpaved roads that challenge their narrow tires. That's what was happening to me. Amity Avenue had turned into Uphill Road, which ran out of asphalt as it climbed alongside highland vineyards. My digital odometer indicated that I had traveled 4.64 miles since leaving Magnet Springs. I was nearing Winimar.

Suddenly I heard the distant, deep bark of a big dog. No canine I knew. But seconds later came the familiar sharp rejoinder I would have recognized anywhere: Abra. My pulse jumping, I scanned both sides of the road. Vineyards rolled away into dunes on my left; a vast empty field fanned out to my right, edged by a forested game preserve. Did the barks come from there? Or from Winimar? According to Leo's map, if I turned right on County Road H, I would come upon the cursed estate.

It was unmistakably Abra who barked again, sounding playful—not plaintive. Then the other dog chimed in. With a shudder, I imagined Leo's glossy legacy roaming the rapidly darkening Schuyler family land. Had she buried the crown there? Had Tammi? I didn't expect Abra to lead me helpfully to her stolen prize. Or to meekly follow me home. If I knew Abra—and, alas, I did—she would rather be a fugitive who danced in the dark with her canine stud. Then I flashed on my own silly fantasies about Nash Grant. For one brief, but humiliating, moment, I saw myself as more ridiculous than that crazy Affie.

And then I saw the Affie. Actually, I saw her boyfriend first as he broke from the cover of the game preserve into the open, unsown field. He was a big blonde god of a dog: a sun-burnished Golden retriever as athletic, strong, and confident as Abra was regal. She burst from the woods right behind him, loping in that signature poetic stride: a curving wave of a run, head and tail held high, glossy curtains of fur swaying, pompom feet stroking the air but barely touching the earth.

God, they were beautiful together. And I knew, even from that distance, from my flawed and limited human perspective, that they belonged together. Abra had found her Nash Grant. Or better yet—her Leo.

My cell phone rang. I fumbled for it, unwilling either to take my eyes off the canine spectacle or dismount from my wobbling ride.

"Hello!" I barked.

"Whiskey? This is Faye. Are you all right?"

"Fine. Are you?"

"I'm okay. It's still only Sunday, remember."

"What's up?" I kept watching the bounding dog duo.

"Uh … Jenx called. She's a little worried about you."

"No need. I'm fine."

"That's good. There's … something else, though."

There always is, I thought. "What?"

"I'd better let Deely tell you. Hold on."

My cursed intern passed the phone to the Coast Guard nanny, who announced, "We have a situation."

The last time she'd used that expression, Leah and Leo had been in trouble. Big trouble.

"It's not the twins," Deely added quickly. "It's Abra."

"Abra?" I echoed, confused. "I'm looking at her right now!"

"You probably are. Jenx just got a call that someone living on Uphill Road saw her with a Golden."

"I think they're in love!"

"Be that as it may, ma'am, Abra must have been here earlier today."

"How is that possible?'

"Well, you know she's fast when she wants to be. We've clocked her coursing speeds at almost—"

"That's not what I mean! What makes you think she was at the house?"

"She left something."

"Fresh scat, you mean? That's probably Prince Harry's."

"No, ma'am, not scat. The Miss Blossom crown. Faye was chasing Yoda through the house and he ran into your bedroom. The crown … is on your bed."

TWENTY-ONE

NEVER MIND THAT THE flying cat had escaped again. My brain was stuck on the image of Abra delivering stolen merchandise to my bedroom. And then ducking out to frolic with her unknown hunk.

"So she left the crown on my bed," I mused. "Probably a hostile gesture, don't you think? Or a pathetic bid for attention? Or is it possible that she was trying to be a good dog and make amends?"

"It's not that simple, ma'am," said Deely. "The gems are missing."

"What?!"

"You know the big, gaudy emeralds that made the crown so ugly? And priceless? They're all gone now. Somebody pried them out. Only the gold mounting remains."

"Uh-oh," I groaned. "Does Jenx know?"

"No, ma'am. She called here because she thought you were going to Winimar, and she wanted Faye or me to stop you. She said you weren't listening to her."

"More like the other way around!"

"Anyway," Deely continued, "Jenx gave us a heads-up on the Abra sighting because she knew you'd need backup. While we were talking, Faye ran past, chasing Yoda. Then I hung up, and Miss Blossom found her crown."

"Or what's left of it," I said.

"You're not going to Winimar, are you, ma'am?"

"Not on my bike tonight." Reluctantly, I slowed Blitzen to a stop. Abra and boyfriend grew smaller and smaller as they dashed in the direction of the forbidden estate.

"Call Jenx and tell her I'm on my way home. She'll probably come straight to Vestige. Oh—and don't touch the evidence. She gets real mad when you do that."

I clicked off and squinted at the now distant golden dots. What a pretty pair. I wondered where Abra had found him.

Time flies on the return loop of a bike trip. Except when you know the police are waiting for you at home. I had plenty of time on that lonely ride back to Vestige to wonder how much trouble I might actually be in. Of course, I was completely innocent of jewel theft, but I suspected that my dog wasn't. And murky though the law may be on certain points, I looked guilty by association. Most likely, I was in very deep doo-doo.

Rounding the bend in the road leading to Vestige, I braced myself for the sight of patrol cars in my driveway: Jenx's and probably one belonging to the state police. Nothing could have prepared me for what I found.

In addition to three cop cars—one each from Magnet Springs, the state cops, and the county sheriff—there were two ambulances: Dr. David's and the kind designed for human patients. The lights atop both ambulances were flashing.

And there was more alarming news.

Next to Jenx's patrol car, I spotted Nash Grant's new Toyota Sienna minivan, purchased—or so I had heard—for the sole nauseating purpose of transporting professor, Avery, and twins as if they were one happy family. I cringed to imagine how happy Avery would be to see her wicked stepmother hauled off to jail. Especially in front of the man I had lusted for and lost.

But first things first: who needed the human ambulance?

Deely must have been watching for me out the front window. She flung open the door before I even reached it. I did not miss the fact that she was sporting a shiner: her right eye was purple-red and swollen nearly shut.

"Is that ambulance for you?" I said.

"No, ma'am. Faye had an accident. I was there too, but I'm fine."

"What happened?"

"I phoned Jenx, like you told me to. Then Faye shouted to me from upstairs that Yoda had let the boys out."

"What 'boys'?"

"The cat boys, ma'am. We thought we had them secured, but Yoda has amazing dexterity. He can pry open doors. It's a Devon rex thing."

"It's a criminal thing!" I cried. "What happened to Faye?"

"I'm getting to that. She was trying to round up cats, and I ran up the stairs to help her. I reached the top just as Faye came around the corner. We collided." Deely pointed over her shoulder to the narrow, railed overlook atop my staircase that ran the width of the living room below. But I was looking at what lay below. Two paramedics were bent over a girl on a backboard. Guess who?

"You got a black eye—and Faye went over the rail?!"

"Yes, ma'am. She'd built up a lot of momentum. Plus she had cats in her arms, so she couldn't grab the banister."

"It's that damn curse!" I croaked. Then I must have swayed, for Deely steadied me.

"Faye's conscious," she assured me. "And the cats landed on their feet—like they're supposed to!"

"Faye's not going to die, is she? Or be paralyzed? It's still only Sunday!"

"It's a good sign that she's alert," Deely said. "Looks like she has a broken arm and a dislocated shoulder, but that's probably the worst of it. I'll ride along in the ambulance."

"Thanks," I sighed. "I'd rather not make another trip."

"You can't, ma'am. You've been banned. By official order of the County EMTs."

"Whiskey! What the hell were you thinking—filling our babies' room with *stray cats*!"

The whiny voice of my stepdaughter wafted down the stairs like a stink. In fact, a bad odor accompanied it; those litter boxes needed cleaning already.

Before I could reply, Nash Grant interceded. He moved toward me with a conciliatory smile.

"Deely told us about your Statement of Intention to Assist," he drawled. "We understand it's temporary. I'm hoping that the twins will stay at my house until my sabbatical ends and I have to return to Gainesville."

Even amid chaos, Nash radiated warmth and sincerity. And sex appeal. But no trace of lust for me.

Avery said, "I reserve the right to come back to Vestige with my twins whenever I want to! This was my father's house, and I'm my father's daughter!"

She stuck her tongue out—possibly on purpose, possibly because of her annoying nervous tic.

"Correction: this was the house your father and I owned jointly," I said. "When Leo died, he left his half to me. Avery, I've done my best to help you and your children. *You* moved their things out of here! Without even notifying me."

"And you couldn't wait a day to fill their room with vermin!" she shrieked.

"Keep it down!" bellowed the same paramedic who had confiscated my phone the day before.

"He means it," I warned Avery.

Deely narrowed her eyes at my stepdaughter. "Dr. David filled the babies' room with 'vermin.' And I helped."

Her Fleggers defenses were kicking in. We could be headed for a cat fight, and not the kind Dr. David knew how to stop.

"Whiskey!" Jenx called from the family room. "I need a word with you!"

The chief was flanked by Dr. David and a sheriff's deputy. I was only too glad to talk to someone other than my crazed stepdaughter, even if it meant getting arrested.

"What's up?" I asked, resisting the urge to hold out my wrists for shackles. Better later than sooner on that score.

Jenx introduced the deputy, whose name flew right past me. When stressed, I can't retain trivia.

"Brady's following up on a lead we got from Vito Botafogo," Jenx said. "The sausage vendor remembered something that might help us."

"More than Mrs. Brewster seeing Tammi pick up Abra and the crown?" I asked snidely.

The deputy frowned at Jenx. "What's she talking about?"

"Tell you later," the chief said. To me she added, "You'll be glad to know that Vito forgives you for not leashing your dog."

"Nice to have one less enemy than I expected. What's happening upstairs?"

"The state cops are guarding what's left of the crown and keeping an eye on that cat Yoda. We don't need any more injuries. When their forensics team gets here, they'll dust for prints. Not just the tiara but your whole house and all your outbuildings. Including Abra's kennel."

I looked at Dr. David. "Speaking of the devil, are you going to bring her in?"

"Yes," the vet said. "Jenx has asked me to execute a double apprehension."

The chief checked her notes. "As you know, Abra's in the vicinity of Uphill Road and County Road H. With a Golden of interest. There are APBs out on both of them."

"So Abra's lover is a felon, too?" I asked. "I should have known she'd fall for a bad boy!"

"It's not like that," Jenx said. "Abra's wanted for jewel theft, but her boyfriend's wanted because he's valuable. If he's the Golden we think he is, he's a trained companion dog, and his owner needs him back. Dr. David's leaving immediately."

The vet nodded bravely.

"But it's dark out!" I said. "And they're near Wini—"

"Whiskey! Dr. David knows where they were last seen," Jenx said through clenched teeth. Did Attorney Sweeney's gag orders also apply to giving directions?

The vet vowed that he was a trained professional who almost always got his dog. When he tried to calm me, it came out sounding like "Pweez wewax." I knew I couldn't do that.

Then I had an inspiration.

"Now hear this," I announced. "For the first time ever, I am publicly taking responsibility for that demon she-dog. As Abra's legal owner, I insist on accompanying Dr. David."

"But—" the vet began.

"I strongly advise against it," Jenx said. "Don't you have enough troubles without looking for more?"

"That's the point!" I cried. "Tomorrow's Monday, which is getting close to Wednesday. So I'm taking a stand against destiny. And against Wee Sweeney and Tammi LePadanni, too. And anybody else who gets in my way! As God is my witness, Faye will never be cursed again!"

I thought I sounded awesome. But Jenx and Dr. David sighed in disgust, and the sheriff's deputy looked spooked.

"Scary lady," he remarked.

Jenx said, "Wait'll you meet her dog."

TWENTY-TWO

GIVEN THE COPS, THE curses, and my tendency to freak out around medical personnel, I was grateful that the EMTs let me have a word with Faye.

"I'm going to make Vestige safe for you," I vowed as they slid her into the back of the people ambulance.

Ever the trooper, she assured me that she would be all right.

"Look at it this way," she said. "I'm probably safer at CMC than anywhere else."

I forced a smile although I knew that hospitals, especially that one, could be deadly.

Miss Blossom's last words, before they banged shut the doors, were "Don't let Yoda out!"

I didn't intend to.

When I re-entered my house, Nash Grant was nowhere in sight. Avery and Deely were still going at it in the living room, arguing about human rights versus animal rights and whether or not cats qualified as vermin. It chilled me to hear Avery expressing the same opinions I held; in her voice they sounded so self-serving. Although I couldn't embrace the Flegger philosophy, coming from Deely it seemed almost appealing.

Then Avery noticed me and snarled, "If Dad had known you'd care more about stray cats than about his grandkids, he wouldn't have left you a dime."

I wanted to say, "If he'd known what a raging bitch you'd turn out to be, he wouldn't have married your mother."

I didn't go there, though. Not because I was noble, but because Nash Grant was coming down the hall from the direction of my library, formerly Leo's office; he was carrying a very fat cat.

"Out of the corner of my eye, I saw this devil scoot past," Nash drawled. "He probably went over the rail with Faye and thought he'd got away scot-free. No such luck, li'l buddy. I'll just slip you back in your pen."

"No!" Avery barked. "Let Whiskey do it. The cats are her problem, not yours."

"I don't mind," Nash said, starting up the stairs.

"I SAID LET HER DO IT!" roared Avery.

Nash froze on the second step. Very slowly he turned around, a practiced smile on his lips. "Now, sweetheart darling—"

"Don't 'sweetheart darling' me! Listen up: you're *not* helping Whiskey with those damn cats! Do you understand?"

Nash lowered his eyes and nodded once. His shoulders sagged, his skin paled. Suddenly he looked more like a pussy-whipped husband than the man of my dreams. Where on earth did Avery get the power to push around a good-looking guy? Or … was that all there was to Nash Grant: just good looks, a sexy Southern accent, and a Ph.D. in advertising? What the hell kind of a degree was that, anyway?

Without meeting my eyes, he stepped forward to hand off his hissing burden. Thank God, Deely interceded. I'd had all the cats—and cattiness—I could stand for one day.

"Ready to go, Whiskey?" Dr. David hustled past. In addition to his battered black medical bag, he was toting two big mesh nets attached to telescoping metal poles. The kind used by dogcatchers—in cartoons.

"You can't be serious," I said, pointing to his gear.

"I'm completely serious. It's all we've got."

"I hope we've also got good flashlights."

Not to mention good luck. We were off to Winimar. After dark.

Expertly restraining the spitting fat cat, Deely managed to blow a kiss to Dr. David. He blew one back, and we boarded the Animal Ambulance.

"Are you planning to keep that flasher on?" I asked. The pulsing red light made me feel like I was in the cast of a TV cop drama, but I'd forgotten to pick up my script.

"Only while we pass through town," Dr. David said. "It gives the human community peace of mind to know we're on the job. Are you worried that the flasher will freak Abra out?"

"No. I'm worried she'll see it coming a mile away and give us the slip. Again."

Dr. David assured me that he was in touch with Brady and the local emergency dispatcher. He said they would relay any reports of a prancing Affie and her retriever companion.

"She won't elude us for long," he concluded.

"But now that it's dark out, who's going to see her?" I asked.

"You'd be surprised. Most farms have excellent security lights."

And I was absolutely certain that Abra would avoid them all.

Apparently everyone in Magnet Springs knew not only about Abra's latest caper but also that Dr. David had been enlisted to bring her in. As we passed slowly through town, our flasher flashing, children ran alongside the Animal Ambulance cheering us on. I wasn't sure whether to feel heartened or humiliated.

Dr. David turned to me, his jaw set. "See that, Whiskey? Magnet Springs is counting on us."

"They still think Abra has the historic Miss Blossom tiara," I said. "And we know she doesn't."

"She might have the jewels," said Dr. David.

"You think she pried them from the crown with her own pointy teeth?"

"No. Somebody expertly removed them, probably for resale. But that person might still be using Abra."

"How?"

The vet considered my question. "Perhaps to transport or conceal the jewels."

I had a very hard time imagining my diva dog following orders, especially since I'd last seen her engaged in what looked like doggie foreplay.

"Or maybe she's supposed to distract us," Dr. David mused.

"She's good at that. How many dogs do you know that can throw a whole town into panic?"

"Just one. I hate to admit it, but your dog may be a public menace."

I must have looked hurt because Dr. David quickly added, "We all know you're doing your best to curb her criminal tendencies."

"I keep hiring keepers!" I cried. "First Chester, then Deely! They've tried everything from Dogs-Train-You-dot-com to The System. Nothing works!"

"Correction: Nothing works *yet*. You hired Deely to babysit the twins. She's only been able to work with Abra on her breaks. If she could concentrate full-time on your dog, you'd see amazing results."

"You think? I hate to speak ill of your girlfriend, but she's the one who let Abra off leash for a run yesterday. That's how this whole mess began."

Dr. David sighed. "You don't understand The System, Whiskey."

"Yeah, yeah. And most other things. Deely said she was working on Abra's 'Learning Challenge.' If I'd known the curriculum, I could have predicted it would land one of us in jail."

"Don't jump to conclusions," the vet said sharply. "I didn't want to mention this until we had more evidence, but I strongly suspect that someone is tampering with The System."

"What do you mean?"

"I think we'll find proof that Abra has been … corrupted."

"We know that already! She has a police record!"

"I mean, her training has been corrupted. *Subverted*, if you will. In my opinion, someone in this town is deliberately undermining Deely's fine work. A little bit of knowledge is a dangerous thing."

"Especially a little bit of knowledge about Abra," I agreed. "That dog steals for the sport of it. Plus, she has a libido that won't quit."

No doubt she was giving the Golden the ride of his life. Talk about corruption. It saddened me to think that somewhere someone needed the services of a trained companion dog who had been seduced by my blonde bimbo.

"What kind of assistance does the Golden provide?" I asked.

"I don't know the circumstances," Dr. David said. "Companion dogs can be trained to very specific skill sets. Some assist with complex activities; others serve to alert or soothe their humans. Or provide balance when they walk."

In my mind's eye, I saw the ruddy sun glinting off the Golden's coat. "Aren't assistance dogs supposed to wear backpacks?"

"Not necessarily. The only thing I know about the dog we're looking for is his name."

"Which is—?" I expected something on the order of Jake or Max.

"Norman."

"No way! That dog is too gorgeous for a geek name! Besides, Abra wouldn't date a 'Norman.'"

"What's wrong with 'Norman'? It happens to be my middle name."

I refrained from further comment. We had passed through the northwest corner of Magnet Springs and were now on Uphill Road. Dr. David turned off our flasher. The moon was a pale silver crescent in the night sky—purely decorative, like the exterior lighting at Providence. Except for the occasional far-flung security lamp, the countryside was pitch black.

"What's the plan?" I asked Dr. David.

"Plan?" He pronounced it *pwan*, which did not inspire confidence. "We're going to stop where Abra and Norman were last sighted: near the intersection of County Road H and an unmarked, unpaved lane two-tenths of a mile east of Uphill Road."

The exact spot where Leo had marked **NO!!!!** in red on my map.

"And then what?" I said breathlessly.

"We're going to get out of the ambulance and look for them."

TWENTY-THREE

ALTHOUGH I DIDN'T LIKE a thing about Dr. David's plan, I couldn't come up with a workable alternative. There was simply no way to catch a dog, let alone two of them, without leaving the vehicle.

"We're not splitting up, are we?" I said anxiously.

Dr. David frowned. "We don't have that kind of relationship."

"I mean, we're going to stick together as we look for the dogs. Right?"

"If we were doing this in daylight, I'd recommend fanning out," he said. "But in the dark, we'd better stay close."

Not to mention in the dark on a cursed property. Suddenly I had to know what he knew. Gag order or not, I needed to find out what Dr. David could tell me about Winimar. So I asked him.

"I heard about the place soon after I moved to town," he recalled. "Nobody wanted to talk about it, but everybody knew about it."

"Everybody except me! I just learned about Winimar *yesterday*!"

Dr. David said, "We hear only what we choose to hear. You're very good at denial."

"Thanks," I said, not sure he'd intended the remark as a compliment. "So what do you know?"

"The usual mix of rumors and legends. It's impossible to say what's real."

"But what do you think? Is the property really cursed? Why did three Schuyler women get their throats slit? Is it true that other people have died here, too? And are former Miss Blossoms doomed if they don't leave town?"

"In my opinion," the vet said, "there's no way to answer those questions, except maybe by reading the books Brady ordered. I'm on the waiting list, right after you."

We slowed, and Dr. David carefully guided the Animal Ambulance through a ninety-degree turn.

"This is County Road H," he said.

We held our collective breath as the odometer clicked off two-tenths of a mile. I scanned the north side of the road for an unpaved lane. A dense hedge of trees and shrubs loomed like a solid shadow wall.

"There it is!" Dr. David announced, applying the brake. He had rolled down his window and was playing his flashlight beam along the berm. I had to strain to see what he saw. The opening was barely wide or high enough to admit a charging Volkswagen Beetle.

"Can we pull in there?" I asked, even though I already knew the answer. Call me a cock-eyed optimist. Or, more accurately, a coward. I loathed the notion of leaving the safety of our vehicle for the vast and dark unknown.

In response, Dr. David parked the Animal Ambulance and handed me a Magnum flashlight. "Step around to the back. I'll get out the dogcatcher nets."

Frankly, I was grateful for the oversized butterfly net on the wobbly pole. Not that I expected it to prove useful. But its ridiculousness helped defuse my fear. I mean, how much evil could befall two people who were so naïve about the art of self-defense? Then I remembered that the Victorian-era Schuyler women had had their throats slit, and suddenly I couldn't swallow.

Though proud to brand myself a feminist, I demurely followed Dr. David down the narrow lane. The night was windless and faintly fragrant with the earth's fertile exhalations of early spring. Muted scuttles were the only woodland sound, probably mice or other equally small and harmless creatures. Or so I prayed. The vet and I swung our flashlight beams aimlessly, picking up nothing but tree trunks and branches. And more branches. After a few dozen yards, the path narrowed to less than half its width, trees pressing in on all sides. Gnarled black fingers clawed at our scalps and faces.

We didn't speak. I couldn't estimate how far or how long we continued that way—footfalls fast and light, breaths shallow. Our path seemed to curve endlessly, its twists and turns confusing my sense of distance and direction.

Then we both heard it: the far-off, piercing howl of either a wolf or a dog. Definitely not Abra. We froze simultaneously in mid-step.

The cry came again. Anguished.

Dr. David's light flickered out.

"David?" I inquired sharply.

"Over there," he hissed.

"Where? What is it?" My skin was suddenly clammy, the flashlight slippery in my grip.

I heard but didn't see him bolt, crashing off into the woods ahead and to my right.

And this is where it all went strange: the flashlight slid from my fingers and tumbled to the ground, its beam bouncing wildly, blindly. I dropped the dogcatcher's net and lurched forward, my only goal to recapture the rolling light. I stumbled, pounced upon it, fumbled for it, and finally seized it in both hands as if it were a live thing trying desperately to flee. Panting hard, I swung the beam toward David. Or where he ought to be. I tried two directions. Three. Then I spun in a complete and infinite circle. Around. And around again.

"David?!" I shrieked. "Where the hell are you?!"

There was no sound save the blasted insolent scraping of those tiny creatures of the night. I swept the forest as if spraying an invisible enemy with pure white light. My jerking beam illuminated trees. Skeletal and still, they offered nothing.

"DAVID!" I bellowed. "You said we wouldn't split up!"

The canine wail came again, louder and more plaintive. And then a second howl: Abra's. It was her cry for help, the voice she'd used the night Leo died.

I could see no one, neither man nor beast. But the dogs were close.

Dr. David Norman Newquist was as absent as if he'd never been here.

Abra barked again, sounding frantic, sounding precisely like I felt. If I could have made as much noise as she did, I would have, but I was hyperventilating, which ruled out howling. I got off one good scream, however.

My trick for fighting back panic was to ask myself out loud, "What's the reasonable thing to do next?"

The answer: *Follow David. Go the way you think he went. Move toward the dogs. Move toward Abra.*

I scanned the ground for the ridiculous dogcatcher's net. It was all I had besides my light. After scooping it up, I forced myself to stop and draw three deep, restorative breaths. Then I started off-trail toward the howls and yaps.

What if my light goes out? I wondered. And then wished I hadn't.

How would I find my way back to County Road H? I'd have to wait until dawn—assuming I could survive the night. Luckily, it was so early in the season that the woods hadn't yet leafed out. Winimar wasn't the tangled jungle it would become in another month. That thought consoled me; I refused to believe I could end up hopelessly disoriented, wandering in fatal circles like those foolish city kids in *The Blair Witch Project*.

I kept telling myself, *This is just a forest in Lanagan County, Michigan.*

And it was just a coincidence that Dr. David's flashlight had fizzled and he had vanished and now he refused to respond to my cries.

Oh sure …

The dogs turned silent at exactly the same instant I saw the light: ahead shone two small ovals of white like blank eyeballs staring back at me through the trees.

Windows, I thought. *Oh please let them be windows. Either that or Leo should have told me what he saw so I'd know how to save myself.*

He'd tried to "save" me by making sure I didn't find out what he knew about Winimar. And by marking a blood-red **NO!!!!** on the county map.

Of course, Leo couldn't have known then that he wouldn't be here to protect me now. When I needed him. What did he see at Winimar two years ago? I longed to believe it was only a coincidence that Leo died one year after that … when his aorta burst as he drove past this place—me in the seat beside him, Abra in the back.

TWENTY-FOUR

MY SKIN PRICKLING, I continued through the woods toward the two white ovals. Troubling new questions dawned: If those were indeed windows, who was on the other side? Did someone live here? How could there be electrical power on this estate? According to Wee Sweeney, the last Schuyler throat-slitting was in 1875, and no one, besides squatters, had resided at Winimar since.

Suddenly the ovals were gone. Blinked out. I had the completely irrational notion that the monster of the forest had gone to sleep or—more terrifying—was now playing possum. Then came the crash of running human footsteps somewhere to my left. Wildly, I zigzagged my flashlight.

"Whiskey! It's all right! I'm over here! Shine your light over here!"

I was never so glad to hear Rs and Ls confused with Ws.

"David!" I cried, willing the convulsions in my arm to stop so that I could focus the light on him. "What happened to you?"

He entered the path of my beam and jogged straight to me, panting hard.

"I'm all right. Let's get the hell out of here."

"But—what about Abra? And Norman?"

"We'll come back for them. In daylight."

"Maybe *you* will," I snapped. "I'm totally freaked out!"

"I know. I heard you scream."

"I saw eyes," I babbled. "Great big cat eyes with no irises! They were open and then they closed!"

Dr. David gently grasped my arm. "Let me take the flashlight. You can't hold it steady."

I gladly surrendered it along with all responsibility for saving our lives.

"Did you see the eyes?" I persisted.

Dr. David hadn't seen anything that looked like white eyes or windows. He said he tripped and tumbled into a shallow ravine. By the time he got back on his feet, I was screaming. He concentrated on following my voice.

"Why did you run off like that?" I demanded.

"I heard urgency in Norman's howl and went to assist. Then I heard your distress and turned back. Sorry if I frightened you, Whiskey. It's how I'm trained to respond."

I would have appreciated someone trained to stay by my side, but I didn't say so. Having him back was an immense relief.

"Can you get us out of here?" I said"

Dr. David shone the light on a compass he withdrew from his pocket. "I know it's rough walking, but if we keep going south, we'll get to County Road H."

And so we picked our way southward across the forest floor, dodging trees, shrubs, stumps, and fallen trunks. The muted skittering sounds continued. But there were no more howls.

"Why do you keep looking back?" Dr. David asked.

"For the eyes! I want you to see them, too. But they're closed now. I mean gone."

I could feel him studying me. "You know, Whiskey, extreme fright can cause hallucinations."

"I did not hallucinate! They were probably two lighted windows, not eyes. I know that!"

"So … you think someone's *living* here?" His tone implied that was preposterous.

"I think someone's here … probably in the old house, wherever that is … with some kind of light. That's all."

Dr. David said, "Didn't you know that the Schuyler mansion burned to the ground in 1903?"

"I don't know anything about Winimar! Haven't you figured that out?"

When he didn't answer, I asked a better question: "What do you think happened to Abra and Norman?"

"I'm concerned that Norman may be injured," he replied. "Abra sounded alarmed but unhurt."

She sounded, I thought, the way she did the night Leo died. As if trying to summon help. Both dogs had quieted suddenly. I asked Dr. David what their abrupt silence might mean.

"It could mean many things. They might have sensed a predator. Or moved beyond our range to hear them. Or been rendered unconscious—perhaps by a tranquilizer."

Or they could be dead.

I didn't say that out loud because I didn't want to hear it. Following the bouncing beam of light toward a nice public highway, I wanted to focus on hope, not doom. This was spring, after all. The season of renewal.

Why, oh why, was my life brimming with death and damnation?

When we finally stepped out onto a real road, the Animal Ambulance was nowhere in sight.

"Over there!" Dr. David said. His flashlight beam revealed the outline of a vehicle parked far to our right.

"You're sure that's yours?" I asked.

"There's nothing quite like it," he replied. "Except another ambulance."

So we hiked down the road. Fortunately, it was the ambulance we'd come in. And it didn't appear to have been tampered with. Even better, it started right up when Dr. David turned the key in the ignition. The time? Almost eleven. I suggested we keep the flasher off and take the long way home so as not to attract attention. I loathed the thought of explaining to late-night well-wishers that we had failed.

No one was waiting up for me at Vestige. My sprawling home stood empty—save for forty or so cats. Chester had planned to keep Prince Harry overnight, barring a puppy-pee-or-poop incident so severe that Cassina pitched him out. Apparently, that hadn't happened. Hooray for our side.

I paused in the kitchen to pour myself a very tall glass of Merlot. In fact, the glass I selected was designed to hold iced tea—about twelve ounces of it. After chugging half the wine while standing over the sink, I refilled the glass. Physically exhausted, I knew that my nerves were frayed to the point of flickering. A little more vino was just what I needed, not only to encourage sleep but also to distract me from the sour smell of cat litter wafting down my wide staircase. Grimly I considered that the messes of one recalcitrant puppy, though aggravating, were minor compared to the nonstop output of a herd of cats. Especially a herd of cats corralled two doors down from my own bedroom.

As I passed the barricaded doorway, I held my breath and willed myself not to glance inside. Still, I couldn't miss that devilish Devon dubbed Yoda. He was hanging from the screen by all four feet, his curved claws penetrating the mesh like small but lethal metal hooks. Despite his piteous yowls, I felt only revulsion. Safely inside my own room, I tried to lock the door. Fumbling with the latch, I remembered that it no longer closed properly. I needed to either make the time to fix it myself—*ha!*—or turn the problem over to my property manager, Luís. Another "to-do" for my endless mental list.

Exhausted, I inhaled the rest of the Merlot, splashed water on my face, yanked off my clothes, pulled on a cotton nightshirt, and collapsed into bed.

I dreamed that Nash Grant was lying next to me in the dark, silently stroking my right arm, and nuzzling my hair. After a moment, he began massaging my breasts, gently at first and then with an almost frenzied intensity. The dream was so vivid that I could feel his soft breath in my face as his tender hands slid my nightshirt up over my hips. He made an erotic sound, a low purr of pure pleasure. Something firm and insistent pressed against my welcoming groin. Something exactly the right shape and size …

Except that it was furry. I opened my eyes.

I had been mounted, but not by Nash Grant. In the dim light from my bathroom, I peered into the luminous yellow orbs of an overweight cat. The very same fatso that Nash had retrieved from the first floor after Faye's accident. He was kneading my breasts with obscene energy, eyes staring, jaws slack. A string of saliva dangled above my cleavage as his thick tail wedged itself between my legs.

"You can't even buy me dinner!" I roared, giving the obese feline the heave-ho. He screeched and scrambled for the partially open door. That damn Yoda must have let the troops out again. Tomorrow I would beg Deely to help me contain the criminals. And I would order Luís to fix my latch. For now I jammed a chair under the door knob and let the rest go.

Through the wall I heard noises coming from Avery's bedroom next door. Noises that could mean only two things:

First, I was not the only human in the house.

Second, Nash Grant really was having sex under my roof. But not with me.

TWENTY-FIVE

I awakened to shouts and curses in the hallway outside my room. Since it was still dark, I knew I didn't want to get up yet. That turned out not to be an option.

"Whiskey! Get out here now!" shrieked my stepdaughter. "Your damned cats are taking over the house!"

"They're not *my* cats, they're stray cats," I muttered, covering my head with two pillows. It didn't help. At that point, Avery must have flung open my unlockable door; not only did her singularly unpleasant voice grow louder, but a couple cats bounced onto my bed.

"Get up and do something!" Avery bellowed. "NOW!"

"Why can't we just ignore them till it's light out?" I mumbled, yanking my quilt over the two pillows that already covered my head. How I wished I were invisible. Or—better yet—in another country. Preferably one that banned cats.

Apparently, my hiding-under-the-covers routine royally pissed Avery off. She ripped the pillows and duvet from my bed, revealing a sight that chilled my blood. Besides the fact that she loomed above me, a wild-haired female Attila the Hun, Yoda was attached to her neck. He looked like a living gargoyle.

"Get this thing off me," Avery screamed, "before I kill somebody!"

I would have obliged. If I didn't, I assumed she'd whack me first. But the grotesque little cat chose that instant to bare his needle-sharp teeth, the sight of which sapped my strength.

"Hold on, sweetheart darling!" Nash Grant called from my bedroom doorway.

I knew he didn't mean me, but I was happy to hear from him all the same.

He darted in, performed some kind of fancy three-step maneuver, and—a moment later—was holding Yoda high overhead. Then he pitched the cat into the hall and barricaded the door with a bigger chair.

I almost cried, "My hero!" Miraculously, however, the part of my brain that sometimes controls insane outbursts was working, so I was spared complete humiliation.

But I couldn't stop staring at Nash's bright red bikini briefs, which strongly resembled a Speedo. Don't get me wrong. He was built well enough to carry it off. Still, seeing a man my age in my bedroom dressed like that and taking orders from Avery was too much to bear. I shot into my bathroom and bolted the door.

No cats. No stepdaughter. No Nash.

A sanctuary. It lasted almost a whole minute. Then Avery started pounding.

"You can't hide in there, Whiskey!" she shouted.

"Why not? The lock works!"

"It's not up to Nash and me to round up all these cats!"

"I didn't say it was. I didn't even say you could spend the night! So why don't you two get the hell out of here? And let a few of the felines follow you home!"

Nash said something *sotto voce* to Avery. I couldn't hear his comment, but I had no trouble catching what she said to me: "You're so jealous, it's pathetic. My man can't get enough of me. You can't even get a man!"

I had been standing with my back against the cool tile wall next to my shower. Now I let myself slide all the way down to the floor. Maybe if I kept perfectly quiet, she would eventually assume I was dead and leave me to rot.

I was able to make out Avery's and Nash's voices but not what they were saying. They seemed to be having an urgent private conversation. Maybe even a dispute. After a few moments, Avery loudly said, "Whiskey, since you can't talk civilly to me, I'm going to let Nash try reasoning with you."

She stomped out of my bedroom, slamming the non-latching door behind her. A moment passed. Then Nash cleared his throat.

"Y'all right in there, Whiskey?"

When I didn't immediately respond, he said, "Knock once for yes. Twice for no. Three times if you hate Avery."

I rapped thrice. He laughed, and I decided that he would sound warm and sexy even if I didn't know he was nearly naked.

"I'm sorry about all this," he said softly.

"All what?" I asked. "You didn't let the cats out, did you?"

"No. I'm sorry for staying the night at your house. It looks disrespectful, and that was not my intent."

Emboldened by the door between us, I said, "I assume your intent is to bed my stepdaughter as often as possible. It's your motivation I can't fathom. Where are the twins, by the way?"

"They're at my house, with Deely. She spent the night."

"And where's your new family-size minivan? If I'd seen it when I came in, I would have been spared the middle-of-the-night surprise. Well, one of them."

"Sorry. It's on the guest parking pad. By the side entrance."

"Of course."

Nash sighed. "Please believe me, Whiskey, when I tell you that I did not intend for this to happen."

"Boys will be boys," I quipped. "Give you an inch and—"

"It's not like that." Lowering his voice so that he was almost whispering, Nash said, "The truth is … I'm not really turned on by Avery."

At that point, I crawled across the cold bathroom tiles on my hands and knees just to press my ear to the keyhole.

He sighed, "It's complicated."

"More complicated than sex?"

"Much more. You see, my ex-wife left me … because I couldn't have children. She wouldn't consider adoption or alternate methods of fertilization."

She's an idiot, I thought. But I kept my mouth shut and my ear against the doorknob.

Nash went on, "I'm afraid I disappointed her. How I loved that woman. Her departure devastated me."

"Really?"

I tried to imagine Nash Grant devastated, but the image wouldn't come. Somehow he lacked sufficient depth for that emotion. Disappointment, sure. A brief bout of depression, maybe. But devastation? *Nah.*

"What does this have to do with Avery?" I asked.

"Isn't it obvious? Avery gave me babies! She proved I wasn't shooting blanks, after all. For that reason alone, I feel compelled to make her happy."

He's an idiot, I thought.

"You don't love her?" I asked cautiously.

A long silence ensued. I surmised that Nash was checking the hallway. Finally, he replied, "The truth is I don't even find her appealing. I can't tell you how much I wish another woman had borne my children. Any other woman. You, for instance. You could be quite attractive, Whiskey, if you fixed yourself up. Why, when I'm with Avery, I have to fantasize I'm with someone, *anyone*, else just to—"

"Okay!" I said, pushing myself into a standing position. "Tell you what, Nash. Why don't you go round up a couple dozen cats—or die trying? And then you and my unappealing stepdaughter can mosey on back to your place! I just realized that I've seen more than enough of you *both*. Now that you've moved the twins out of my house, I'd like to get on with my own life. Y'all take care now, ya hear?"

Silence from the other side. I timed it using my bathroom clock; Nash Grant needed an entire minute to formulate his lame response: "Whiskey! I never meant to offend you!"

"Offend me? You can't offend me because I don't give a damn! Move along, li'l doggie. And please—take your bitch with you."

"Did she just call me a *bitch*?" Avery was back. I had to admit the girl had timing.

"As a matter of fact, I did!" I shouted through the bathroom door. "Doesn't that make you mad? Don't you just want to get the hell out of here?"

Apparently, it did, and she did. Because they did. Without bothering to round up a single feline first. Oh well. I planned to enlist Deely's help. She'd be getting off nanny duty very soon.

TWENTY-SIX

I COULDN'T FALL BACK to sleep after the fracas with Nash and Avery—even though it was barely five AM when they made their noisy, self-righteous exit. I returned briefly to my bed, but Yoda and who knows how many of his cronies wouldn't stop scratching at my unlockable door. When the yowling and scrabbling became intolerable, I made the only choice I could: to meet them head-on rather than lie there awaiting the inevitable breach. I flung open my door armed with my best Screeching Avery imitation. It terrified them. Cats scattered in every direction. Even Yoda the Instigator disappeared down the hall.

Straining to ignore the now overpowering stench of soiled litter, I made my way to the kitchen for a cup of coffee. A moment after I snapped on the overhead light, my doorbell rang. The wall clock said 5:19. Who the hell visits at that hour?

A familiar yip instantly identified the callers. Forgoing the peephole, I opened my front door. Unfortunately, I forgot about the little matter of forty free-roaming cats. Not to mention the natural antipathy between felines and canines. In other words, I created chaos. Or—to be precise—Chester and Prince Harry's arrival did. Before I grasped what was happening, Abra's son had bounded upstairs after a herd of cats, and about a half-dozen frenzied felines had achieved liberation by charging out the front door. I slammed it after them. Then I counted fourteen cats clinging for their nine lives to my custom-made silk shantung draperies.

"I was walking Prince Harry and saw your light come on," Chester explained, gaping at the mewing multitude. "I didn't even know you liked cats!"

"I don't."

He considered that and offered this bit of advice: "Then maybe you should start with one or two."

It was probably the look of defeat on my face that inspired Chester to whip out his cell phone.

"Do you want me to call Deely?" he asked.

I nodded. He sent me to the shower, and I enjoyed a long hot one. When I emerged, a mug of steaming coffee was waiting on my bedside table. I practically inhaled it, gratefully recognizing Chester's unique brew. Following Cassina's latest world tour, he had learned to make her new favorite cardamom-spiked blend. I suspected that it was part of Chester's plan to convince her to let him keep Prince Harry. So far, it had earned the kid part-time ownership. Heaven knows I was rooting for him.

From down the hall came the unmistakable rasp and rattle of cat litter being cleaned, a sweet sound if ever I'd heard one.

"Whiskey?" Chester stood respectfully on the other side of my door.

"Yes?"

"Deely's here. Dr. David, too. Are you receiving visitors?"

Since I was still wrapped in my fleecy robe, I asked him to give me five minutes.

"You also have an appointment in Grand Rapids," my young neighbor reminded me.

Wee Sweeney at ten! I'd almost forgotten.

"How did you know about that?" I asked Chester.

"We all know," he replied. "But it's my job to remind you."

"Wait! It's Monday. Shouldn't you be at school?"

"It's 6:15, Whiskey. My driver doesn't leave until eight."

Then he slid a folded newspaper under my bedroom door and advised me to drink a little more coffee before I read it.

"Why?" I said. But he was gone. I followed directions, figuring Chester was usually right.

The weekly edition of the Magnet Springs *Magnet* featured this headline:

SHE'S AT IT AGAIN!!!!!

Next to the inch-tall type was a stock photo of Abra taken on the last day of her purse-snatching trial the previous August. Mandated to doggie counseling rather than jail—or euthanasia—and surrounded by curious tourists, she'd happily posed with a designer bag in her chops. Below the main headline, a boldface subhead read:

Local Realtor's Dog Steals Crown, Returns Crown, Steals it Again

I skipped the three-column article. My eyes had jumped to another photo, bisected by the page fold. This one was snapped Saturday by Fast Eddie Fresniak: Yours Truly giving Magnet Springs
the finger from the back of Faye's ambulance. The caption read:

Whiskey Mattimoe responds to reporter's questions.

Since the *Magnet* was a family-friendly newspaper, the third
digit of my right hand had been pixilated like the face of an under-
age criminal. Who were they kidding? Even young readers would
know I was flashing the universal sign of disrespect.

I steeled myself for a phone call from Odette, demanding to
know why I was hell-bent on sabotaging our profits. The least I
could do was show contrition by wearing one of her camisoles.
But the first was still in my laundry hamper, and the second should
have been; it was blood-stained from cat scratches.

"Ma'am?" Deely waited outside my unlatched door.

"I'll be right there," I called, tossing the *Magnet* onto my un-
made bed.

"I brought you something," she said.

"I already saw the paper …"

"No, ma'am. This is something to wear."

She slid a flat brown-paper bag under my door and retreated.
Inside was a new black camisole.

"Thank you!" I called after her, uncertainly. Why would the
Coast Guard care about improving my sex appeal? When I emerged
from my lair a few minutes later, I found Deely wearing an identical
camisole.

"You inspired me," she whispered as we passed in the hall. Toting two industrial-size bags of cat litter, she must have had a bit of dust or dander in her eye; either that, or … she winked.

I trotted downstairs just as Dr. David came through the front door carrying two kicking cats under each arm.

"NO MORE CATS!" I cried.

"These aren't 'more' cats; they're the cats that got away—when you let Chester in this morning," he panted. Passing me en route to the Cat Room, he asked, "You're wearing a camisole on our mission to Winimar?"

"I'm wearing a camisole for my appointment with Wee Sweeney at ten. Hey, it couldn't hurt."

When he didn't reply, I called over my shoulder, "I know you know I'm going to Grand Rapids! Everybody does!"

"But everybody doesn't care the way I do," Chester chimed in, refilling my coffee mug. "Would you like English muffins or toast with your eggs this morning?"

"Since when do I have food in my house?" I asked.

"Since I brought some from the Castle. I cooked breakfast for Cassina. I'm trying to soften her up."

He nodded meaningfully toward Prince Harry, who zipped past us in the wake of two cats.

"Good plan. How goes the housebreaking?"

Chester shrugged. "Cassina liked the breakfast."

I found it hard to believe that his musician mother would be up at this hour. He explained that she and Rupert sometimes enjoyed a plate of eggs on their way to bed, which was usually just before sunrise.

"Rupert takes his over easy," Chester said, "but Cassina likes hers scrambled with cheese."

I didn't usually eat breakfast, not because I was on my way to bed at that hour, but because I rarely kept anything edible on hand. While I was showering, Chester had made two trips back to the Castle and returned with enough food for Deely, Dr. David, and me.

"We're going to need our strength," the vet said as he helped himself to a third blueberry bagel. I noticed that he and Deely refused Chester's tastily prepared eggs. Probably a Flegger policy: "Don't eat anything an animal gave up unless you're sure that animal had an attorney-negotiated contract."

Chester was intrigued by Dr. David's appetite.

"Big day at the clinic?" he asked.

"Something like that." Dr. David cast me an ominous glance. I gathered that he didn't want to discuss what had happened last night. Fine by me. I preferred not to contemplate those big white eyes again, either. At least not until the sun was up.

"How soon do you want to get started?" I asked.

"How soon can you put something on over that camisole?"

April mornings in Michigan are brisk, though full of promise. Dressing in layers is the key. Over the camisole I pulled on a couple sweaters of varying thickness; I also wore jeans and hiking boots. For the quick pre-Grand Rapids change, I grabbed a tweed skirt and matching jacket as well as clean tights and semi-dressy boots. Today I would put Odette's theory to the test: that a black camisole works anytime, anywhere.

Miraculously I had remembered to recharge my cell phone last night. Now, as I slipped it into my leather shoulder bag, it buzzed.

"Good morning, Whiskey. I'm sorry to call so early."

Judge Wells Verbelow was on the line. I winced, guessing that he had read this morning's edition of the *Magnet*.

"About that photo," I began. "I didn't mean to give everyone the finger. Just Fast Eddie."

Wells chuckled. "That's not why I'm calling. I heard that Abra and a Golden were seen near Winimar last night, but they eluded you and Dr. David."

Apparently all my personal failures were public knowledge.

The judge continued, "If you're going back out this morning, I'd like to lend you Mooney. He has a knack for finding Abra."

I pointed out that he had found her once and failed to find her once.

"Batting .500 is an impressive average," Wells declared. "Especially where your dog's concerned."

True enough. I was deep into a no-hitter myself.

TWENTY-SEVEN

I TURNED MY PHONE over to Dr. David so that he could speak to Wells about Mooney. When he finished, I wondered aloud how the judge had known we were heading back to Winimar.

"He talked to Jenx," the vet said. "It's Flegger policy to keep local law enforcement informed. So I told the chief what we were doing, and she told the judge."

Dr. David made it sound so straightforward. Yet Jenx didn't want to listen to anything I said. I'd supplied reports about Brandi's temper tantrum, Dock's dented truck, Faye's antique hair jewelry, and Tammi's involvement with Abra and the crown. Still, the chief seemed more interested in what everybody else had to say, especially a certain sausage vendor. I wondered if Vito Botafogo had remembered anything important. And if he liked the roses I'd sent.

Again I rode in the Animal Ambulance as Dr. David steered it toward Winimar. Driving into the glare of the rising sun, our mission seemed less dramatic than it had the night before. We just needed to get the job done. Once again, the vet turned his flasher on as we passed through town. Clumps of kids en route to school chanted, "Get Abra! Get Abra!" Last night they had sounded like a cheering section. This morning they reminded me of a lynch mob.

We parked along County Road H near the narrow opening through which we had started last night. Wells Verbelow and his Rott Hound were waiting for us. Upon Dr. David's advice, I'd brought along Abra's favorite pillow, which Mooney sniffed longingly before we started. Although we pretended not to notice, Abra's scent sexually aroused the Rott Hound. It was an awkward moment. Being a professional, however, Mooney quickly calmed himself and began the work at hand—or paw. Wells shook my hand, wished me luck and promised to phone me later. I thought I detected subtle signs of sexual interest on his part, too. Toward me, I mean. We'd attempted courtship many months earlier, and I'd felt no chemistry. But with the camisole, who knew? It might be a whole different story.

Dr. David had brought along those ridiculous dogcatcher nets. When he held out mine, I didn't take it.

"I'm electing to let Mooney do the work of my net," I said.

The vet was not pleased. I wasn't in such a great mood myself. Frankly, I didn't even know if I wanted Abra back. What if she'd permanently chosen a life of crime? Her reputation could ruin Mattimoe Realty.

Such was my mood when I followed Mooney and Dr. David through the woodsy portal into Winimar. Although the sun was tickling the horizon, we stepped into midnight darkness. I paused, disoriented. Despite the still-leafless flora, the dense latticework of branches above and around us obliterated most light. I had the brief but disturbing sensation that Winimar could entrap me.

Shuddering, I gave thanks for my multiple sweaters since shadows also preserve chill. My hiking boots were a wise choice, too; the dewy ground was spongier underfoot than I remembered from last night.

Unlike me, Mooney seemed instantly invigorated by his new surroundings. Drool flying from his flapping jowls, he accelerated to a jog and, seconds later, veered off the trail. Dr. David trundled after him, his dogcatcher's net snagging on twigs and trunks.

"He's going the wrong way!" I called out, gamely bringing up the rear.

When the vet scowled at me over his shoulder, I tried again: "This isn't the direction the dog sounds were coming from last night!"

"It's Mooney's show now," Dr. David panted. "He's a professional tracker. You're just a realtor."

What the hell was I doing here? Then I remembered that I'd intended to check the place out before agreeing to list it. Better that I had company—even this company—than that I was here alone.

Suddenly a cloud enveloped us. Actually, it was a blanket—a dense, wet, suffocating quilt of fog rolling in from Lake Michigan. The blinding, muffling stuff of a coastal spring.

I couldn't see Mooney at all. Dr. David, just a few yards ahead of me in his bright yellow FLEGGERS RESCUE jacket, was almost invisible, too.

"David!" I cried out.

"Right here, Whiskey!" he called back. "Stay with me! I think Mooney's onto something!"

But I couldn't see either of them at all.

"Keep talking! Please! So I can follow your voice!"

Neither of them made another sound.

I halted, sure that I'd crash into something if I didn't. Cautiously, I extended my arms, groping the nothingness. Fog obliterated even my own hands. I inched forward, reminding myself to breathe and call. *Breathe and call.*

Nobody answered. But I nearly lost an eye on a branch I didn't see coming.

My boots, also out of view, made squelching sounds in the gooey, gluey terrain. This was not the route we'd taken last night. Baited by the howling dogs, we'd veered *right* off the trail. Today Mooney had bolted *left*, toward Lake Michigan. Or so I thought. We'd meandered a bit before I lost contact with man and dog, but I believed—perhaps wrongly—that I was still headed west. Dr. David was the only member of our party carrying a compass. I might as well have been blindfolded.

Then I remembered: Although I didn't have a compass, I did have a cell phone in my pocket. Fully charged.

I fumbled for it, realizing only then how hard I was shaking. Through the mist, the small screen glowed indistinctly. Good enough! I didn't need to see in order to speed-dial Dr. David.

But I did need a signal. There was none. Like the would-be elevator passenger who doesn't want to believe the out-of-order sign, I punched every button repeatedly. Nothing. This was a dead zone.

I tried to think positive. The good thing about fog is that it's temporary. Even the densest stuff burns off as the sun climbs the sky. My question was … what if sunlight couldn't penetrate this place?

I resumed calling Dr. David's name and inching forward. If I concentrated, I believed that I could continue moving in the same essential direction (westward?). Of course, I had no way of knowing if that was the way the vet and Mooney were still going. If they were still going anywhere.

When I paused, I became aware of profound stillness. It was a spring morning, after all. There should have been bird songs and faint rustles of chipmunks foraging for food. Like my confusion, the silence was total. And terrifying.

Until I heard the howl.

TWENTY-EIGHT

I KNEW THAT BALEFUL, guaranteed-to-raise-the-hair-on-your-neck *basso profundo* moan. It belonged to Mooney, the Rott Hound. He had the lung power to push out the loudest sound and keep it hanging in the air until everyone listening desperately wished he would shush.

Trying to determine where he was howling from, I turned in a slow circle. His sound was everywhere and nowhere; it filled the fog.

My cell phone buzzed, and I literally jumped. Whereas moments earlier I'd had no signal, suddenly I had a real live caller. The fog was too thick, the light too low for me to read the incoming number. No matter; I would have been thrilled to make contact with anyone. Even Avery.

"Hello!" I shouted.

"Whiskey! It's David! Where are you?"

"Lost in the fog! Where are you?"

"I'm with Mooney. We've found … something."

Either the damp air had finally penetrated my clothes, or I was coated in a cold sweat. I shivered uncontrollably.

"Abra?"

"No," Dr. David said. "Not a dog."

"Oh God. You mean ... a person?"

"A lawyer. Kevin Sweeney."

"Here?" My brain somersaulted. "But I have an appointment with him at ten o'clock—in Grand Rapids!"

"Not anymore you don't."

"You mean he's—?" I couldn't bring myself to say the D-word.

"He's down a well shaft, crying for help. I think he's badly hurt."

"But not dead, right?"

"Not dead yet." Dr. David sounded exceedingly grim. "Mooney found him. I called an ambulance, but it won't be easy for the paramedics to reach us. They're going to try to follow Mooney's howl."

"I'm trying, too! I think you're somewhere to my right—"

"Whiskey, listen to me!" Dr. David had to shout to be heard over the Rott Hound. "If there's one abandoned well shaft, there could be more. Walk very carefully!"

"You think Wee Sweeney just happened to be here at Winimar and fell in a hole?" I asked.

"I don't know what to think. He seems to be going in and out of consciousness. I can't see him down the shaft, but he was able to tell me his name."

"How long till the EMTs get here?" I asked, choosing a direction and stepping gingerly.

"Hard to say. Apparently, we're the only ones still fogged in."

Why did that not surprise me?

Except for three brief interruptions when he put me on hold to take calls from Jenx and the paramedics, Dr. David stayed on the line. Within minutes and with deep relief, I heard the approaching sirens.

Mooney, the sound guide, never let up. His howls, which increased in volume and spookiness as I drew near, gave me a thumping headache. Still, I desperately needed his audio beacon, as did Sweeney's rescue crews.

I was close to Howling Ground Zero when something caught the corner of my eye. By now the fog had thinned to broken streams of haze, most of which hung about chest high. To my left, back among the denser trees, I thought I glimpsed a figure. Tall and straight, she stood in profile, her hair glinting gold-brown against the morning gray. She was there; then she was gone. But I was half-sure I'd seen a woman.

"Hello!" I called. Mooney's deafening howls drowned my greeting. I tried again. No response. And she did not reappear. My brief desire to follow her vanished in the next puff of mist.

Jenx had arrived with the sheriff's deputy I'd met last night. The guy jumped when I emerged from a fog bank in front of him.

"Sorry," I said. "Didn't mean to scare you."

His eyes darted wildly around. "Is your dog here, too?"

"Just Mooney. As far as we know."

The deputy asked Jenx if we could turn Mooney off now that everyone was in place. The Chief looked to me for assistance. I couldn't help, having left my handy wallet-sized Dogs-Train-You-dot-com Guard Dog Commands Card in my purse. Fortunately, Dr. David pronounced the magic word: "ENOUGH!"

Mooney promptly shut it. And the fog faded.

The ensuing silence was deafening. We all stared at a ragged, partially overgrown hole, approximately four feet in diameter.

"Kevin Sweeney!" a firefighter shouted into the depths. "Can you hear me?"

No reply. He called again. From very far below our feet came an unintelligible moan.

The fireman brightened. "That's good, Kevin! My name's Tim, and I'm here with a bunch of other folks. We're going to get you out!"

Mooney woofed his support.

I watched, fascinated, as the rescue experts did what only they could do. Using cables, a harness, and a complicated winch, they lowered Fireman Tim out of sight. Someone aimed a large spotlight into the abyss.

Minutes ticked by as the cable continued to roll. How deep was the shaft? How badly hurt was the attorney?

When my eyes met Jenx's, I saw two more of my own questions reflected there: (1) What had brought Sweeney to Winimar? and (2) Was his fate part of the curse?

While we waited for answers to those and other mysteries, Dr. David sidled up to me. "I don't want to worry you, Whiskey, but Mooney found something else of interest."

He held out his hand, palm up. In it lay Abra's broken rhinestone collar. So help me, I fought back tears.

"You think she's … dead?" I asked.

The vet seemed surprised. "To the contrary, Mooney and I believe she left this as a clue for us."

I turned to the Rott Hound, who—I swear—was studying my reaction.

"*Rrrrrhhhnnngg*," he gurgled insistently, whipping his intimidating tail back and forth as if to affirm Dr. David's interpretation.

"But how did she remove her own collar?" I said. Mooney seized the dog necklace in his juicy jaws and began rubbing it against the spiky, desiccated root ball of a fallen tree.

"He's demonstrating how she broke the clasp," Dr. David explained. "Notice how near this was to where Sweeney fell."

"You think ... she pushed him?" I asked, accepting with horror that my dog was not only a jewel thief but a would-be killer.

"No!" The vet gave me a disapproving glare. Mooney joined in with a low growl. "We think she was trying to save him, possibly with Norman's assistance."

Jenx, who had been listening, chimed in. "Abra may be a material witness to an attempted murder. One more reason to bring her in."

"But where is she?" I said. "And why, if she's innocent, does she keep running?"

"You said yourself she's in love," Jenx replied. "Or we could go with the Tammi LePadanni Corruption Theory ..."

"Finally! You're listening to me!"

"Let's just say we're keeping an open mind. Some of what you've said jibes with Vito's observations."

The sausage vendor again. "Why would Vito Botafogo know more than I know?"

"Maybe, for starters, because he's been selling sausages at every Miss Blossom crowning since 1929. Vito's seen a few things ..."

"But can he remember any of it?"

"They're coming up!" announced one of the firefighters. "Stand clear of the opening!"

All but the most essential personnel took two giant steps backward. I didn't breathe again until Fireman Tim's head inched up over the edge of the hole. Harnessed to him on something that looked like a cross between a sling and a hammock was a limp figure. Though covered in mucky slime, it appeared to be wearing a three-piece suit.

"That's Wee Sweeney, all right," muttered Jenx, moving off to consult with the firefighters.

"Uh—Ms. Mattimoe?" The uneasy sheriff's deputy stood before me. "Mind if I ask you a few questions?"

"Should I have a lawyer present?" I said.

He laughed as if he'd never heard that one. "Why would you need a lawyer? Dr. Newquist mentioned that you saw something odd out here last night. Could you describe it for me?"

I glanced at the vet, who nodded his encouragement.

"You're going to think I'm nuts," I began.

The deputy shrugged as if to say he was already on board that bus. I told him about the two white ovals that looked like giant glowing eyes and how they'd suddenly blinked out. Oddly, he didn't seem surprised. At all. In fact, he grinned and nodded as if enjoying my account.

"You think that's funny?" I asked, too tired to be anything but annoyed.

"No way." He cleared his throat and pointed past my shoulder. "I think your 'eyes' are over there."

TWENTY-NINE

I LOOKED WHERE THE deputy was looking. As if on cue, the last gauzy remnants of fog rolled back like a theater curtain, revealing a small wood structure a couple hundred feet away. About the size of an enclosed gazebo, the forlorn building stood clear of all trees, its sagging roof a lopsided hairline. There was no door on the side facing us. But high on the wall were two oval windows.

My legs buckled.

"Easy!" Dr. David said, grabbing my right elbow so that only my left knee went all the way down to the ground.

"What is it?" I said.

"Probably a bathhouse," replied the deputy. He pointed to a broad, leaf-filled hollow to the right of the structure. A row of trees lined one edge. "Used to be a shallow pond there, I think. Years ago, it might have been a halfway decent swimming hole."

"That must be where I fell last night!" Dr. David exclaimed. "Only I came at it from the other side."

Suddenly I understood how he could have tumbled through the trees without seeing my white "eyes."

The vet added, "We were this close to the well shaft and yet we missed Sweeney."

I was grateful we'd missed falling down the hole.

To the deputy I said, "Could the bathhouse have electricity? I'm sure there were lights on in there last night."

He frowned in that way people do when they're trying not to laugh. Then he motioned for us to walk with him.

I said, "You've been inside it already?"

"No …"

From his breast pocket he withdrew two papers folded together and passed them to me.

Opening them, I saw at once that the first page was the cover sheet of a fax—from none other than part-time Magnet Springs Police Officer Brady Swancott. Time-stamped earlier that morning, the message read:

> I'm faxing a map of Winimar downloaded from the Internet. Can't verify its validity, but it may be part of the book-in-progress about the estate. More info ASAP. Proceed with caution.
>
> —B.S.

Fleetingly I thought that Brady's initials could undermine his credibility—if one didn't know him. My personal experiences with the cop-slash-grad student had all been positive, however. I slowed to study the second page. Then I stopped.

"What is it, Whiskey?" Dr. David said. When I didn't answer, he walked back to where I stood and read what I was reading. The deputy, whose name I'd finally learned was Clifton, waited while we took it all in.

To call the page a map was a gross exaggeration. At best, it was a crude hand-drawn picture with many notes penned in a cramped and nearly illegible hand. Dr. David indicated a small square near the lower right corner labeled BATHHOUSE. Next to it was an arrow and a cartoon-type bubble in which someone had scribbled something. We both squinted, uncomprehending, at the message. The deputy rejoined us.

"'I tried to work here,'" he translated. "'Until she came for me.'"

I shuddered with a profound chill that had nothing to do with the damp April morning.

"Who's … 'she'?" I asked.

Deputy Clifton pointed to a stick figure wearing what appeared to be a long skirt. The figure had no label, only a question mark.

I inhaled deeply to steady myself. This was not a map; no legend, no distance scale. Not even a title or date. More than likely, this was an online hoax or game, the work of an over-imaginative, under-employed teen.

The figure had been placed not far from the spot labeled BATHHOUSE. Probably not far, also, from the spot where, earlier this morning, I'd glimpsed what I thought was a woman.

Had she come for Wee Sweeney? Had she come for us?

I opened my mouth but didn't know what to say.

"Did you see something else around here?" the deputy asked me.

I nodded once.

"A woman?" he guessed. "Like on the map?"

"Maybe …"

Dr. David's turquoise eyes grew round. "Where? When?"

I motioned vaguely behind us. "When I was following Mooney's howl through the fog … for just a second … I thought I saw someone. But she was gone before I could even blink, and she didn't answer when I called out. It was probably just a tree."

The men said nothing.

"Yup," I sighed. "She was a tree."

We all stared at the paper that wasn't a map. Specifically, at the cartoon bubble next to BATHHOUSE. The longer I studied it, the clearer the cramped writing became. I shifted the page, trying to find decent light.

"'Beauty ends—'"

"What did you say?" Jenx tramped up behind us, her heavy boots stirring dead leaves. Mooney accompanied her; though drooling, he looked very alert.

I repeated myself. The chief stared.

"What's the matter?" I asked.

"You brought me that yesterday," she said.

I thought she meant the paper. "This is from Brady. Today."

"No, those words. They were on the note Faye got at the hospital. With the hair jewelry."

She was right. Mrs. Slocum Schuyler's note about the *memento mori*. Remember-to-die jewelry.

I deciphered the rest of the scribble: "'Beauty ends. Vengeance is never satisfied.'"

"Is she going to faint?" I heard the deputy say. I didn't know who he was asking, but I knew he meant me. I couldn't answer because I was concentrating on not dropping the paper. Or dropping over.

Jenx said, "Better faint than puke. But I don't think she'll do either. Breathe, Whiskey!"

I did. And then I breathed again. Mooney offered his sturdy tail as a handrail in case I needed one. But I didn't. After a moment, all was well, or at least I was still vertical.

"I'm good," I said.

The deputy looked doubtful.

"How about you sit here on this dog while we go see about the presumed bathhouse," he said.

"Are you nuts?!" I cried. It felt good to be the person saying that for a change. "I'm not staying behind!"

"Mooney will protect you," Jenx said. Low in his throat, the Rott Hound made a reassuring sound and assumed bench position. The "bench" looked solid enough, although one end leaked.

"What's the matter?" said the deputy, his eyes twinkling. "Afraid she'll come for you?"

He and the others walked away. Instead of answering, I scurried after them, Mooney right by my side.

THIRTY

Catching up to Jenx, I said, "How bad is Sweeney hurt?"

"He's unconscious, and the EMTs think he lost a lot of blood," she replied.

"Blood?" I blanched. "Falling down the well?"

"Who said he fell? More like he was dumped. After he was stabbed."

"Somebody stabbed Kevin Sweeney?"

"You're a little slow today, aren't you?" the chief observed.

"You mean she's not usually like this?" said Deputy Clifton. He and Dr. David were yards ahead of us, halfway to the presumed bathhouse already. The deputy's self-confidence seemed to be mushrooming. At my expense.

Jenx said, "About that woman you told the deputy you saw . . ."

"Could have been a tree," I reminded her. "Probably was a tree."

"Let's say it was a woman. Just for the hell of it. If it was a woman, what color hair did she have?"

"Blonde. Or brown. Probably, though, she was a tree."

"How tall was she? This tree-woman?"

"Hard to say at that distance, in the fog. Maybe … about my height."

"Pretty short for a tree," Jenx said.

"Pretty tall for a woman," I said.

"It works for you," Jenx said.

Silence reigned during the rest of our short walk to the bathhouse. I can only speak for myself, but I couldn't have uttered a word if I'd wanted to. The building held me in thrall. Though ordinary enough, I suppose, for a broken-down bathhouse on a reputedly cursed estate, there was something eerie about the place. Foreboding, even.

And there was something else, which I spotted at the same instant Mooney broke into a howl: a human leg. A foot and a calf, to be accurate. The partial leg lay on the ground at the corner of the presumed bathhouse, sticking out from the other side. I immediately chose to believe that there was an intact and living body still attached. I had to believe that or … barf *and* faint.

The foot was wearing a well-worn hiking boot. Man-sized. The calf was clad in denim, as in jeans. Faded, lightly frayed, tight-fitting jeans.

I stepped aside to let law enforcement do whatever they wanted. My real estate license wasn't relevant here.

Dr. David turned to me. "Recognize that foot?"

"Should I?"

He shrugged. "I was just wondering."

We both stayed back a respectful distance; Mooney did the same, even though he was trained to be of some help. I concluded that he was waiting for a specific command or, at the very least, an invitation. Ditto Dr. David. I knew he wasn't hesitating because he was squeamish; after all, he was a vet. If we'd found a paw instead of a booted foot, no doubt he would have rushed right in.

The deputy placed a call for paramedics. Then Jenx reappeared, moving briskly toward us.

"He's alive," she announced.

"Is he anyone we know?" I asked.

"Not in person."

"What does that mean?"

She pulled a small, well-worn paperback from her hip pocket and passed it to me. I'd seen this book once before, or another copy of it. My part-time handyman Roy Vickers had been carrying one the day he applied for work at my office, straight after being sprung from jail.

I read aloud: "*Seven Suns of Solace: Finding Peace in Your Personal Galaxy*. By Fenton Flagg, Ph.D."

"Turn it over," the chief said.

On the back was a close-up color photograph of a ruggedly handsome middle-aged man. He appeared to be wearing a denim shirt.

"That's the rest of him," Jenx said.

"What do you mean?"

"The guy on the ground over there. I'm pretty sure it's Fenton Flagg."

"Was he carrying the book as ID?"

"This is my book. Hen's making me read it."

Of course. In addition to her massage therapy practice, Noonan worked as a certified Seven Suns of Solace tele-counselor, so called because she conducted most of her business over the phone. Tourists who stopped in for a massage and loved her touchy-feely advice kept calling back to hear more. With the meter running.

I'd managed to steer clear of that whole seven-steps-to-self-actualization claptrap, but you'd be amazed how many locals hadn't. Henrietta Roca, Jenx's partner, for one. Peg Goh, our acting mayor, for another. And then there was Avery. As much as I would have liked to finger her as Noonan's single glaring failure, I had to admit that all improvement is relative. Even Avery's life was better than it used to be.

"Fenton Flagg is *here*?" I asked.

"He's right over there," Jenx assented. "At least the guy on the ground looks like him."

"Why is the guy on the ground?" asked Dr. David.

Jenx shrugged. Then she had an idea. "You got medical training. Maybe you should take a look at him."

The vet hesitated.

"Worried about liability?" I wondered.

Dr. David shook his head. "It's been a long time since I studied human anatomy. I was trying to remember how it works."

Apparently, it came back to him because he examined the guy on the ground and announced that he seemed to be suffering from DKA.

I'd heard of DKNY, which had something to do with fashion.

"What's DKA?" I asked.

"Diabetic ketoacidosis."

I knew that couldn't be good. "Are you sure? Humans aren't your specialty."

"The symptoms aren't that different in animals: fruity breath, vomiting, unconsciousness."

"What causes it?" I said.

"Severe insulin deficiency. Mr. Flagg—or whoever that is—is in a diabetic coma."

Fortunately, the EMTs found us faster this time, and we didn't need to wait for firefighters to pull anyone out of a well. I stayed clear of the medical action, killing time by playing with my cell phone. Oddly or not (we were at Winimar, after all), even when I stood in one place, sometimes I had cellular service, and sometimes I didn't. My signal strength went from five bars to dead zone and back again, seemingly at random. Spooky.

As I messed with my phone, it buzzed. Caller ID said Chester was on the line. I made up my mind to sound cheerful. No sense scaring the kid.

"Whiskey!" he exclaimed. "Are you all right?"

"Just peachy, Chester. How about you?" My voice couldn't have been chirpier. Or faker.

"I'm fine. I went to school, but I've been listening to my portable police scanner. Sounds like a lot of trouble going on where you are."

"I'm at the office, Chester," I lied brightly.

"No, you're not, and I wish you wouldn't try to deceive me. I know you and Dr. David went to Winimar."

"Did Deely tell you?" I demanded.

"She didn't have to. Everybody in town knows you guys are trying to catch Abra and her boyfriend. When your cell phone stopped working, I got worried."

"Pish posh!" I said, unable to imagine where that phrase had sprung from. "Dr. David and I are having a wonderful morning."

"Really?" Chester's tone was suspicious. "Are you drunk?"

Chester knew what drunk sounded like. I'd seen his mother in that state even though she, her son, and her handlers vigorously insisted that she imbibed only Tahitian shark fin tea.

"Of course I'm not! Just getting a lot of fresh air." I inhaled noisily for his benefit and regretted it. Traces of Fenton Flagg's vomit hung in the air. "It's a beautiful morning in Michigan!"

"Since when does that matter to you?" Chester asked.

"The point is I'm fine! Sober, too. Go back to class—or whatever it is you do at that fancy academy."

Chester had shared some strange stories regarding what passed for "individualized instruction." Portable police scanners might well have been part of the curriculum.

"You should call Faye," Chester said. "She's in the hospital, you know. And she's got that curse on her head."

A cold wave of guilt nearly knocked me over. In the background, on Chester's end, someone was speaking a foreign language.

"Is that your teacher?" I asked, eager to change the subject.

"It's my personal assistant," he said. "She's serving my mid-morning snack."

I promised that I'd call Faye immediately—provided the curse didn't kill my phone first. Chester and I had barely said good-bye before Faye called me. That was a tad awkward given that I was her temporary guardian, and she had fallen over my banister trying to round up cats that I was responsible for. Really, when you thought about it, the girl had every right to expect *me* to check on *her*.

Yet she sounded her usual sunny, mature self.

"Whiskey? Are you all right?"

Funny, that was exactly how Chester had opened his call.

"I'm fine," I said. "Let's talk about *you*!"

"But you're at Winimar! Somebody out there called for *two* ambulances and lots of backup!"

"Do you have a police scanner, too?"

"No," Faye said. "But I'm surrounded by nurses, and they always know what's up."

I'd read somewhere that it's bad form—or is it bad luck?—to talk to sick people about other sick people, so I refused to have that kind of conversation. Instead, I adroitly turned the topic around to focus on Faye.

"What's new with you and your injuries?" I said gaily.

"Interesting you should ask. The attending physician referred me to an orthopedic surgeon. Guess who?"

"You don't mean … Brandi's dad?"

"Yes!" Faye chirped.

"I'm on my way over—just as soon as I can find a path out of here! Don't let Dr. LePadanni come near you!"

"Not a problem," Faye replied. "He never showed up for work today. And he's not answering his calls or pages."

THIRTY-ONE

FAYE EXPLAINED THAT SHE had been assigned another orthopod. I heaved a sigh of relief. It was about time that poor girl got a break—as in better fortune, not bones. Although I wanted to believe that the hospital was the safest place for her, common sense and personal experience suggested otherwise. I told her I'd be there by noon; it was now almost 9:40.

Mentally I replayed the weird scene I'd witnessed at Providence on Saturday night: Brandi LePadanni angrily smashing her rose bouquet as her father blandly looked on. Then someone had come and gone, leaving the entire estate in darkness, the pit bulls barking frantically inside. Now, thirty-six hours later, the esteemed surgeon was MIA. I had learned a few things in the meantime: that both Tammi and Brandi were having sex with Dock Paladino, and just hours before my visit to Providence, Tammi had taken Abra and her stolen crown for a ride.

The second team of paramedics worked furiously on the man who might be Fenton Flagg, Ph.D. Placed on a backboard, he was attached to various tubes and apparatuses, and then carefully carried through the woods to the rescue vehicle waiting on County Road H. So far this morning, we'd had two calls for that kind of ambulance and no need for Dr. David's.

"What do you think happened to Abra and Norman?" I asked the vet.

"Check this out!" Jenx interrupted. "Norman was here, all right!"

She waved us over to the bathhouse. Mooney followed in a slight zigzag, his broad wet snout to the ground.

As we approached, the sweet-sour stink of sickness grew stronger, an ominous overlay on the musty morning air. I noticed that Deputy Clifton had wandered off a ways and seemed to be studying the trees.

To my surprise, the far side of the structure was not completely enclosed. The bathhouse was actually a modified gazebo partitioned into an open area and a sealed-off room.

"There," Jenx said, pointing into the shadows. I stepped uncertainly in the direction she'd indicated.

"Just look. Don't enter!" the chief barked.

I stopped abruptly, squinting into the shadows. Inside the open-air portion of the bathhouse, tucked into a gloomy corner, was a large low-sided bowl—unmistakably a dog dish. Empty.

"What makes you think it belongs to Norman, the missing Golden?" I asked.

With the steel toe of her boot, Jenx adroitly spun the bowl so that we could see its other side where *Norman* was lettered in a fancy script.

"He couldn't live here," I mused.

"Nope. He probably lives with Fenton Flagg," Jenx said. "That was the guy on the ground, all right. We recovered his ID."

"And where does Fenton Flagg live?"

"According to his driver's license—Wimberley, Texas. But we have reason to believe he's been working here."

"Here? As in … Winimar? You mean—"

"Yup. I think Flagg's writing the book on it. The latest book."

"How do you know?"

"Well, he's a New Age writer," Jenx said. "And Brady's seen his name mentioned online as an authority on cursed properties."

I scanned the bathhouse. Aside from the dog bowl, the only other signs of human occupation were a battered leather shoulder bag, partially unzipped, and the largest Coleman lantern I'd ever seen. Those items were on a narrow built-in plank bench, attached to an inside wall. My eyes slid to the interior door. Though ancient and weatherworn with a heavily tarnished brass latch, it sported a shiny new combination lock.

"Did Fenton Flagg happen to be carrying the combination?" I asked Jenx.

"Not on him. But I haven't searched the shoulder bag. The deputy insists we wait for the state boys." She spoke that last part through clenched teeth. Jenx hates working with the state boys, a.k.a., the Michigan state police. Although their equipment and training are top-grade, they tend to abide by a strict protocol. In other words, when they come in, Jenx is out.

"Look at this," Dr. David said. A few yards off, he was bent at the waist, his back turned to us.

Jenx and I went to see what he saw. On the ground at Dr. David's feet lay a blue leather leash.

"You think it's Norman's?" I asked. "You think Fenton Flagg let Norman off leash and then reported him missing?"

Dr. David said, "I think Flagg knew he was in trouble and sent Norman to get help. Somebody else reported Norman missing. Somebody who saw him with your dog."

"Somebody … like Sweeney?"

In lieu of answering, Dr. David whistled, and Mooney was back on the clock. The Rott Hound sniffed the blue lead so hard I feared he might inhale it. Then he looked meaningfully at the vet, who said, "GO!" Mooney bounded off into the woods.

"Last night Norman sounded like he was hurt," I reminded Dr. David.

"He sounded like he was in distress," the vet corrected me. "He was probably agitated on behalf of his master, frustrated that Flagg was too sick to respond."

Almost exactly one year ago, late at night on County Road H, Abra had wailed for precisely the same reason. Leo lay dead next to her—next to me—in our car, which was wedged sideways in a ditch. I was hurt too badly to extricate myself, but she managed to wriggle free and stand in the middle of the road yelping until she attracted a passing motorist. Abra the rescue dog. Abra the runaway. Abra the felon. Hardly a blonde bimbo, she was deeper than I dared to contemplate.

Jenx said, "It can't be a coincidence that Sweeney and Flagg were both here at Winimar. I think Sweeney knew what Flagg was up to. As for Norman, I'm guessing he was trained to remind Flagg to take his meds and to go get assistance if necessary."

"So you think Sweeney came out here to stop Flagg? Or to help him?" I asked.

"I don't know," Jenx said. "What with all his gag orders, it's hard to believe Sweeney would permit Flagg to write a book about Winimar, let alone make friends with him."

"Unless they had some kind of connection," I offered. "Is there a surviving Schuyler descendent on whose behalf Sweeney manages the trust?"

Jenx shrugged.

"Well, somebody stabbed Sweeney," I pointed out. "Was it Flagg?"

"Flagg got sick way before Sweeney got stabbed," Dr. David interjected. "No way Flagg would have had the strength to attack Sweeney, let alone throw him down a well."

"How did Flagg and Sweeney get here, anyhow?" I asked. "Anybody seen any cars?"

"There's something over there!" shouted Deputy Clifton, pointing through the trees.

We all peered in that direction. A dark hulk lurked like a large crouching predator amid the infinity of gray.

"Is that a truck? Or a van?" Dr. David said, squinting.

"Neither." Although I couldn't see the vehicle more clearly than anyone else, I knew what it had to be. "That's a Hummer."

Dr. David stayed behind to wait for Mooney while the rest of us picked our way through the woods to Sweeney's car. I confidently assumed it was the attorney's for three reasons: (1) Jenx had told me Saturday that the attorney drove a black Hummer; (2) We'd found Sweeney in the abandoned well shaft, so he had to have gotten here somehow; and (3) This was Winimar, object of his administration and subject of his many gag orders.

The Hummer's vanity plate provided a fourth reason to believe the vehicle belonged to Wee Sweeney; it read TRUSTEE.

I was just about to claim the credit due my superior powers of detection when Jenx said, "Hey, Whiskey, did you notice the blue paint on the front bumper?"

Not yet I hadn't. As soon as I moved from the rear of the vehicle to the other end, I saw it. The left underside of the bumper, though unwrinkled, bore a clear scrape of light blue paint, distinct as a decorative stroke across the gleaming black.

"Same color as Crystal's car?" I asked.

Jenx was crouched in front of the grille, head cocked, square jaw jutting. "Could be," she replied. "Same color you saw on Dock Paladino's truck?"

I crouched, too, for a closer look. "Could be. You think they both ran her off the road?"

"I think both vehicles deserve a closer look," the chief said. "But I don't know what the state boys are gonna think. Technically it's their case now." She growled the word "their."

"Can you test the paint, anyway?" I said.

"Nope. Forget about authorization. I don't have the budget or the equipment." Jenx gazed at me with mild interest. "But *you're* welcome to snoop some more. Unofficially."

"How do you mean?"

Jenx peeked around both sides of the Hummer to ensure that Deputy Clifton couldn't hear us.

"See what else you can find out about Sweeney and Dock. I'm going to keep tabs on Tammi and Brandi. Brady's busy speed-reading those first two books on Winimar. They came in this morning's mail."

I told Jenx what Faye had said about Dr. LePadanni failing to show up for work.

"Who's going to look into that?" I demanded.

"I will, just as soon as I can. You thought something weird was going on between him and his daughter on Saturday night," Jenx recalled.

"Right! But you blew me off in favor of Vito Botafogo!"

Jenx leaned close to my ear. "Before Abra knocked him down at the Miss Blossom contest, Vito saw some things I need to investigate."

"Such as?"

"For starters, Emma Kish called somebody."

I remembered seeing the sharp-featured blonde accept her second runner-up bouquet and then whip out her cell phone. It hadn't struck me as all that strange.

"Maybe she's one of those folks who's always on her phone," I suggested.

"You mean, like a realtor?"

I pulled a face. "Vito's old. He probably thinks public use of cell phones is rude."

"Vito got the impression Emma was checking in with someone. Telling them what was happening where she was. Maybe giving the 'go' sign."

"She probably called a friend to say the pageant was a joke and where was everybody getting together tonight."

Jenx cleared her throat. "Vito also saw what happened to Miss Blossom's prize check."

That caught my interest. "What happened to it?"

"When the steps collapsed and she went down, the check flew out of Faye's hand. Guess who stepped in to retrieve it?"

I would have guessed Abra, except I knew she'd gone for the crown instead.

"Who?"

"Vito's estranged great-grand-nephew, Dock Paladino."

THIRTY-TWO

"*THAT* WAS THE BIG revelation Vito struggled to remember?" I asked Jenx. "One of his relatives picking off the prize check?"

"I think he had a crisis of conscience," the chief explained. "Even though the Botafogos haven't spoken to the Paladinos for two generations, Vito wasn't ready to rat out one of his own."

"What changed his mind?"

"He heard that Tammi LePadanni put a curse on Faye. Those old Italians respect the evil eye. Scares the shit out of 'em. Vito already knew Dock was banging Tammi. When he found out Tammi had cursed Faye, he didn't want Dock getting away with taking Faye's check. Looked to him like the locals were ganging up on her. And it's not like she's an outsider. Faye's half-Italian, you know."

I didn't know.

"Vito thought the poor kid was getting a raw deal," Jenx said. "So he decided to point a finger."

"Vito knew Dock was banging Tammi?" I repeated.

"Whiskey, you're the only person in town who didn't know that."

"Did everybody know he was banging Brandi?"

Jenx nodded.

"And Crystal?"

She nodded again.

"But not Noonan, right?" I said. "Nobody knew about Noonan and Dock until Noonan told us at the Goh Cup."

"*Noonan* and Dock?" Jenx looked as stunned as I must have when I heard the revelation. "Are you sure you were supposed to repeat that?"

I stared at Jenx. "I finally know something everybody in town doesn't already know, and you expect me to keep it to myself?"

"I thought you respected Noonan."

"Of course, I respect Noonan! That doesn't mean I can't talk about her behind her back! Anyway, it's not like it's a secret. Peg and Odette know about Noonan and Dock, too."

"But they can keep their mouths shut," Jenx said.

Changing the subject ever so slightly, I said, "I didn't even know Dock was at the Miss Blossom event. I've never met him."

"That's because you're not into boating. If you hung around the marina or the bars down there, you'd know Dock."

"He must be a major hunk to attract all those women …"

Jenx frowned as if trying to imagine herself in someone else's steel-toe boots. Or someone else's stilettos.

"Do you like Brad Pitt?" she asked.

"Dock Paladino looks like Brad Pitt?"

"Nope. Pretty much the opposite. Dock's big, dark, and beefy. And he sweats a lot. Don't get me wrong, I like that look—just not in a man."

"Do you think Dock attacked Kevin Sweeney?" I said.

"If we're talking 'could he?'—no problem. Dock's strong enough to overpower our little lawyer, stab him, and toss him down a well. But why would Dock do it?"

"Maybe Sweeney was putting the moves on one of Dock's girls," I theorized.

Jenx shot me a look. "I'm no expert on hetero-relations, but something tells me those two wouldn't have the same taste in women."

She peered inside the locked Hummer, moving from tinted window to tinted window.

"Can't see much of anything in there," Jenx mumbled.

"Where did the deputy go?" I asked. Not that I liked the guy, but when you've just found two unconscious people on a cursed estate, and your canine bodyguard is off on a mission, there's comfort in numbers.

"Who knows?" Jenx said, turning in a complete circle to look for her uniformed peer. She bellowed, "Hey! Clifton! Where the hell are you?"

No response.

"Oh jeez. Now I'm gonna have to call for backup," she sighed.

"I thought the state boys were on their way," I said.

"A couple state police detectives and a forensics team," Jenx sneered. "I need somebody who's not afraid of ghosts."

"Ghosts?! Who said anything about *ghosts*?"

"Forget that," Jenx snapped. "Let's just say I need backup that can think nonlinearly."

"Brady and Roscoe?" I suggested.

"Bingo."

Jenx roused her part-time officer and his canine crony. Brady said he was deep into the first book about Winimar, but he and Roscoe were on their way. They would reach us within thirty minutes.

When my cell phone rang, I gasped. Part of my brain was still stuck on the word *ghosts*.

"Whiskey, it's Wells. Are you all right?"

I tried to sound a lot less rattled than I was. "Peachy. Just standing here in the middle of nowhere trying to figure out how Sweeney got his car this far into the forest and what happened to Deputy Clifton. He was here, but now he isn't."

I was thinking, but didn't add, *Like that woman I thought I saw.*

"Trust me," the judge said, "no matter what's going on, Mooney will protect you."

"I believe that … except Dr. David gave Mooney an assignment, and—being the good dog he is—he accepted it. Mooney's long gone."

Briefly I recapped our discovery of Sweeney and Flagg. When Wells asked no questions, I assumed he'd already heard the latest news from Winimar. Probably on his police scanner.

"I can assure you, Whiskey, that Mooney will return, and he will keep you safe. That is one highly trained Rott Hound."

"Okay. But who's protecting Mooney while he's out there following orders? Even in daylight, this place is too creepy for words. So far today two dogs have vanished, and two people have required emergency medical care!"

"Abra and Norman haven't 'vanished,'" Wells said. "That's one of the reasons I'm calling. My clerk lives on County Road H near Downhill Road—one mile east of Uphill. Her husband just phoned to say there are two dogs matching Abra's and Norman's descriptions out by their barn. He's going to try to contain them until Fleggers or Jenx can get there."

"With all due respect, Wells, this is Abra we're talking about. Nobody can contain her."

"I think this man can."

"Why? Is he a professional dog wrangler?"

"Close enough. He used to be a rodeo clown, back in the day."

I visualized Abra bucking like a wild-eyed eighteen-hundred-pound bull. If this guy was trained to deflect lethal moves, he just might be able to corral my dog.

"What are Abra and Norman doing by the barn?" I asked suspiciously.

Wells said, "They're grooming each other."

Foreplay, I thought. But all I said was, "Sweet."

THIRTY-THREE

ON A WHIM, I asked Wells if he was friends with Dr. LePadanni. One high-level local professional with another, don't you know.

"Stanley and I have played golf together a few times and had drinks afterwards. That's about it."

"*Stanley LePadanni*?" I asked.

"That's his name," Wells said.

I had forgotten that the surgeon's first name almost rhymed with his last. Just as Tammi's and Brandi's did. A too-weird family tradition.

"How can Dr. LePadanni play golf? He's morbidly obese. I can hardly even imagine him walking …"

"He uses a cart," Wells conceded. "But the man has a killer swing. Why are you asking about Stan?"

I relayed Faye's news that the surgeon was a no-show. Then I took a deep breath and told Wells what I'd seen Saturday at Providence, omitting the little matter of my trespassing. I made it sound as though my intention had been to stop in and offer my part-time agent congratulations on her daughter's second-place win.

"When nobody came to the door, I walked around the back and peered in," I said. Never mind that I hadn't actually rung the bell.

Wells was silent for so long I thought my cellular service had died again.

"Hello?" I said.

"Whiskey, something about this story doesn't add up."

I hoped he was referring to Brandi's tantrum, the pit bulls, the mysterious visitor, or the abrupt lights-out—and not my lie about why I was there.

"What, Wells?" I asked innocently. "What doesn't add up?"

"Stanley LePadanni offering no comfort to his daughter while she was in distress. He would move heaven and earth to soothe Brandolina. I've heard Stan say he'd kill anyone who made her unhappy."

"Nice talk from a man who took the Hippocratic oath," I murmured.

That was the second time in as many minutes that Wells had linked a form of the word *kill* to the surgeon: *Killer* golf swing. Would *kill* anyone who made his daughter unhappy. A figure of speech? Or did the judge know something I didn't, namely that Dr. LePadanni had a murderous streak? Although I'd gone to Providence for the express purpose of checking Tammi's black Lincoln Navigator for blue paint, I hadn't gotten that far. When I peered into their four-car garage, two vehicles were missing and two more—black, of course—were inaccessible.

Since direct questions are often the shortest route to straight answers, I asked Wells the Big One: "Is Dr. LePadanni capable of murder?"

I heard the judge inhale sharply. "Stanley's a healer."

"Sure, sure. But—if provoked—could he fly into a fatal rage?"

"Couldn't most of us?" Wells said calmly. "Confronted with the need to defend home or family?"

"True, but there's self-defense … and then there's defense of ego. I mean, there's thinking your life's on the line, and then there's being too vain or proud or greedy to let someone take something away from you. If you know what I mean."

"I know what you mean. I'm a judge, remember?"

"Sorry."

"No need to apologize. Frankly, I'm concerned about Stan. Has Jenx talked to Tammi or Brandi this morning?"

"Not yet. Jenx is still here with me—I hope."

I glanced around and was profoundly relieved that the chief, unlike Deputy Clifton, hadn't vanished. Even better, Dr. David was now at her side. They appeared to be conferring.

Still sounding placid, Wells said, "Stay close to Jenx. At least until Mooney returns. And keep your phone on."

I started to explain that my phone was always on but only sporadically working when the line went dead. Several attempts to reconnect with Wells—or anyone in the outside world—proved fruitless. So I hot-footed it over to where Jenx and Dr. David stood talking behind the Hummer.

"Any sign of Mooney? Or the deputy?" I interrupted.

"Not yet. We're still waiting." Dr. David used his smooth voice, the one he generally saved for distressed animals.

"What's going on?" I demanded, my eyes darting back and forth between the vet and the chief. "Do you two know something I should know?"

"Settle down!" Jenx said. "You're acting like a caged animal."

I felt like one.

"We're trying to figure out where Sweeney entered the property," Jenx explained, "assuming it was Sweeney who drove the Hummer this far. Deputy Clifton has the internet diagram that Brady faxed. We can't remember if it showed another driveway besides the one we hiked in on from County Road H. Can you?"

I couldn't. But I was able to share Wells's news about the Abra-and-Norman sighting over on Downhill Road. Dr. David looked especially relieved.

He said, "I'll head over there in the Animal Ambulance as soon as Brady and Roscoe get here."

"You should wait for Mooney and take him along," Jenx said. "With Abra, you'll need all the help you can get."

I reported that the farmer who'd spotted the dogs was a retired rodeo clown, skilled at corralling bucking bulls and broncos.

"So he can probably handle Abra," I concluded. Brady and Jenx just laughed.

Everybody had faith in Mooney. My fear, though I didn't voice it, was that both he and Deputy Clifton had fallen under some kind of evil spell. While waiting for Brady and Roscoe to come rescue us, I studied the ground leading up to the Hummer. There had probably been a lane here, once upon a time. Not quite wide enough for a super-sized SUV, however. I noticed that the sides of the vehicle bore a number of long, nasty scratches, probably from forcing its way through dense, jagged overgrowth. Who would do that damage, willingly, to a ride as new and expensive as this one?

I retraced about forty feet of the Hummer's curved route, glancing back every few yards to make sure Jenx and Dr. David were still in sight. They were once again deep in discussion, my presence or absence apparently irrelevant. I could detect the Hummer's wide tire tracks although to my untrained eye they weren't obvious. It had been a dry spring in Lanagan County; thus the trail, such as it was, consisted of squashed vegetation rather than ruts. I knew from the sucking mud I'd traversed earlier that there were wet spots on this property. But the driver, whoever he or she was, must have known—or at least gambled—that the Hummer could get through anything. I supposed that was why people drove Hummers. In addition to proclaiming that size really does matter, owning a Hummer means never having to say you're stuck.

A series of sonorous barks and woodsy crashes announced the welcome approach of Officers Roscoe and Swancott. Jenx, Dr. David, and I hooted a variety of greetings, ranging from "Hello!" to "Over here!"

I wanted to cry out, "Please save us!" But I was cool.

No sooner had Brady and Roscoe arrived than Mooney gamboled in from the opposite direction, his thick club of a tail happily beating the air. Something soggy flapped from his quivering jowls. Jenx donned a pair of surgical gloves before removing the item. I knew that was protocol for handling evidence, but I also figured it was the only way to keep one's hands dry in the vicinity of Mooney's mouth.

"What is it?" I asked Jenx.

She addressed her reply to Brady: "It's the diagram you faxed Deputy Clifton before he met us here."

"What are you talking about?" Brady said. Jenx handed him a severely wilted piece of paper, rendered almost translucent by Mooney's drool.

"I didn't send this," Brady said.

"Yes you did," I told him. "We all saw the top sheet. It had a note from you."

"Saying what?"

"Something about how you weren't sure it was reliable, but you'd downloaded this map of you-know-where from the Internet. You thought it was part of the 'book-in-progress.'"

Jenx added, "'Proceed with caution,' you said."

Brady peered closely at the bottom edge of the page, which was mostly gone. When he glanced up, his usually laconic features wore a tense expression.

"Chief, look at what's left of the originating phone number. It's not ours."

Jenx read it and groaned. "Somebody pretending to be you sent this to the sheriff's office!"

"Or," Brady said, "somebody's pretending to be from the sheriff's office. How well do you know the missing deputy?"

THIRTY-FOUR

JENX ADMITTED THAT SHE didn't know the missing deputy, having met him last night when he'd answered the call to Vestige. That was following Deely's discovery of the crown *sans* jewels and Faye's plunge over the banister.

"You didn't know the guy, so you just assumed he was a deputy?" I asked.

"He had the right car, badge, name tag, and uniform," Jenx snapped. "Did *you* think he looked like a phony?"

"No, but then I'm trained to evaluate foundations and floor plans."

At that instant we all heard a cry for help. Mooney and Officer Roscoe were the first to spring into action. Good thing, too, because I, for one, no longer trusted my sense of direction. And my confidence in our local two-legged police force was flagging.

Everyone jogged along behind the two canines, who had unofficially paired up. I thought it was cool that Officer Roscoe accepted without question the aid of a trained volunteer—of mixed breed, no less. There was a job to be done, and they didn't need to discuss it. We humans could probably take a page from that playbook: working smoothly together despite race, creed, or income-tax bracket.

Uh-oh. I'd just gone temporarily Fleggers in my head. There was no time to contemplate my philosophical lapse. We accelerated, sailing—or stumbling—over, around and between various forms of jagged vegetation.

The cry for help came again, distinctly the voice of the missing deputy.

"He could be trying to lure us into a trap," Brady warned.

"Should we … divide to conquer? Break into two teams?" Dr. David panted.

In the worst physical condition of the group, he was falling behind fast.

"That's an idea," Brady said, glancing back. "How about it, Chief? You and I go ahead, and Dr. David and Whiskey stay behind?"

"Oh no!" I cried. "Our team needs an officer who's armed to the teeth!"

"You want Roscoe?" Jenx asked.

"Only if he can use a gun."

The chief slowed to a brisk walk. "Brady—you go ahead with Roscoe and Mooney. I'll stay behind with the unarmed humans. Call for backup if you need it. Don't be a hero, and don't let the dog-boys try that trick, either!"

"Right on," Brady said, resuming his pace.

"You think Clifton's messing with our heads?" I asked Jenx.

She shrugged. "Somebody is. Probably more than one somebody."

"What do you mean?"

"People lie. Fact is, most folks have something going on they'd rather not talk about."

"Like what?"

"Sex or money. Everybody feels guilty about something. Or knows they should."

I considered that in light of my own suspicions. "You think Sweeney was up to no good and somebody tried to stop him? Or was it the other way around?"

"Or," Dr. David suggested, "was Sweeney in the wrong place at the wrong time? Maybe he saw something he wasn't supposed to see."

"Like Whiskey's tree-woman, you mean?" Jenx asked.

Just then a car engine roared to life. We three stared at each other stupidly, our faces saying, "Do you hear that, too?"

Finally I spoke the two words that didn't need pronouncing: "The Hummer!"

Jenx and Dr. David broke away toward the sound. I scrambled after them like a little sister scared of the bogeyman.

By the time we figured out where the vehicle had been, it was long gone. Brady raised Jenx on her walkie-talkie to ask if that was the Hummer he'd heard leaving.

"Affirmative," she said sadly.

But there was good news. Brady had located Deputy Clifton, who appeared to be authentically injured.

"He says somebody sneaked up from behind and clobbered him on the head. The guy definitely needs stitches."

Jenx said, "Maybe he agreed to get hurt in exchange for payment. Maybe his job was to lure us away from the Hummer …"

"Unlikely," Brady replied. "His IDs all check out. I called the sheriff's office, and he's a real deputy. Just not the sharpest knife in the drawer."

Jenx decided that we should wait where we were and let Roscoe and Mooney lead the human officers back to us. Brady said they were on their way. In the meantime the state police forensics unit finally arrived, most unimpressively. The four men found us by shouting "Hello!!! Where is everybody?!" as they wandered noisily through the trees. I would have expected better tracking from Cub Scouts. Still, I was relieved to see them. The more the merrier when you're waiting on cursed earth.

When Brady and shaky Deputy Clifton returned, Jenx announced that Dr. David and I were cleared for departure. With compass in hand and Mooney at our feet, we headed for the Animal Ambulance parked out on County Road H. Time to round up Abra and Norman. Or such was the plan.

We had no trouble finding the farm in question on Downhill Road. Unfortunately, only Norman and a middle-aged man in overalls appeared at the end of the long gravel driveway. The Golden heeled as the farmer limped over to meet us.

"Where's the Afghan hound?" I asked, fervently hoping that the man's bad leg was the result of a long-ago rodeo accident and not this morning's encounter with a bucking blonde dog.

"She threw me off balance, and I fell," he said, working the words around an impressively large wad of tobacco. "Nearly busted my knee replacement when she got away."

"Which way did she go?" asked Dr. David as if we'd wandered into a low-budget Western.

The farmer pointed south down the road toward town. Then he winced and rubbed his shoulder.

"Damn dog nearly busted my shoulder replacement, too. And I think she threw my back out. Got any pain meds in that ambulance?"

We didn't, but I offered him a large bottle of ibuprofen from my purse. He shook out six tablets and swallowed them without water, the tobacco still lodged in his cheek. Then he slipped the bottle into the bib pocket of his overalls.

"Who the hell owns that she-devil, anyhow?" he said.

I cleared my throat. "The man who owned her died a year ago. She hasn't been right since."

"No shit." The farmer spat a golf-ball-size wad that landed on the toe of my right shoe. Without comment, I scuffed it off on the grass. He could spit in my eye if he'd promise not to litigate.

As the farmer described Abra's antics, Dr. David arched his eyebrows, and the boy dogs wagged their tails. Though unnerving, the vivid account included nothing I hadn't seen for myself. I already knew that my dog could dodge, weave, and leap with the best of them. Finally, Dr. David opened the rear doors of the Animal Ambulance, and Norman and Mooney leapt in. Despite their competing feelings for Abra, they behaved like gentlemen. Norman probably knew that Mooney was no threat, and Mooney, most likely, just wanted another glimpse of Abra.

I reboarded the Animal Ambulance without having disclosed either my name or my relationship to the canine fugitive. We started down the driveway. I figured I had flown under the radar ... until the farmer shouted, "Wait! Come back here!"

In the sideview mirror, I saw him hobbling after us. Dr. David hit the brakes, and we spewed gravel. So much for my escape. The farmer sidled up to my window, which I reluctantly rolled down. So reluctantly that I made him rap on it first.

"Yes?" I asked.

"Almost forgot to tell you," he panted. "We don't get much traffic on Downhill Road. Mostly neighbors. But just before that crazy dog ran off, I saw a big black SUV go by in a hurry. You know, the kind that looks like a tank."

"You mean … a Hummer?"

"Yeah. Something about that car made your dog go nuts."

"Who said she was *my* dog?"

"Well, *you* sure as hell tried not to. We may live in the sticks, Mrs. Mattimoe, but we can read."

He withdrew a folded copy of the *Magnet*'s front page from his hip pocket and pointed to the photo of my pixilated middle finger. Nodding, he said, "I did the same thing when the bitch took me down."

THIRTY-FIVE

Dr. David thanked the farmer for his information because I was too embarrassed to do so. Then he pointed the Animal Ambulance southward on Downhill Road.

"Well, that jibes with Yolanda Brewster's story about Abra jumping into a black SUV," I said. "Only Mrs. Brewster insisted that Tammi LePadanni was driving, so I assumed the car was her Lincoln Navigator, not Sweeney's Hummer."

"Abra may have been trained to respond to both," Dr. David said. "Or to have a generalized response to large black vehicles."

"Including Dock Paladino's Dodge Ram pickup?" I asked.

He nodded.

"Great. So now she's trained to steal jewels *and* chase cars."

"Just big black ones."

I had promised Faye that I'd visit her at CMC by noon. Since it was almost eleven-thirty, Dr. David offered to drive me straight to the hospital. I had qualms about pulling up in the Animal Ambulance, but he promised not to turn on the flasher. When we approached the visitors' entrance, an alert security guard waved us toward the EMERGENCY access. I rolled down the window and waved back, shouting, "It's okay. He only helps animals."

The guard frowned and then spoke to someone on his walkie-talkie. I advised Dr. David to get the hell out of there.

"How will you get home?" he asked.

"This won't take long. Drive around for a while. I'll call you on my cell phone when I'm ready. You can pick me up out on the highway."

I didn't like the situation; through the floor-to-ceiling glass of the hospital's foyer, I spotted two more security cops jogging our way.

"Better burn some rubber!" I advised. Dr. David peeled away, and I turned to face a uniformed trio. "Hi, guys! Do you happen to know which room Miss Blossom is in?"

They did. The hospital security staff had been clued in about The Curse. One guard was assigned to protect her or maybe to protect the hospital from her; I wasn't clear which. Although he was on his lunch break, he was willing to walk me to Faye's room … once I explained the Animal Ambulance. The guards had thought I was trying to impersonate an EMT. I assured them I had more than enough real emergencies already and didn't want access to more.

A replacement security guard slouched outside Faye's third-floor room. His nametag read TROY T. I decided to make him my ally.

"Hey, Troy." I smiled warmly and reached into my bag for one of my business cards. "I'm—"

"Stop right there," he ordered in an icy voice.

"But I'm just—"

"I said STOP!"

So I did. He told me to put my hands up. I did that, too.

Then Faye called from her room, "It's all right, Troy! That's the woman I told you about. Believe me, she's harmless."

"Yeah?" Troy sounded unconvinced. "You sure she isn't packing?"

"Only business cards and a cell phone," I said. "I even remembered to turn it off."

Troy let me pass. Faye looked healthy for someone with her head bandaged, her arm in a sling, and two days left to live.

"Don't let the head wound scare you," she said. "I needed a few stitches, that's all. But the shoulder needs surgery."

She described a cracked rotator cuff and some kind of double fracture. I assured her that Mattimoe Realty would pay all her medical bills. It was the least I could do. Fortunately, the hospital had lined up an orthopedic surgeon *not* related to the LePadannis. He had already examined Faye, and she liked him. Her surgery was scheduled for first thing tomorrow morning.

There was a knock on the open door. Troy said, "Package for Miss Blossom. I mean, Miss Raffle."

He held out a box identical to the one she'd received yesterday: made from white cardboard, it measured about five inches long by six inches wide by three inches high. A small attached envelope was addressed to MISS BLOSSOM. The block letters were written in red ink, probably with a Sharpie. We'd seen that printing before.

"Oh god," I moaned. "No more creepy hair jewelry!"

Faye reminded me that the threats were creepier than the jewelry. I urged her not to open the package unless Jenx or Brady was present. But you know teenagers; even the good ones don't always listen. Faye insisted that Troy qualified as protection. He stood a little straighter when she said that. To her credit, she donned surgical gloves before popping open the lid.

The tissue-lined box did indeed contain hair jewelry. But this time it was hair we knew. Faye instantly recognized the honey-brown locks clipped from the left side of her own head during yesterday's Aqua Net attack. They were woven—rather intricately, I had to admit—with the blonde hair of a certain Afghan hound. The finished product appeared to be a dog collar. An entirely inappropriate gift for Miss Blossom, but one that my missing canine could use. If we ever found her.

Finally Faye opened the envelope. I held my breath as she silently read the message inside. Then she turned the card for me to see, keeping it safely beyond my fingerprints. Chester would have been so proud.

This time there was no spidery writing on antique vellum. Printed in red Sharpie ink on a plain white card were the words:

GET READY TO GIVE UP YOUR CROWN OR DIE TRYING. WHAT'S YOUR LIFE WORTH, BITCH?

THIRTY-SIX

THE B-WORD DIDN'T FIT Miss Blossom, although it did apply to a certain collarless dog. I assured Faye that Miss Blossoms generally survived their reigns. And most people survive orthopedic surgery. Faye's odds seemed especially excellent now that she had a surgeon unconnected to the curse.

She agreed that I should take the latest hair jewelry to Jenx and Brady. Troy the security guard wasn't so sure.

"I don't think you're supposed to remove evidence from the scene of a crime," he said slowly.

"What crime?" I asked. "This is just a suspicious package. The police will want to see it."

"I don't know," he said. "I watch a lot of *Law & Order*, and I don't think Lenny Brisco would want you to do that."

"Lenny Brisco's dead," I reminded him.

"The actor who played Lenny is dead," Faye clarified. "I think Lenny is supposed to be alive and well and living in Florida."

"I don't know," Troy said. He was frowning at his walkie-talkie as if it just might connect him to Lieutenant Brisco.

"You're really good at your job, Troy," Faye said brightly. "But Whiskey's trying to follow police orders. Chief Jenkins wants to see *everything* that might be connected to the curse. Whiskey needs to take the hair jewelry."

Troy nodded and slouched back out into the hall. I gaped at Faye.

"You could make millions selling real estate! Let's cut a deal: I'll train you one-on-one, starting the day you get out of here."

She smiled. "Thanks, but I promised my parents I'd go to college."

"We can work around that."

"Okay, but could Odette train me?"

That hurt. I sucked it in, though, and promised to have my star salesperson call her. Egos aside, recruiting Faye Raffle to sell for Mattimoe Realty would be a coup … with two minor provisions. First, that she survived beyond Wednesday. And, second, that as a former Miss Blossom, she wouldn't have to leave town or die.

I was in the hospital lobby, my cell phone set to summon Dr. David, when I realized that Wee Sweeney and Fenton Flagg had to be at CMC. I could look in on them both. This was one of those rare occasions when a lawyer wouldn't bill me for stopping by. And I seriously wanted to talk to the writer. If our dogs were in love, we were practically in-laws.

As I waited for the elderly volunteer at the Information Desk to look up from his crossword puzzle, I noticed the front-door security guard watching me. I smiled and waved, which prompted him to use his walkie-talkie.

Faking a tubercular-sounding cough, I finally won the attention of the Information Desk guy. He scowled and pointed down the hall.

"How do you know what I'm about to ask?" I said.

"With a cough like that, you'd better be looking for the ER."

"Actually, I'm here to visit Kevin Sweeney and Fenton Flagg."

"We don't let sick people visit sick people," he said flatly.

"I'm not 'sick,' just sick and tired of waiting for you to acknowledge my presence. What rooms are they in?"

The volunteer tried to peer around me, no doubt in hope of catching the security guard's eye. I made that into a little game, shifting my weight from right to left and back again, successfully blocking his view.

"You think you're pretty cute, don't you?" he said.

"Not really. Now where are Flagg and Sweeney?"

The old guy gave up the game too soon for it to be fun, but I got the information I needed just as the security guard was approaching. I waved to them both and took off.

Flagg and Sweeney were in ICU, which didn't bode well for visitation. But I figured I could at least leave messages. I introduced myself to the unit clerk, who told me that Sweeney was in surgery. She directed me to the waiting room while she checked for an update on Flagg. There I picked up a magazine and quickly became engrossed in the cover story about Brad Pitt, a.k.a. the Anti-Dock-Paladino. Suddenly someone said, "Whiskey! What are you doing here?"

I looked up to see my favorite massage therapist. And my brain started ticking. Noonan: as in Noonan and Dock; Noonan and the Seven Suns of Solace; Noonan and … Fenton Flagg?

"You're here to check on Fenton, aren't you?" she said, sitting next to me. "I heard you were one of the people who found him. Thanks for being open to the Light that led you where the Universe needed you to go."

"Uh, right." I cleared my throat. "So—you, uh, know Fenton Flagg? Personally? Or just through the book?"

Noonan smiled. "Of course I know him. I'm married to him."

That was the most shocking news of the day. Which is saying quite a lot. Noonan fetched me a glass of water and then rubbed my back while I tried to absorb what she was saying. She had met Fenton Flagg eighteen years earlier while attending a reincarnation retreat in northern Idaho. They'd felt an instant connection—no doubt from previous lives—and debated whether to be soul mates or marriage mates.

"We made the wrong choice," Noonan conceded. "But our destinies are forever intertwined. We know that's true."

Maybe it was her earlier Dock Paladino revelation that had set me up to be stunned by this one. I said so.

"Oh, Fenton and I have been separated for *years*," she explained. "In fact, we only lived together for about ten months. We realized that we could never spiritually divorce, so what was the point of legally divorcing?"

As a divorce graduate, I felt impelled to point out its benefits. But Noonan seemed to live in a slightly altered reality. So I changed the subject.

"Did you know Flagg was writing the book on Winimar?"

She blinked at me. "Of course I knew it. He was staying at my place."

Which technically was *my* place because Noonan rented her cottage from me.

"Why didn't you tell anyone?" I said.

"No one asked me."

I was pretty sure Brady had asked her about Winimar, and I said so.

"Yes," Noonan said. "Brady asked what I knew about *Winimar*, but not about Fenton. So I told him about the history of the place. I'm sure I violated Sweeney's gag order."

That seemed to please her. I understood why—screwing lawyers, at least metaphorically, could be fun.

"How long has Fenton been working on the book?"

"Six months, give or take."

"Fenton Flagg has been at your house for six months?"

"Only when he needs to do primary research. Otherwise, he lives in Texas … and runs seminars in Taos, New Mexico."

Noonan sighed. "Fenton has a full life—and a very full calendar. Sometimes he forgets to take care of himself. That's where Norman comes in."

She explained that Norman was trained to remind Fenton to take his insulin and to fetch help if necessary.

"When I heard that Norman was on the loose without Fenton, I knew something had gone terribly wrong."

Yeah, I thought. *Norman met Abra.*

An ICU nurse appeared and asked Noonan to step into the consultation room. Noonan invited me to join them; I wasn't sure if she needed my support or just wanted to prove that she was keeping no secrets. The nurse explained that Flagg was stabilized but unlikely to regain consciousness for a few more hours.

I asked Noonan what I could do to help.

"Think powerfully positive thoughts," she said. "And don't let Norman run away after Abra."

I promised to do my best. Back out in the hospital lobby, both the Information Desk guy and the security guard scrambled to look busy when they spotted me. But I knew they were watching my every move. So I waved merrily and raised Dr. David on my cell phone.

"Norman and Mooney are bonding!" the vet enthused.

We agreed to meet on the highway in front of the hospital in five minutes. Walking down the wide entrance drive, I checked over my shoulder. A uniformed security guard I hadn't seen before was fifty paces behind me. I waved; he didn't. Presumably, he was making sure I exited the premises. I may not have gotten all the answers I sought, but I had definitely left an impression.

When the Animal Ambulance pulled up on the berm, Mooney and Norman were sharing my seat.

"Where am I supposed to sit?" I said, half-joking. Both dogs thumped their tails, but neither offered to move.

"This is a major breakthrough, Whiskey," Dr. David announced. "Two male dogs in the prime of their lives, both with hero complexes and the same love interest. And yet they can unify!"

"That's nice," I said. "Now tell them to get out of my seat."

The vet gave me a pleading look. "Would you mind—?"

Suddenly I understood. "Oh no. I'm not riding in the back so these guys can play copilot."

"Please, Whiskey … I think Norman gets carsick. Somebody puked back there."

"Too bad! I'm your human passenger, remember? This is an Animal Ambulance. The four-leggers are *supposed* to ride in the back!"

"Technically, that's true," Dr. David hedged, "but only if they're sick. These guys are healthy."

"You just said Norman puked!"

"He's fine now. As long as he rides in the front …"

THIRTY-SEVEN

IN THE INTEREST OF winning back my rightful place in the Animal Ambulance, I mentioned that I'd uncovered the mystery of Fenton Flagg. Hearing his master's name, Norman whimpered piteously. The poor dog became so agitated I was sure he was going to pee on my seat.

"Okay, *now* he has to move," I declared, "because I'm not going to wipe up a mess."

Too late. The seat was already slimed, courtesy of Mooney.

"All right, I'll ride in the back." I aimed a sour face at Dr. David. "But you'll never guess who was in ICU to see Fenton Flagg. And I'm never going to tell you."

"Noonan?" the vet wondered.

"Okay …" I said, deflated. "But you'll never guess *why* she was there to see him. Never in a million years!"

"Are they married?"

I stared at Dr. David. "Are you putting me on?"

"I'm wrong?" he asked.

"No, dammit, you're right. You're absolutely 100 percent right! Did Noonan tell you?"

"I just guessed."

"You *guessed*? How could you *guess*? I can never *guess*. Never, never, never!"

"That's okay, Whiskey. We all know you lack intuition. It's part of your charm."

"My 'charm'?"

"The way you have to learn everything the hard way." He smiled sympathetically.

I told him to take me to Vestige. *Pronto*. Then I slammed the passenger door and marched around to the back. The rear doors were harder to operate. I struggled until I pried them open, then crawled in and yanked them shut. It should have been satisfying to relax back there while the dumb males panted, drooled and whined up front. Unfortunately, I managed to sit down in Norman's puke. There's always an upside, though: the squalor made it much easier for me to sulk.

I was in a slightly better mood by the time we reached my house. Until I got out and noticed that I had company. Avery, to be precise. I had caught her in mid-move. That is, she was in the process of hauling out the last of her stuff, which would have been wonderful except that "her stuff" included some of Leo's stuff. Which was now technically *my* stuff.

Our conversation, such as it was, accelerated from zero to sixty in about ten seconds.

"Put that down!" I yelled. "Or better yet, back where it belongs!"

I was referring to the Mission-style floor lamp Avery had removed from Leo's former study.

"Dad knew I liked this lamp. He would have wanted me to have it," she declared and flicked her pink tongue.

"If so, he would have left it to you in his will. But he didn't!"

"Because you wouldn't let him," she snapped. "I know my father. He wanted me to be happy."

"I knew your father, too," I said. "He wanted you to learn to make yourself happy!"

"Trust me—taking this stuff will help!"

She inserted the lamp into the back of Nash Grant's mini-van, which already contained an assortment of Leo's—now *my*—small furnishings. I lunged for her.

"Down, girl! Down!" Dr. David cried.

I wasn't sure who that command was intended for, but neither of us obeyed. We were two crazed bitches fighting over what was left of the last decent male. And I'm not talking about Nash Grant.

Lucky for me, Avery's hair was longer and therefore easier to pull. I got a couple handfuls although I should be ashamed to admit it. I knew we were out of control when I heard Dr. David call in Deely for backup. Inside the Animal Ambulance, Norman and Mooney howled; I chose to believe they were cheering me on.

To break us up, Dr. David tried every command from Dogs-Train-You-dot-com and The System. I'd like to blame my bad behavior on the fact that I didn't know the lingo. But the truth is I went after Avery because I wanted to.

Leo and I had often discussed her chronic whining and sense of entitlement. He hoped she would outgrow it; now twenty-two, she showed no sign she ever would. Although Leo had spoiled his only child in the mode of many divorced fathers, he held fast to the belief that we must each find our own path to peace. I was sick of being the pebble that Avery kicked around on her personal dead-end road.

I'm not sure how long we'd been rolling on the ground together in the classic embrace of hate before Deely drove up, brakes squealing. She probably expected more blood. I know I did. Sure, both my nose and Avery's were bleeding, and we both had split lips. I had more scratches than Avery thanks to her expensive artificial nails. But I'd landed a few good punches; she would soon have two doozy shiners, and her nose already looked nicely swollen. I was sorry I couldn't hang around for her complete discoloration.

After Deely separated us, Avery sputtered something about calling the cops and opened her cell phone. When I pointed out that *she* was trespassing, she snorted and dialed Nash Grant. By then Deely was leading me toward the house, but I could tell by Avery's curses that Nash wasn't as sympathetic as she needed him to be.

Ever an expert at damage control, the Coast Guard nanny wasted no time fixing this mess. First she put a few walls between me and Avery. Then she produced a first-aid kit and told me how to use it. She said that Dr. David was doing the same for the other team. Finally, while I lay on my bed with an ice pack pressed to my face, Deely went back outside and—with the vet's help—retrieved every single item that wasn't positively, absolutely, legally Avery's.

"I never knew your late husband," Deely said, slightly winded from her exertions. "But I'm sure he wouldn't be pleased. The time has come to make sure nothing like this ever happens again."

"You mean put out a contract on Avery?"

"No, ma'am," Deely said. "Change your locks."

"Excellent idea!" I perked right up. "Except I've got to go see the cops about some hair jewelry … if I can find it."

Where had I dropped the sicko Faye-and-Abra hair collar? Before I could bolt out of bed, Deely produced the white cardboard box.

I thanked her and added, "Would you mind calling Larry the Locksmith? He's an old pal of my ex-husband, but I'm not sure he likes me. Better tell him Jeb Halloran sent you."

Deely promised to take care of it, along with the forty cats still in residence down the hall. Nervously I glanced around my bedroom for signs that Yoda had led another mutiny. There were none. In fact, the second floor was ominously quiet.

"I reinforced the barrier this morning, ma'am," Deely said. "And fixed the latch on your bedroom door. I also changed the litter and put out fresh food and water. And facilitated two feline recreation breaks culminating in catnip. Dr. David will begin the surgeries tomorrow."

Then she reminded me that she was due to start her shift at Nash's house in one half-hour. Suddenly I realized how desperately I needed her. Even assuming that the cats would soon be gone, how on earth would I cope if she worked full-time for Nash and Avery? Horror of horrors: what if she moved to Florida with them at the end of his sabbatical?

"Deely!" I called after her. "Would you consider a career change?"

"To what, ma'am?"

"How about being a personal assistant instead of a nanny?"

"Is there a difference?"

"It pays better."

I promptly offered her half again what she was currently earning. Deely wasn't motivated by money, however. She studied me in silence and finally said, "You need me more than the twins do."

THIRTY-EIGHT

AND SO DEELY JOINED my payroll. She insisted, however, that Avery and Nash deserved two weeks' notice. How could I disagree? I knew deep down that I was mostly vexed by the loss of Leah and Leo. I'd been deprived of their company without warning.

Examining myself in the bathroom mirror, I decided that low-wattage lamps were my new best friends. Shadows, too. And solar eclipses. Also wide-brimmed hats. I grabbed one of those and headed to Police Headquarters, the latest hair jewelry tucked into my shoulder bag.

The outer office was deserted when I walked in.

"Helloooo!" I called.

"Hey, Whiskey." Brady's faceless rejoinder came from the kitchenette. "Need some ice for your shiner?"

"How do you know I have a shiner?"

"Avery just phoned." Officers Swancott and Roscoe appeared in the kitchenette doorway. They both looked sympathetic.

Brady said, "Need some ice for your upper lip?"

"Maybe I want to look like Angelina Jolie."

"Well, you don't."

I sighed. "Is Avery pressing charges?"

"I talked her out of it. But that doesn't mean she won't sue."

"At least I won Deely."

"Huh?"

Too tired to explain, I handed over the box of hair jewelry—now bearing my prints. Brady wasn't nearly as pissed about that as Chester or Jenx would have been. Or maybe he just went easy on me because of my big lip.

He dangled the hair collar by its brass buckle so that Roscoe could sniff it. The canine officer moaned obscenely.

"Definitely Abra's hair," Brady confirmed. "That's the sound Roscoe always makes when he smells her."

Brady dropped the hair collar into a plastic evidence bag. "Hair of the missing dog braided with hair of Miss Blossom. I told you Faye would receive a second package."

"But what does it mean?"

"I'm still learning. I was speed-reading the first Winimar book and eating my lunch when you walked in."

Lunch? How many hours had passed since I'd wolfed down Chester's breakfast? As if I'd asked my stomach, it growled.

"I made a big pot of chili," Brady said. "It'll be better tomorrow, but it's edible today. You're welcome to join me."

He motioned for me to follow him into the kitchenette. On the battered Formica table was a slender blue cloth-bound volume, heavily worn and water-spotted. He picked it up and showed me the spine. Faded gold letters spelled out *The Curse of Winimar* followed by a familiar last name: **Sweeney**.

I blinked at Brady. "How—?"

"Sit down and have some chili," he said. "You're going to need strength."

What he offered was fire. The chili powder and cayenne pepper made my split lip scream and my eyes water, but I didn't complain. Brady wouldn't talk till I'd consumed half a bowl. His arms folded on the tabletop, he waited for me to wipe my eyes and mouth with a paper napkin before he began.

"The first book on Winimar was published in 1912. Author: Keenan Sweeney, Wee Sweeney's great-great-grandpa." He smiled modestly. "Online genealogical research isn't that hard."

Brady used the fingers of both hands to count off generations.

"Wee Sweeney's great-great-great-great-granddad was Jonathan Sweeney, Mrs. Slocum Schuyler's lawyer. She consulted *him* to create the trust that endures to this day."

"The one that gave Magnet Springs the butt-ugly Miss Blossom crown?"

"That's the one."

"So who was Keenan Sweeney? And why did he write the book?"

"Ah." Brady grinned mischievously. "As near as I can tell, Keenan was the family rebel. While both his brothers became lawyers, like Sweeney men were—and are—supposed to, Keenan was a writer. There's been a century and a half of attorneys in that family! Talk about a tradition: one Sweeney always kept the family practice alive, refusing to retire until another younger Sweeney passed the bar exam and carried on."

"That's not a tradition," I said. "That's a curse!"

"The question is why do they do it?" Brady tapped the antique book. "I'm hoping the answer's in here."

"And if it's not?"

"Then maybe it's in this one."

He reached around to find something on the counter behind him and produced a second book—a fat, frayed paperback. The cover was half gone. What remained of the title read *I'm Cool, But You …*

"… *Have a Curse on Your Head,*" Brady said. "That's the rest of the title. Honest! Publication date: 1976. Author—"

"Another Sweeney?" I guessed. The writer's name had been ripped away.

Brady said, "Murray McCready."

I was disappointed. "Not a Sweeney or a Schuyler."

"No, but you might recognize him, all the same." Brady flipped to the last page and then handed me the book. I studied a small black-and-white headshot of a precociously young, almost too-handsome man.

"How would I know Murray McCready?"

"I didn't say you knew him. I said you might recognize him."

"Well, I don't."

"Are you sure? Look again."

Brady was beginning to annoy me.

"Yes, I'm sure! Why would you think I should?"

"Because you met him today. Sort of."

"I met Murray McCready *today*?"

And then it hit me. The double initials should have been a clue. Likewise, the brief bio: "Murray McCready is a motivational speaker and spiritual guru. Originally from east Texas, he now lives in northern Idaho."

In unison Brady and I said, "Fenton Flagg."

THIRTY-NINE

"THIRTY YEARS LATER MCCREADY's writing the sequel to his first book? Using a pen name?"

"Fenton Flagg's his real name," Brady said. "Murray McCready was the pseudonym. And the current project's not a sequel."

"Then what is it?" I said.

"A history. The first one was a self-help book. Flagg used Winimar as an analogy."

"Speak English, College Boy." Jenx had appeared in the kitchenette doorway. "Hey, Whiskey! Sexy upper lip. I like a gal who looks like she's been in a fight."

"Whiskey *was* in a fight, and you'll never guess with whom," Brady said.

"Avery already called me." Jenx sounded bored. "And, no, Whiskey, I don't think she's gonna sue. Now what's this about Flagg's new book?"

"I saw the notes that the forensics team found in Flagg's bag this morning," Brady said. "This time he's trying to sort the facts from the fiction about Winimar. In his first book," Brady indicated the ragged paperback. "—he used Winimar and its curses to illustrate how R.A. works."

"What's R.A.?" I asked.

"Reactional Analysis—a psychological approach popular back in the '70s. Still used by some counselors to show how our reactions color our world."

"You're losing me," Jenx said. She had removed a quart carton of chocolate milk from the mini-fridge, opened it, and was about to pour it directly down her throat.

"R.A.'s just a fancy way of saying that you believe what you want to believe," Brady explained. "Basically, we choose our own truths."

"You mean, it doesn't matter if somebody puts a curse on your head … unless you believe in the curse?" I said.

Brady held up Flagg's first book. "That's his thesis."

"You said the state cops opened Flagg's bag. Did they find the combination to the lock on the bathhouse door?"

"Nope," Brady said. "Maybe Kevin Sweeney has it."

"Or maybe he *had* it," Jenx said, using the back of her hand to wipe away her chocolate-milk mustache. "Maybe that's why somebody stabbed him. He's out of surgery, by the way. I just got the update. They think he'll make a full recovery, but it's gonna take time. Hey, what's with the blonde-and-brown hair jewelry? They make that stuff with highlights now?"

When I told her, she said, "I'll bet you can't wait to look into that."

"Why?" I sensed something in the offing. Probably something not so good for me.

"Because I don't have the manpower to run it down," the chief said. "But *you* have a vested interest. Faye's counting on *you*."

I groaned. "So … I should put 'Investigate hair jewelry' on my To Do List, right under 'Investigate blue paint on Sweeney's Hummer'?"

"You can cross off the blue paint," Jenx said. "I'm looking for Sweeney's Hummer. But your dog's mixed up with the hair jewelry, so that's your department. Unofficially."

"Wouldn't Sweeney be in charge of the original hair jewelry? It's part of the Schuyler estate."

"Maybe. Maybe not," the chief said.

"In police work, you can't afford to make assumptions," said Brady. "Study the chain of custody: Who owned the hair jewelry? When and where? Even if Sweeney had it, somebody else could have borrowed, stolen, or sold it and then sent it to Faye."

"Well, I can't ask Sweeney," I said. "He's sick."

"He's a lawyer with gag orders. He might not tell you, anyhow."

"So what should I do?"

The chief was searching the fridge for something edible. Brady was back at the stove, stirring the chili. For a minute, I thought they'd forgotten me.

Finally without looking up, Jenx said, "Rico Anuncio sells antique jewelry in his gallery. He might know who owns what … or who wants to own what."

Rico owned a black SUV. A Lexus RX 330, like mine, except mine was white; I was one of the Good Guys. Rico had returned from his around-the-world cruise just in time for Miss Blossom's crown to go missing. Or rather, for it to be stolen by my dog, who—according to

Mrs. Brewster—delivered it to a black SUV. Even if Tammi was at the wheel, Rico could be involved.

"Is the West Shore Gallery open on Monday?" I asked.

But both officers had left the room. Brady was back at his desk with the Keenan Sweeney book, the index finger of his left hand tracing a vertical path through the text, his right hand poised to flip pages.

"You can really read that fast?" I asked. Without glancing up or losing a beat, he replied, "That's why they call it speed-reading. You're going to love the stuff about the death of the first Miss Blossom."

"Can't you just tell me?"

He turned the page. "I'm reading, Whiskey. See you later."

Officer Roscoe, now nestled under Brady's desk, thumped his tail once for good-bye.

Jenx was furiously taking notes, the phone receiver jammed between her ear and her shoulder. One of my skills as a realtor is reading upside-down. As I passed Jenx's desk, I saw what she had printed at the top of her notebook page: DOCK PALADINO. I wondered who was on the other end of the line.

———

The West Shore Gallery was two blocks down from the police station. During its proprietor's long vacation, the shop had been open only on weekends. Now, I supposed, Rico Anuncio would be anxious to re-establish regular hours, which might or might not include Mondays. I didn't have to wait until I reached the gallery to find out. Rico very nearly collided with me as he exited Bake-The-Steak.

"Well, if it isn't the woman with The Finger from today's front page!"

He fluttered his own digits, all ten of which sported sparkly rings. Then, feigning secrecy, he stage-whispered, "Frankly, Whiskey, I'm not sure telling Magnet Springs to go fuck itself was a good business move."

No doubt I owed my staff, if not the entire town, an apology. But first I had questions for the man some dubbed "Mr. OGP" (Obnoxious Gay Pride).

"Rico, do you sell antique jewelry?"

He took a giant step backward and formed his hands into a view-finder, through which he scanned me from head to toe.

"Who knew you were an antique jewelry kind of girl? Then again, who knew you owned a black camisole! How's that working for you, by the way? Better than the big hat, I hope."

"The jewelry's not for me. Could we go to your gallery?"

"*Avec plaisir.*" He bowed toward his establishment, half a block away.

The West Shore Gallery was the largest and most eclectic of the three galleries in town. Two bright, spacious rooms morphed every month or so from Postmodern to Whatever, according to Rico's mood. Although I appreciated the pickled plank flooring and stark white walls, precisely illuminated by recessed halogen lamps, the art *du mois* often left me shaking my head. Today was no exception. The featured artist was someone named Zolfo who had apparently run out of every color except red. His canvases featured scarlet splotches of varying sizes and shapes on a white background. The smallest picture I could find sold for $2,700. The largest was $8,000.

"Zolfo also takes commissions," Rico said from across the room.

"What's his going rate on wallet-size?"

Rico cleared his throat. "My antique jewelry is over here."

I joined him in front of a tall glass case. A quick scan revealed nary a piece of hair jewelry. I must have looked disappointed because Rico said, "Not what your imaginary friend is looking for?"

"Is any of this Victorian?" I asked.

Rico unlocked the case and extracted several ugly pieces, which he described in detail. They included a brass-domed brooch with five layers of Bohemian rose-cut garnets, and a black enamel and seed pearl mourning bracelet.

"'Morning'?" My ears perked up. "As in time of day? Or time of sorrow?"

I should have guessed. When Rico began recounting how Queen Victoria wore mourning jewelry after Prince Albert died, I had to interrupt: "Sold any hair jewelry lately or know anyone who has?"

"Funny you should ask. Saturday Kevin Sweeney brought in a couple pieces for me to appraise."

My pulse jumped. "What did he have?"

"Mid-nineteenth-century earrings and a bracelet—in beautiful condition."

"Worth much?"

"Only historically. I could tell by the engraved initials that they were part of the Slocum Schuyler estate. I half-expected Sweeney to make me sign a gag order."

"Did he say why he wanted them appraised?"

"I assumed he was updating the value of the estate." Rico arched a carefully plucked eyebrow. "You're not suggesting that the hair jewelry had something to do with Sweeney getting stabbed, are you? I just heard about that!"

I told him, quite honestly, that I didn't know. And that was all I told him. But I asked one more question: "Ever do business with the LePadannis?"

He shook his head and then amended the reply. "Tammi took a weaving course I offered here last fall. That was before she went to work for you. I think she had too much time on her hands."

FORTY

I HAD BARELY SET foot inside the foyer of Mattimoe Realty before the part-time receptionist said, "Odette's looking for you."

Mumbling that I was busy, I made a beeline for my private office, where I intended to sequester myself. Except that Ms. Mutombo was already perched on the edge of my desk, filing her nails with way too much energy.

"Show me the finger," she demanded without looking up.

"Huh?"

"I never knew until this morning that the third digit of your right hand was pixilated. Is that why you like to wave it around?"

"Odette, that caption was completely out of context. I was giving Fast Eddie Fresniak the finger. I like most of Magnet Springs!"

"Except, apparently, your late husband's daughter and her lover."

"Did Avery phone *you*, too?"

"She didn't have to. She phoned everyone else in town. Heads-up, Whiskey: she may sue."

"*She* was trespassing! And burgling!"

"So you beat her to a bloody pulp."

"Did not!"

"I understand she phoned Fast Eddie to photograph her wounds. Can't wait till next week's edition."

Groaning, I cradled my head in my hands.

Odette said, "And before I forget, there's more bad news: Tammi LePadanni failed to show up for her appointments yesterday. And she's still not answering her home or cell phone."

I sat up straight. "You mean she's missing?"

"Missing in action, at any rate. We now have several pissed-off high-profile clients."

"I'll call them," I said, wondering if Dr. and Mrs. LePadanni were missing together or separately. "Tammi left no word with anyone?"

"None."

"Do we have her daughter's cell phone number?"

"Miss Non-Winner, you mean? You'll have to ask Tina."

I buzzed my office manager, who immediately started whining.

"We're getting complaints about Tammi! She missed four appointments yesterday and one this morning. I'm pretty sure she came in here either late last night or early this morning because her coffee cup was in the sink, and it looked like she'd picked up her messages. But she's not taking calls, and Brandi's not answering her cell phone, either. I even called her school. Brandi's absent!"

So all three LePadannis were MIA. I told Tina to prepare a list of the offended clients and their phone numbers so that I could start the reparations. Then I tried calling Tammi at home and on her cell, and got voice mail in both cases. Next I called Brandi; I reached her voice mail, too. Not surprisingly, her outgoing message sounded like a series of questions: "Hey? This is Brandi? I can't talk now? But like maybe later? So like leave a message?"

I like did. I identified myself and said I was worried about her mom. I asked Brandi to call me back or have Tammi call me herself.

Odette had stopped messing with her perfect nails and was paying close attention as I concluded the call.

"You suspect foul play, don't you?" she said.

"Yeah, and I have a sinking feeling that it's the LePadannis who are playing foul. What does your telephone telepathy say about that?"

"It says if Tammi stays gone, I'll take over her client file."

"Of course you will. But who stabbed Sweeney? Who killed Crystal Crossman? Where's Abra? And where are the LePadannis?" Odette lowered her eyelids, a rare look of concentration tightening her usually seamless face. "Something is very wrong at Providence. Jenx or Brady should check it out. And if they don't, you will."

Odette was psychic, all right. When I called Jenx, she suggested I add Providence to my To Do List.

"Just one question," I said. "What are the police doing right now that's more important than looking for a missing family? And don't tell me Brady's reading a book!"

"He finished the book," Jenx said. "In fact, he finished both of them. He and Roscoe are out in the field."

"And what are *you* doing?"

261

"Connecting the dots. That's what police work is." She hung up.

Tina brought me the names and numbers of clients offended by Tammi's absence. I phone-schmoozed 'em all, offering to personally handle whatever needed handling. Without exception, they requested Odette.

I needed to return to Providence. Only this time, I needed to get inside. Once I confided, unofficially, in my office manager, Tina murmured something about looking under Tammi's desk, where I found what appeared to be an extra set of house keys.

That left only the alarm system to crack. Tina to the rescue again: when she coughed what sounded like the word "phone," I lifted Tammi's and found an index card with what looked like two numeric codes. Possibly Tammi's email or ATM passwords. But I chose to believe they'd get me past the alarm and into the house. I studied the index card. Was this the same printing as on the hair-jewelry notes? Without a side-by-side comparison, I couldn't be sure.

Next was the little matter of the pit bulls. Were they contained or not? Tina couldn't help me there. I was mulling over my options when the receptionist rang: "Call from Yolanda Brewster on line two."

I punched the button and exclaimed, "Mrs. Brewster! How are you?"

"I'm fine, Miz Mattimoe. Mighty flattering photo of you in this morning's paper."

I scrambled to explain my erect middle digit, but Mrs. Brewster didn't care. "For a woman who can't say 'shit,' you making progress. And here's something to help you make mo' progress: I just saw that dog of yours again. She was under my porch."

"Doing what?"

"I couldn't get my chair out there in time to see. But I can guess. That black truck was back, too. I think Tammi LePadanni had your crazy dog, and your dog got away! Abra come out from under my porch and run toward downtown. I don't know which way the truck go."

I asked Mrs. Brewster if she was sure it was the same vehicle she'd seen before.

"Black trucks ain't like black men, Miz Mattimoe. Black trucks all look about the same. If that wasn't Tammi LePadanni, then we got us a coincidence. And I don't believe in those."

That's when I remembered that Mrs. Brewster had a personal connection to the LePadannis. I asked if her nephew DuMayne followed up on his pit bull sales. My tenant archly replied that Du-Mayne loved those dogs, so of course he checked up on them.

"I know that Tammi keeps the dogs indoors … as pets," I began.

"Of course she does!" Mrs. Brewster exclaimed. "Or DuMayne never would've let her buy 'em. It's in the contract."

"What contract?"

"The contract DuMayne's customers have to sign when they buy his dogs. They *got* to keep them inside. And they got to have a special room in their house just for the dogs. That's how come DuMayne only sell to rich people."

From her tone, I could tell she thought DuMayne's clients had more cents than sense.

I reflected on what I'd observed during my Saturday night visit to Providence: vicious, big dogs gone mad inside a pitch-dark house where only moments before a teen-queen wannabe had pitched a fit in front of her impassive father. Someone had come and gone, presumably taking Brandi along. And they'd turned the lights out when they left. All the lights. As if the power were cut. *The power …*

Although I rarely used my own, I knew enough about alarm systems to understand that the security provider would have registered a power outage and tried to reach the client. If no one answered, the company would have called the police. Thus Jenx would have gotten a call that night to check on Providence.

I thanked Mrs. Brewster for the Abra Update and apologized if my dog had made a "mess" under her porch.

"Not so fast, Miz Mattimoe! You tell me what kind of 'mess' that might be! You need practice using the big-girl word."

"Ah," I sighed. "*Shit.*"

Next I phoned Jenx, wondering how many realtors had their local police chief on speed dial. I could tell that Jenx's calls were being forwarded to her cell phone. When she picked up, I quickly asked if she'd been notified by the alarm company to check on Providence Saturday night.

Annoyed, she said, "No. And if you don't mind, Whiskey, I'm working."

So I speedily summarized my theory about the power going out.

"Did you *hear* an alarm?" Jenx asked with fake patience.

"No, but—"

"Most alarm systems run on batteries if AC power is cut. You probably would have heard the LePadanni's alarm go off *if* it was triggered. Unless they have a silent alarm."

"But—"

"No buts, Whiskey. I didn't hear from the alarm company, and you didn't hear the alarm. Either it didn't go off, it was silent, or somebody inside Providence answered the alarm company's call. Maybe the power didn't even go out. Got it?"

She hung up before I could tell her about Abra's probable shit.

FORTY-ONE

JENX'S LACK OF INTEREST hardened my determination to solve whatever mystery lurked at Providence. Subdivisions as upscale as Pasco Point are nearly deserted in daytime, save the hourly workers hired to maintain the place. On my way there, I rehearsed my cover story, should I need one. I would tell the truth, mostly: that I was checking on my missing employee. Was anyone who worked with Dr. LePadanni investigating his whereabouts? I phoned the surgeon's office myself.

Once again, I got voice mail—a message hastily recorded by a rattled office manager. The mature woman's voice said, "Due to circumstances beyond our control, this office is closed until further notice. We are telephoning patients to reschedule appointments. Please bear with us. Thank you for your cooperation."

I decided to approach Providence head-on, acting for all the world as if I had every right to be there. I figured I'd attract less attention that way than if I attempted to sneak in. Thus, shortly after three o'clock I sailed past the stone sign at the entrance to the subdivision and into the elegant world manicured by landscapers and cleaning services. If only my mission were as straightforward as theirs.

What the hell was I doing? Besides hoping to avoid a couple pit bulls with their own bedroom? Basically, I was here to snoop because the cops didn't think the LePadannis were important enough to check out themselves—even though Ma, Pa, and Baby Girl were all either in trouble or playing hooky. I wondered if one of them was driving Wee Sweeney's car.

My heart raced as I turned in to Providence. Passing the phallic fountain, I pulled around to the back and parked in front of the four-car garage that matched the Mediterranean-style mansion. After killing the engine, I sat very still, willing myself to become bold. Then I opened my door and listened. No barking. That was odd. Even Abra set up a racket when I had visitors.

Pasco Point was silent mainly because it was still too early in the season to mow. Next door a two-man landscape crew was hand-spreading pre-emergent herbicide. My arrival didn't interest them. It didn't interest Tammi's pit bulls, either, if they were still in residence. Or still alive. Had the dogs been fatally neglected? How long could they last if deprived of food and water? I did some quick mental math and realized that just less than forty-eight hours had passed. If I remembered my high-school science, humans could last up to three or four days without water. Was it different for dogs? If the pit bulls had been neglected but weren't dead, then they were either in a weakened condition (point for my side) or royally pissed off (I lose).

The spring sunlight made the house glow; its apricot-tinted stucco suggested vitality. Yet, except for the playing fountain out front and the beds of blooming forsythia, daffodils, and crocuses, Providence didn't breathe. Just for a moment, I had the eerie sense that no one had ever really lived here.

I shut my car door as quietly as I could, and my cell phone jangled. *Damn.* I'd forgotten to turn off the ringer.

"Whiskey? It's Wells. I can hardly hear you."

"Sorry." Tentatively I raised my voice. "Is that better?"

"A little. David Newquist called to tell me about Mooney and Norman. Apparently you had a thrilling morning."

"Especially Mooney and Norman," I confirmed. "And Kevin Sweeney and Fenton Flagg. Did Dr. David give you the human news, too?"

"Indeed he did. That's why I'm calling. What are you up to?"

"Why?"

I scanned the LePadannis' yard for a hidden camera. *Was I on a new reality show … about people poised to commit felonies? Was Judge Wells Verbelow the host?*

He went on, "David said you had a little incident with Avery."

I doubted that Dr. David had put it that way.

"Uh … yeah. Unfortunately, we both lost our tempers. But I'm sure it won't permanently damage our relationship." *Because we've always hated each other.*

"I hope that's true," Wells said. "But if it isn't, I'd like to recommend a good attorney. Even if Avery doesn't pursue legal action, you might want to retain his services in relation to Abra."

"You think I'm going to get sued?"

"I think you're subject to litigation on several fronts."

Wells was trying to be gentle, but there's no way to make pending legal action sound like a picnic. Anyway, there I was, about to break in to Providence, so he might have been right. I let him give me the name of an attorney, and I pretended to write it down.

"Is there any chance you could join me and Mooney for dinner at my house tonight?" Wells asked. "I know this is short notice, but Norman may be there, too. David asked if I could keep him for a while. I have an extra kennel, so I don't see why not."

I thanked Wells for the invitation and told him I'd have to get back to him since I wasn't yet sure what my afternoon might yield. A felony arrest? A double pit bull attack?

Clumsily steering the conversation around to his missing friend Stan, I asked Wells if the surgeon had ever mentioned his two pet pit bulls.

"Interesting you should bring that up. While David and I were talking about Norman, I recalled something Stan said about his dogs. They're not assistance animals, but they are highly trained and intuitive. Stan said he needed to say only a few key words, and they could practically read his mind."

"You wouldn't happen to know what those key words are, would you?"

"Probably 'kill' and 'halt.'"

When I whimpered, Wells added, "You'd never go near dogs like that voluntarily. Unless the LePadannis were with you. I'm not sure what methodology they used, but if those dogs were trained for security work, you can be sure they were trained to kill on command."

"What if they don't hear the command?" I asked hopefully.

"They could have been trained to kill on sight. Or sound. Some dogs are taught to lie still, watching or listening for the approach of an intruder. Then, when their victim walks within range, they take him down."

By now my knees were so rubbery I had to lean against the side of my car.

Wells said, "Where are you, anyway?"

"Uh … on my way to … call on someone."

"You usually are. Where?"

"Uh. Near … Pasco Point." *Very near.* "Why?"

"I was wondering if you were on your way to see Faye again today."

"Did something else go wrong?!"

"Not that I know of. Her parents called me from Venezuela. They had a few questions about her care in their absence."

I knew what that meant: they were running a character check on me. I wondered if they knew I'd left their only daughter vulnerable to an Aqua Net attack and a head-first fall over my balcony.

"Are they aware that she's in the hospital?"

Belatedly I realized that I should have called Faye's parents myself. Another point deducted from my side.

"Yes. I told them you're checking on her regularly. And they've called her, too, of course, when they've been able to get phone service. The labor strike has made that problematic. The next time you see Faye, please tell her that her parents expect to leave Venezuela tomorrow."

Just in time for her funeral. I didn't say that out loud, of course. I wanted the judge to think I was a competent temporary guardian, my legal problems notwithstanding. Then I noticed that one of the landscapers next door was checking me out. And not in a flattering way. More in a "what-the-hell-is-she-up-to?" way. If they suspected I didn't belong here, I'd have to work fast.

I told Wells I had to go and promised to RSVP him ASAP about dinner. Then I faced the arched, carved mahogany door that was my portal to Providence, and prayed for benevolent pit bulls.

FORTY-TWO

Elegant enough to be a front entrance, the wide rear door was sufficiently recessed to conceal it from the prying eyes of neighbors and their hired help. Fifty yards to my right, the landscape guy was still watching me. But he conveniently faded from both my view and my mind as soon as I stepped onto the LePadannis' terrazzo porch.

Of the two keys I'd taken from under Tammi's desk, one was probably for the detached garage, the other for the front and/or back door. I studied the index card I'd found under Tammi's phone. Assuming that I gained access to the house, my next challenge would either be to dodge raging pit bulls or enter the right code on the alarm keypad. But first I'd have to locate the alarm keypad.

I had sold literally dozens of homes armed with alarm systems. So I knew a few things about electronic security. For instance, a home the size of Providence typically contained several alarm keypads that communicated with the control panel. Generally, keypads were located near the doors used most often. Since the door before me was closest to the garage, I assumed it came with a keypad. But the LePadannis might have decided to place the keypad elsewhere. Or—scarier thought—they might have aesthetically concealed it. In either case, I would have to move quickly. And hope to God that the keypad had a generous delay setting to allow me enough time to find it before activation.

Not knowing the layout of Tammi's house was a distinct disadvantage. Guessing would eat up precious time. Especially when I was trying to keep an eye peeled for pit bulls.

Wishing I had Odette's photographic memory for figures, I willed myself to memorize the two possible pass-codes: 485075 and 041148.

Then I inhaled deeply, slid one of the two keys into the lock, and turned it.

The key clicked obligingly. I pushed down on the solid bronze lever, and the heavy door swung toward me.

I listened for the rapid click-clack of approaching dog claws on tile but heard nothing. Cautiously I set one foot inside as my eyes scanned the wall for a keypad. All the walls. I saw no keypad.

Where could it be? The foyer was spacious as rear foyers go— about ten feet by twenty with a high arched ceiling and creamy stucco walls. I took three long strides to the nearest wall art, a rectangular fabric collage in what I would call warm Tuscan colors, and pulled up a corner. Nothing there.

My eyes leapt beyond the foyer into the immense, sky-lighted kitchen. So many mahogany cabinets, some running from ceiling to floor. Theoretically, the keypad could be in any one of them.

But I doubted it.

Tammi's words rushed back into my consciousness. We'd been at the Magnet Springs Country Club for a fund-raiser last winter. She wasn't talking to me although I knew she wanted me to overhear her comment to a fellow "Mrs. Doctor." The other woman had complained about her state-of-the-art alarm system going off in error and repeatedly summoning the annoyed local cop … who happened to be Chief Jenkins.

Tammi said, "Why deal with alarms that break down when you can have a system that never fails?"

"What's that?" asked the other woman.

"Pit bulls, trained by the best. Stan and I don't need electronics."

At the time, I had thought Tammi meant that they didn't really need the alarm system they already had. Now, though, I believed she meant that they used pit bulls *in place of* an electronic alarm.

I stuffed the index card back in my pocket wishing that I'd brought mace instead. Even pepper spray would have consoled me. Now I clutched that other card, the wallet-sized Dogs-Train-You-dot-com Guard Dog Commands Cheat Sheet, downloaded, printed, and laminated for me by Chester. Although he intended it for use with Abra, somehow I could never get my hands on the card when she was wreaking havoc. Today I had remembered to remove it from my wallet.

Of course, I had no way of knowing if the LePadannis' pit bulls knew Dogs-Train-You-dot-com vocabulary. Odds were good that at least a few commands would translate. Unless the trainer had used Spanish or Korean or some other tongue. No point contemplating that nightmare.

Weighed down by stillness, the house felt eerie and deep. More foreboding than the fog-swathed silence of Winimar. Here the quiet had an artificial quality that unsettled me. I fought the urge to say "Hello!" just to see if the air could carry a human voice.

Slowly I crossed the wide slate-floored kitchen toward the archway leading to the rest of the house. One of the largest kitchens I'd been in, this one was square and measured roughly thirty feet by thirty. One wall was all glass, overlooking a small courtyard lined with daffodils and containing two wrought-iron benches. The kitchen's other walls were mostly covered in cabinetry; one end of the room featured a built-in mahogany banquette that easily seated twelve. In the center of the room stood an S-shaped granite-topped island with two additional stainless steel sinks, bi-level counters, and a black ceramic cooking surface. The room's color scheme, besides rich mahogany, was a mix of ivory and gray with terra cotta accents. Sunshine streamed in from both the skylight above and the south-facing glass wall, making everything shimmer.

I wished I'd remembered to bring gloves. Veering toward the refrigerator, I pulled my sweater sleeve over my hand like a makeshift oven mitt and jerked open the mahogany-paneled door. No light popped on; the air wafting out was only slightly cooler than room temperature and tangy from berries and soft cheese gone bad. The power had been cut Saturday night, for sure.

I spotted a notepad on the granite island. In the same printing I'd seen on Tammi's index card, I read "Feed Romeo and Juliet." In this household, Shakespeare's star-crossed lovers probably had four legs each. And they couldn't have been cats because Tammi disliked felines more than I did.

Ahead of me through the arch was a broad corridor from which two sunny rooms flowed. My eyes followed the hallway to its conclusion: the large central room where Brandi had played out her drama. I could see only a bronze floor lamp, a dense carved coffee table and part of a white leather couch—all pieces that I'd glimpsed Saturday from my vantage point near the garage. Brandi had stood behind the white couch, beating her red rose bouquet against the sofa table while Dr. LePadanni sat immobile in a white leather chair to her left. I couldn't see her table or his chair from here, but what I could see of the room fit my memory.

What had happened to Dr. LePadanni? And where were Romeo and Juliet, the presumed hungry pit bulls?

I started down the corridor, the room ahead opening like a white flower. Just before I took the step that would reveal Dr. Le-Padanni's chair, I inhaled a scent that closed my throat. A uniquely rank combination, it brought to mind the odor that had assaulted me last summer when I'd unlocked my shed to discover a dead raccoon.

I tried to collect myself. Something rattled behind me. I spun around. Two white and tan pit bulls, their squarish heads too big for their bodies, stood shoulder to shoulder less than ten feet away. The rattle came again, louder. It was a stereo growl rising from their deep chests.

FORTY-THREE

MY BODY TENSED AS if electrified. Suddenly aware of every part of myself—from my hair to my toes—I felt completely exposed and vulnerable. Romeo and Juliet's joint growl sounded like approaching thunder.

If only I had paid more attention when Deely and Chester babbled about canine behavior. In a situation like this, were you supposed to stare down the dogs, or avoid making eye contact? I stole a glance at the Dogs-Train-You-dot-com Commands Cheat Sheet. Maybe, just maybe, I could convince Romeo and Juliet not to kill me.

When I glanced back up, the dogs were slowly advancing in a semi-crouched position. Coiled to spring, they resembled a double-barreled lethal weapon.

"Stay?" I said, sounding pathetically lame even to my ears. An icy sweat bathed my forehead, my neck, my armpits. Without thinking, I had begun backing toward the central room. The room with the stench.

Romeo and Juliet never blinked. In unison they continued growling and creeping toward me, four dark eyes fixed on my face. As the seconds ticked by, and I shuffled backwards, the two dogs became one: a single overdeveloped muscle bearing down upon me, pushing me ever closer to my fate. And I was pretty sure I knew what that was.

The stink of the room enveloped me; I gagged just as the back of my right thigh made contact with a solid piece of furniture. Involuntarily I glanced around. Dr. LePadanni sat in the same chair I'd seen him in on Saturday night. Only now his balding head lolled forward, seeming to rest, detached, on his massive chest. I gave silent thanks that I couldn't see his face; one less ghastly detail to repress.

"Doctor?" I asked tentatively. But I knew he was beyond acknowledging that honorific.

I felt a hot breath on my right hand and gasped. Either Romeo or Juliet was sniffing me at close range. The other dog stood back, looking less deadly but still watchful. The growling had stopped.

"Nice doggie," I said, my mouth as dry as if I'd been sucking salt.

Incredibly, the sniffer wagged its tail. The other dog cocked its head at me and whined. I watched, grimly mesmerized, as Romeo and Juliet circled Dr. LePadanni's chair, glancing from him to me as they exhaled one long sorrowful wail.

Dog-trainer dropout though I was, I knew enough to move very slowly as I withdrew my cell phone. All I said to Jenx was "I'm at Providence, Dr. LePadanni's dead, and the pit bulls are loose."

She told me to stay where I was (like I had a choice); she'd be there in less than ten minutes. The wait probably seemed longer because I was trapped in a vile-smelling room with a corpse and two attack dogs. Romeo and Juliet worked out a routine: they took turns watching me and circling their late master; occasionally, Romeo peed along the perimeter of the room. I figured that was territorial marking and not a housebreaking failure. Although the dogs no longer terrified me, I thought it best not to stare at them. So I memorized the pattern of the tile floor and breathed through my mouth.

What—or who—had killed the doctor? I tried not to think about him, which was my grandest feat of denial. Talk about ignoring the elephant in the room …

I'm just proud to report that I didn't faint or puke.

———

"I can't believe you didn't faint," Brady said. "Or puke." He and Officer Roscoe were escorting me out of Providence into the fresh coastal air.

I embraced the compliment even though I knew the truth. I'd stayed conscious for one reason only: pure terror. I'd been afraid, if I fainted, the pit bulls would eat me.

"Does it always smell this good this time of year?" I asked.

Brady and Roscoe tilted their heads and sniffed. Noncommittally, Brady said, "It always smells like mud this time of year."

"It smells like life," I said.

Brady didn't argue. He and Roscoe had seen what I'd seen inside Providence. Jenx and the paramedics were still in there along with three sheriff's deputies—*not* Deputy Clifton—and a couple state troopers. No fewer than seven emergency vehicles lined the LePadannis' long driveway. The landscaping duo next door had given up all pretense of work and now stood staring. Several traveling maid services had also left their posts to gawk. Whenever anyone ventured too near, Roscoe bared his teeth, and the voyeur retreated.

I'd been struck by Roscoe's snobbishness toward Romeo and Juliet. They'd made a friendly, tail-wagging overture; in response, he had literally turned his back. Maybe he was offended by dogs who assumed he'd be their new best friend. Notoriously excepting Abra, Roscoe tended to be aloof—a quality I attributed to his refined breeding and elite education. But with Romeo and Juliet he'd been downright rude. Maybe Roscoe just didn't like pit bulls.

"I don't like pit bulls," Brady remarked.

We were watching the arrival of the Lanagan County Canine Control Unit. Two officers descended from the white van wearing body armor and wire-mesh facemasks.

"But the LePadanni dogs don't seem vicious," Brady continued, "even toward Roscoe. And pit bulls can be animal-aggressive."

I said, "Romeo and Juliet just wanted to take care of their master."

That reminded me I was a caregiver, too. I excused myself to phone Faye.

"Mom just called!" exclaimed Miss Blossom. "They'll be here tomorrow! It was only the second time we've talked on account of the labor strikes."

I recalled Fenton Flagg's first book, *I'm Cool, But You Have a Curse on Your Head*. Maybe we do make or break our own luck. After I finished talking with Faye, I had a question for Brady.

"Didn't you say that Reactional Analysis was about choosing what you want to believe?"

"Right. Murray McCready—I mean Fenton Flagg—says we form our own reality. If you want to believe you're cursed, you're cursed. If you want to believe you're a winner, you're a winner. Some people choose to believe they can do whatever they want."

"What does that make them?"

"Sociopaths."

"Is that what we're looking for? A sociopath? Whoever ran Crystal Crossman off the road did something the rest of us would never dream of doing."

"I see your point, but . . ." Brady chose his words carefully. "There are also crimes of passion. Moments when ordinary people lose their moral center. That makes them wrongdoers but not sociopaths." He leaned closer. "But the way Tammi cursed Faye? Now *that's* sociopathic."

The two Canine Control officers emerged from Providence with Romeo and Juliet on leads; the men had removed their protective face masks. Tails wagging, the pit bulls heeled all the way to the back of the van where they waited obediently for the doors to open.

FORTY-FOUR

MORE THAN AN HOUR had passed since Officers Swancott and Roscoe ushered me out of Providence into breathable air. The canine cop was called back to duty indoors while the human cop and I waited in the north-facing courtyard for Jenx to either arrest or dismiss me. I still owed Wells a *yea* or *nay* on his dinner invitation. Since I didn't yet know whether I'd be heading home or to the slammer, I turned off my cell phone.

By now Brady and I had run out of small talk. Or at least the kind of small talk I liked. I wanted details about the case; he claimed he couldn't give me any. I'd been *sent* here because the police wanted to know what was up and didn't have the manpower to find out. Ergo, I was as involved as Brady ... just not as legitimately. Not legitimately, at all, according to the other law enforcement agencies on site. Both the sheriff's office and the state police were troubled by my B & E.

Brady confided that it would have been better for me to flee the scene before the cops arrived. I explained that I would have happily done so if only Romeo and Juliet had been willing to bid me adieu. Jenx was trying to tap dance our way out of this quagmire.

I closed my eyes and focused on cheerful thoughts. Thoughts that didn't include hiring a high-priced attorney to defend me against criminal charges.

Suddenly the French doors opened, and Jenx said, "Whiskey, you're free to go."

She looked exhausted, leading me to conclude that the state and county boys had given her a rough time. But when I saw the other guys, I revised my opinion. Either Jenx had argued them into a stupor, or they were taking an off-the-record siesta on the nice leather furniture in the family room. Eyes half-closed, bodies slack, they slumped in armchairs and on sofas. Then I noticed something else: the wall art and lamp shades were askew, and the area rugs were rumpled. Even the brass chandelier hung cockeyed. Telltale signs of Jenx's energy run amok. The chief was inclined to disrupt geomagnetic fields if someone questioned her authority. Let alone her integrity.

I issued a collective thanks to the assembled lawmen. Nobody stirred. Curious though I was about the cause of Dr. LePadanni's death, even I could guess that this was not the time to ask.

I was outside already, striding toward my car, when I heard Brady behind me.

"Whiskey, wait!"

He was accompanied by Roscoe, who weaved and staggered as if drugged.

"What happened to him?" I gasped.

"Same thing that happened to the other officers."

"Jenx's magnetism?" I'd forgotten that Roscoe was in there, too.

Brady nodded. "He took a direct hit. Poor guy. When Jenx gets riled, look out."

We watched Roscoe stumble around in a circle and then land on his side, panting. Most of the gawkers had gone. Roscoe's "disorder" alarmed the few who remained; when he fell over, they retreated to the other side of the street.

"Between the books and my online research, plus what I saw in Fenton Flagg's notes, I've reached an astounding conclusion," Brady announced. "There are living Schuyler heirs."

"I thought the family tree ended with Mrs. Schuyler's nephew …"

"Let's put it this way: Mrs. Schuyler's generation was the last to procreate—legitimately."

"Are you saying the nephew had a bastard?" I asked.

"No. I'm saying Miss Blossom did."

I stared. "Mar Schuyler had a baby? With whom?"

"I'm still putting the pieces together. But the case we're working on now looks like the latest chapter in a long, sick story of revenge."

"Starting with the original Miss Blossom?" I asked.

Brady nodded. "If I'm right, Mar Schuyler did what young girls often do: she loved a wild boy, she got pregnant, and she got sent away. The wrinkle was that her mom was nuts. Rich and nuts. A nasty combination. Mom never stopped meddling."

"How?"

"According to the original Winimar book, the first Miss Blossom missed the crowning of the second Miss Blossom because she had consumption. Nobody had seen Mar Schuyler in months;

word was she'd been sent to a private hospital. Mom attended the second annual coronation in her daughter's place and led the crowd in a prayer for Mar's recovery. Then she tearfully donated the custom-made emerald tiara to the village of Magnet Springs. That was in April 1848. In July, Mar died at home. Not from consumption, as you know. She was murdered. Mom fingered one of the Italian tradesmen who'd helped build Winimar. She claimed he was obsessed with Mar and often 'leered' at her. There were no signs of a break-in. Mom insisted the Italian knew how to sneak into the house. Thanks to Mrs. Schuyler's prodigious grief, money, and social connections, the accused was swiftly tried and executed."

I said, "Does the first Winimar book state that Mar had a baby?"

"No. The second one does. According to Murray McCready—a.k.a. Fenton Flagg—Mar confided her pregnancy in one of the maidservants, who was then fired for knowing too much. The maid claimed she would have kept quiet. But after losing her job, she was P.O.'d enough to spread the word before she left town. Mrs. Schuyler promptly countered with the consumption story. And here's where Reactional Analysis comes into play: Everybody who was anybody in Magnet Springs *chose* to believe that Miss Blossom had consumption because they were told to believe it by Mrs. Schuyler, who had way more influence than an Irish maid."

"What happened to Mar's baby?"

"I can't be sure I got it right till I talk to Flagg in person."

"Oh, come on! Who are the Schuyler heirs?"

"Sorry. I need to see Flagg first."

"Why? Do we know the Schuyler heirs?"

I was fishing, but Brady wouldn't take the bait. So I tried a new question: "Who was hanged for Mar's murder? If it's in the books, you know I'm going to read it, anyway."

Brady sighed. "His name … was Antonio Paladino."

FORTY-FIVE

I stared at Brady. "Paladino? As in—?"

"Yeah. Believe it or not, Dock's real name is Anthony."

"Are you saying Dock Paladino is the last surviving Schuyler heir?!"

"I'm not saying *that*!" Brady looked uncharacteristically stern.

"Okay …" I was willing to backpedal, a little. "Are you saying we should go have a chat with Dock's great uncle, the sausage vendor?"

"*That* we should do," Brady agreed. "If Jenx says we can."

He went back inside to check, leaving me and Roscoe in the driveway. We were both disoriented but for different reasons. I assumed that the metal tags on the canine officer's collar had made him extra vulnerable to Jenx's geomagnetic fit. He seemed more alert now, but still cautious about getting back up on all fours. My mind was reeling at the notion that Dock Paladino might be connected to both the curse and the cash of Winimar.

Brady re-emerged, pointing toward his cruiser. "Want to ride with me?"

I declined, preferring to follow in my own vehicle rather than return to Providence to pick it up later. This place was as creepy as Winimar.

Because I'd sent a floral apology after Abra knocked him down, I already knew that Vito Botafogo lived in the two-block zone of Magnet Springs called Little Italy. It should have been called Itty-Bitty Italy. Just north of downtown, but not far enough to count as the true North Side, Little Italy consisted of a dozen tiny houses built close to the street, one rundown post-World War II apartment building, the only Catholic church in our zip code, and two small but excellent restaurants. One specialized in northern Italian *cucina*, the other in southern. I preferred the northern place myself. You can't go wrong when a meal starts with a good Chianti and all the crostini you can eat.

Thinking about food reminded me that I still owed Wells a reply to his dinner invitation. Since it was already after five and I had police business to conduct, I decided to request a raincheck. I reached the judge on his cell phone as I drove south out of Pasco Point, right behind Brady's patrol car.

Wells's disappointment was audible; it stirred a strange blend of feelings in me, starting with guilt—since I had lied yet again about what I was up to—and ending with lust. Yes, *lust*. When Wells lowered his voice to say that he'd see me for dinner tomorrow, he actually sounded … sexy. I wanted some of that. Apparently, Odette's lingerie strategy was having the desired effect. I offered to bring wine, but Wells had a different idea: "Just show up wearing that camisole."

As we cruised into town, Brady buzzed me. "We'll approach from the alley behind Vito's house."

"Why? There's plenty of on-street parking."

"We're not doing a property appraisal, Whiskey. If somebody's up to something at Vito's, we want to catch them in the act."

"The act of what? What do you think's going on?"

"Could be anything. Follow my lead."

I had been mentally prepared for nothing more strenuous than decoding Vito's thick accent. Now another rush of adrenaline coursed through my system. How much of that hormone could I have left?

Passing Christopher Street, I glanced longingly at the Toscana Ristorante. What I wouldn't have given for a glass of red wine.

Behind Brady, I made a right turn into the alley. Dead ahead of us, about halfway down the passage, loomed a gleaming black tank.

I buzzed Brady. "Sweeney's Hummer!"

"Yeah," he replied. "And there might be a vehicle on the other side of it that we can't see from here."

"Dock's truck?" I guessed. "Or Tammi's SUV?"

Brady said, "Back out of the alley, turn your car around, and then back it in behind mine. We need to be able to fly out of here if things get complicated."

Things were already complicated. I followed his simple step-by-step directions, grateful not to have to think too much. Brady and I disembarked at the same time.

"Shit!" he said.

"What's the matter?"

"I stepped in shit!"

He checked the bottom of his shoe. Then our eyes met.

"Look familiar?" he asked. I understood the question.

"It could be hers. I don't know what she's been eating since Saturday …"

Brady nodded, deftly sidestepping the remaining pile to wipe his foot on a discarded brick. He pointed to the little white house nearest the Hummer.

"That's Vito's."

The smell of Italian sausage was a sure clue; it grew stronger with each approaching step. I wondered if Vito cooked the stuff all the time, or if he had cooked it for so long that the alley was permanently scented.

There was another black vehicle on the far side of the Hummer. In fact, there were two: a Dodge Ram truck and a Lincoln Navigator, presumably Dock Paladino's and Tammi LePadanni's. But who had driven Sweeney's Hummer? Or, put another way, who else was here besides Tammi and Dock and—if we'd read the shit right—my dog? I was pretty sure Abra couldn't drive.

Brady reached for his service revolver.

"Are you planning to use that?!" I whispered.

"God, no," he replied. "I was just checking to see if I brought it. It makes me look older."

The urgent bark of a dog split the air. I spun around, and there she was, loping toward us, her blonde tresses bouncing.

Then everything happened at once: a shot rang out; a woman screamed; a door slammed; a man shouted a long stream of words I couldn't decipher.

I knew that couldn't have been Brady's gun going off since he didn't intend to use it. And that couldn't have been me screaming or slamming the door because I hadn't moved. I was still staring slack-jawed at Abra, who kept on coming despite the noise.

"Get down!" Brady shouted.

Now I moved, flattening myself against the ground near the Hummer. Abra sailed past on the other side as a second gunshot sounded, accompanied by shattering glass.

I imagined the bullet piercing Abra. Then someone screamed. That time it was me.

"It's all right," Brady said. "Just stay down."

He had his weapon in hand.

"Do you even know how to use that thing?"

His response was vaguer than I would have preferred: "I've been to the firing range."

He instructed me to call Jenx on my cell phone. "Tell her to send backup. *Now.*"

That should have been easy, but my shaky finger misdialed speed-dial. Twice. When Jenx answered, I panted, "We're in the alley behind Vito's on Christopher Street, and somebody's shooting at us—or maybe at Abra! She's here, too. So's Sweeney's Hummer and Dock's truck and Tammi's SUV!"

Calmly the chief told me to remain on the line and keep breathing. I watched Brady inch along the length of the Hummer, poised to spray bullets.

"Hello!" he shouted toward the back of Vito's house. His voice sounded two octaves deeper than usual. "This is Officer Swancott of the Magnet Springs police. Come out with your hands up!"

I wondered if he said that because he'd been trained to, or because he'd seen cops do it on TV. No way I believed it would work.

Then a man called out, "How do we know you won't shoot us?"

Before Brady could answer, there was yet another scream, this one from inside the house. I heard Tammi shout, "Who let her in? Down! Get down, you goddamn bimbo!"

FORTY-SIX

THE BACK DOOR OF Vito's house swung open, and a man who had to be Dock Paladino stumbled out.

I guessed he was Dock for three reasons: (1) he looked exactly like Jenx had described him—big, beefy, and dark, the opposite of Brad Pitt; (2) he was, after all, related to Vito; and (3) he was followed by Tammi and Brandi LePadanni, who were followed by Abra.

Nobody in that oversexed group was thinking about doing the dirty. Dock clutched his left shoulder, which was bleeding; Brandi cringed in terror as Abra—in rare Attack Dog Mode—lunged and snapped at her; and Tammi looked just plain pissed off.

"Uncle Vito ain't coming out," Dock informed Brady. "He won't even put down the damn gun. Got me once already, and he says he's not done till I'm dead. The old coot can't see worth shit, but he still shoots."

"Can somebody? Get this dog? Away from me?" whimpered Brandi LePadanni.

Her face free of make-up and streaked with tears, she was still stunning. More stunning than usual, perhaps, because she seemed vulnerable. I couldn't help but admire the thick raven hair tumbling over her shoulders, her full lips and flawless bone structure. Brandi LePadanni looked for all the world like a Hollywood starlet trying vainly to blend with the rest of us. She never would.

When I missed my cue, Brandi shrieked, "Help me? Whiskey? You stupid bitch?"

Okay, so she was gorgeous *and* awful. Which did nothing to motivate me. I figured my dog wouldn't listen, anyhow. Then Officer Swancott whistled sharply. In mid-lunge, Abra veered away from the beauty and flew to Brady's side, where she lay down.

"How? Did you?" I began, sounding like You-Know-Who.

"Don't look so surprised," Brady said. "Abra and Roscoe trained together."

"Yes, but I thought Abra was the example of what *not* to do."

"I ain't-uh coming out-uh or putting down-uh the gun-uh until you put that bad-uh boy in hand-uh-cuff-uhs!"

A stooped old man stood on the other side of the screen door, waving a handgun like a surrender flag. When Brady didn't immediately move, Tammi snapped into action.

"Oh, for Christ's sake, I'll do it," she muttered and whipped a pair of handcuffs out of a jacket pocket.

"Freeze!" Brady boomed. "Drop the cuffs!"

Tammi sighed elaborately and let them hit the ground. Training his weapon on her, Brady scooped up the cuffs and tossed them to me. Hardly standard issue, these were lined with faux fur and pink lace. *Ugh.*

When Brady clicked real cuffs in place on Dock's wrists, I observed that Paladino's shoulder was leaking only a thin trickle of blood. Not enough to make even me feel faint. Sirens howled as police cruisers poured in at both ends of the alley, effectively trapping us all.

Vito hobbled into the alley, his empty hands up. Covering her flawless face, Brandi sobbed. Tammi stamped her foot and demanded to know how long this was going to take.

"I've got real estate clients to see!"

"Not anymore," I said loudly enough to cut through the sirens.

Deputy Clifton was one of two sheriff's men on the scene. Although his head was bandaged, he'd insisted on getting right back to work.

"I was glad to take this call," he said. "One of these folks probably cracked my skull."

"And worse," Jenx remarked ominously. "Much worse."

I turned to her. "Do you know something I don't know?"

"Always, Whiskey. Don't get me started."

Brady took Dock to the police station in his car; Jenx took Vito in hers. Clifton and the other sheriff's deputy were assigned to deliver the LePadanni ladies.

With Abra riding shotgun, I followed the four marked cars. Whimpering and wagging all the way, my diva dog couldn't wait to flirt with Canine Officer Roscoe. Reserved though he was, he always let her sniff his ass. I was pumped up, too. Tammi appeared to be in deep doo-doo, and she was one of my agents. Between her, Abra, and Faye, I had too many connections to hang back now. No way was I going home till I had some answers. Or till somebody in uniform made me go home.

Once at the station I hoped to slip into the interrogation room, which doubles as a supply closet. Since there were four suspects, almost every room at the station was put to use, including the kitchenette and both holding cells. And I was barred from the proceedings. That didn't discourage me, however. I was willing to wait for results.

True to her usual prurient drive, Abra made a beeline for Roscoe's rear end, inhaling him as if she hadn't had a whiff of manhood in months. Never mind that she'd been cavorting up and down this side of the county with Norman. Her tangled blonde coat betrayed her wanton ways.

Abra had a curative effect on Roscoe, instantly relieving the last of his geomagnetic hangover. I tried not to watch them. It had been too many months since I'd whiffed real manhood.

"Vito wants to talk to you."

Brady's voice startled me. I must have dozed off while slumped in the lobby.

"Vito?" I echoed.

"Don't worry. It's not about suing you."

Brady held open the swinging entrance gate for me to pass.

"Wait." I scanned the lobby. "Where did—?"

"They're out back. It was getting a little hot and heavy in here, so I put them in separate kennels."

Vito Botafogo was in the kitchenette, the perfect interrogation room for a sausage vendor. I joined him at the Formica-topped table, relieved that Brady had assured me the old man didn't plan to litigate. Otherwise his furrowed expression would have scared me all the way down to my wallet.

"Hello, Vito," I said. "Did you get the roses I sent?"

He nodded. "Very nice. My late wife Rosa, she would have loved them."

I remembered Rosa—a tiny, white-haired woman who could out-shout any vendor at a public event. She had died years ago. So Vito and I shared a common bond: we were both widowed.

"I want to tell you something," he said. "Something about your late husband Leo."

My heart lurched. Was this yet another revelation, or did Vito hold the key to what Leo had seen at Winimar?

"Leo, he was a good man," Vito began. "He had respect for other people's business, you know? When he saw something he was not supposed to see, he knew what to do about it."

I crossed my arms on the table to keep them from shaking.

"Vito, what did Leo see?"

Slowly the old man ran his tongue over his lips. He probably tasted *salsiccia fresca*.

"Every year, the new Miss Blossom, she got to have her picture painted at Winimar."

"Her picture? You mean, her portrait?"

He nodded nervously. "But not just a portrait. Is special. Must be done in a … certain way."

My mind flashed back to my earliest suspicions that something kinky was going on at Winimar. Crystal Crossman had firmly denied it, and I'd willed myself to believe her. Then she had died.

"What do you mean, 'in a certain way'?"

"The new Miss Blossom, she must dress up in the clothes of the first Miss Blossom. And there's more …" He winced as if telling the story caused him physical pain.

"Go on," I coaxed, wondering what any of this could have to do with Leo.

"She must pose by the grave of the first Miss Blossom."

"Mar Schuyler is buried in the Magnet Springs cemetery. I've seen her crypt."

Vito vigorously shook his head. "Crypt is empty. Her mama wanted to keep her body close to home."

"Why?"

"Because … her mama killed her."

I stared. "Mrs. Schuyler murdered her own daughter? Why?"

"Because she loved the wrong man, and she had his baby. Mar, she wanted to marry her lover and raise their child at Winimar. But Mrs. Schuyler, she said no, she made Mar go far away to have the baby and give it up. Then Mar came back, but not alone. She was with her baby and her husband, Antonio Paladino. Yes, they were married! Mrs. Schuyler, she said they could stay one night. And that night, Mrs. Schuyler went crazy. She killed her daughter in her sleep, and she tried to kill the baby and his father, too, but they ran away. Mrs. Schuyler, she had told everybody her daughter was sick with consumption. Now she called the sheriff. She said her daughter came home from the hospital. And Antonio Paladino, he broke into the house and killed her! Mrs. Schuyler never, never told nobody about the marriage. Or the baby."

"How do you know all this?" I demanded.

"Is part of our family legacy. You see, Antonio, he couldn't save his wife. But he saved their baby. Before he was arrested, he told his brother what happened. And the brother told their sister, who knew how to write. She wrote everything in the family Bible, and she saved it for the Paladino baby. Who passed it on to the next baby, and so on. This is what makes the Paladinos stronger than the Schuylers."

The old man trembled with pride.

I said, "How did Mrs. Schuyler get away with murder?"

Vito laughed ruefully, rubbing his second and third fingertips against his knobby thumb.

"Nobody questions the richest family! Nobody can afford to!"

"But who murdered Mrs. Schuyler? And her nephew's wife?"

"We will never know," Vito said sadly, "but me, I think it was Antonio's brother, Alessandro. I think he did it to avenge his brother. Family against family."

Beauty ends. Vengeance is never satisfied.

"What happened to the baby?" I said.

"Ah, the baby. The night when Mrs. Schuyler went crazy, Antonio, he gave the baby to his brother. And his brother, he gave the baby to their sister, who lived in Grand Rapids. She raised that baby."

"Was it a boy or a girl?"

"A boy! A fine, strong boy! Mar, she named him after his father, Antonio. From then on, every Paladino boy is named Antonio."

"But you're named Vito," I pointed out.

"That's because I am a Botafogo, son of Giuseppe. My father, he come to this country when he was thirty years old. He make rule at our house: we speak Italian always. It is my first language. It was my sainted late wife's first language, too."

"That explains your accent," I said. "But not Dock's name."

"My mother, *she* was a Paladino," Vito said. "The Antonios, they are the *sons* of Antonios."

"I see. So the name Antonio is part of the curse."

Vito bristled. "That is no curse! That is a Paladino *tradition*! The curse is on the Schuylers and the things they owned: Winimar and the big, ugly crown. I tell you now about the curse."

And he did. What I really wanted to know was what any of it had to do with Leo. Vito told me that, too …

FORTY-SEVEN

BEFORE WE DISCUSSED THE gritty details, Vito Botafogo insisted that we eat. He was an Italian sausage vendor, after all, and we were stuck in the police station kitchen at dinner time. Vito made magic using a can of minestrone, Brady's leftover chili and a handful of questionable items found in the fridge.

"Your husband Leo, he was half-Italian, no?" asked Vito.

Actually, Leo was a hundred percent Irish. I wasn't sure that was the right answer, however. So I smiled noncommittally over my steaming soup bowl.

Vito smiled back. "I thought so. Leo, he understood about honor. We talked about Winimar. I told him I cared nothing for Sweeney's damn gag orders. I knew how bad that place was. I knew it was no good for nobody. And I was not afraid to say so. Leo, he was not afraid, either. He did the right thing."

I waited while the old man noisily slurped his soup. Finally, he said, "There is a very old tree at Winimar. On the trunk of that tree is carved a heart and the words 'Antonio Paladino loves Mar

Schuyler.' Leo knew that I am part Paladino. So he came to me first … before he went to the police."

"Leo went to the police because he saw a heart carved into a tree?"

"No! Leo saw Miss Blossom pose in the old dress by Mar Schuyler's monument. It marks her grave, deep in the woods. Is big and bronze and very beautiful."

The 'tree-woman' I saw in the fog? I wondered. *The female figure who "came for" the creator of the crude map faxed to Deputy Clifton?*

Vito went on. "Leo, he already knew something was not right. Every year, Miss Blossom must leave Magnet Springs after she gives back the crown or … bad things will happen. Or so she believes. Is the curse of Winimar. When Leo saw the secret grave, he knew the trust did not give full disclosure. Leo, he wanted to protect innocent Miss Blossoms from the poison of an old secret. And he wanted to protect you, too."

I squeezed the elderly man's bony hand. "Vito, this is an important question: Are you the only Schuyler heir?"

"I am the oldest living heir, but not the only heir."

"How many are there?"

He raised two gnarled fingers.

"You … and Dock?"

Vito's face darkened. "Yes. Antonio—Anthony—who calls himself 'Dock.' The man who runs with married women and their daughters. The man who steals the prize check of poor Faye Raffle. *Bah.* He is a bad Paladino! Sometimes, the Schuyler blood, it shows up again. This Paladino has the bad blood in him!"

I waited a moment for the sausage vendor to calm himself.

"You said the curse was on the Schuylers and all they owned. Aren't you, as an heir, entitled to some of that wealth?"

He laughed until he choked. "No! The trust, it was set up for the glory of the Schuyler name. I do not have that name. No descendent does since Mrs. Schuyler's nephew. But the oldest living heir, he or she is entitled to make a decision. He or she decides if the youngest living heir gets a special privilege."

Vito sneered.

"Which is—what?"

"If the oldest living heir says yes, then the youngest living heir, he or she can tell the judges how to vote for Miss Blossom."

"You mean—rig the contest? How can that be?"

"Is part of the trust—and the gag order. Is the only power Mrs. Schuyler gave to heirs who are not named Schuyler. But we Paladinos never stoop so low! Until *this* Paladino."

"I'm guessing you didn't let him exercise that right."

"No, I did not," Vito declared. "He is a bad man. Only interested in sex and money. Mostly money. He said Mrs. LePadanni would help him if her daughter won the contest. He threatened me. But I refused. Today he came again to my house. He said he would not leave until I give him my money. He said he needs to run away. And Mrs. LePadanni does, too. I think they hurt somebody. They have nasty tempers. The daughter, she has a temper, too. Beautiful, but very bad. *Bah.*"

"Do you think Dock and Tammi tried to kill Kevin Sweeney?" I said.

"Maybe. Dock, he is a Schuyler heir, so he sees things."

"You mean … hallucinations?"

"I mean every Schuyler heir sees Winimar with the lawyer. Is in the trust. The lawyer must show us the estate. So we can see how much wealth the Schuyler family had. Ha! We see what evil looks like."

"Does it look like two white eyes that glow in the dark?"

Vito stared at me. "Yes! That is what remains of Mrs. Slocum Schuyler!"

A shiver shot down my spine. "Do you mean … Mrs. Schuyler's remains are in the bathhouse? Behind the locked door?"

"No! Her memories are there."

Vito explained that after Mrs. Schuyler killed her daughter, she placed Mar's best things—including her dresses and jewelry—in a vault within the bathhouse, where Mar used to spend her leisurely summer days. Only the lawyer had access, but he was obliged to show the contents to all Schuyler heirs.

"What's the point?" I said.

"It was Mrs. Schuyler's way to keep her daughter alive. The same with the portrait. She made sure that every year the new Miss Blossom is painted. In the same pose and the same dress as Mar Schuyler. But the new Miss Blossom can never tell. You have seen the original portrait, no?"

"You mean … the one that hangs in the Town Hall?"

I recalled an untitled oil painting of a young woman in a rose-colored gown. Never in all my comings and goings through the Town Hall had I wondered about the people in the half-dozen portraits displayed there. I assumed they represented Magnet Springs' wealthy founding families, and, being a second-generation Springer myself, I didn't much care who was here more than a century before me.

"Yes," Vito said. "That is Winifred Margaret Schuyler, age eighteen. Her mother believed no other girl will ever be so lovely. She thought she could prove that by making sure every new Miss Blossom posed for the same portrait, only smaller and in Mar's very old dress. In front of her statue."

"Where are the portraits? And who paints them?"

Vito sighed wearily. "I am not supposed to tell. But I am an old man sick of secrets. According to the trust, the Schuyler lawyer must hire a different artist every year. The artist must be from out of town and not very good. Also, he is sworn to secrecy. The paintings are stored in the bathhouse."

"You're saying … here are over a hundred and fifty paintings in there?"

"Small ones, yes, they are stacked everywhere. I have seen them; they are quite poor." He made a face. "The lawyer for the trust, he tells the girls there is a curse on the winner if she stays in Magnet Springs. Mrs. Schuyler, she believed that a girl who goes away will soon be forgotten. But the image of her dead daughter hangs in the Town Hall. And so Mar lives forever."

I recalled the feel of Mar Schuyler's hair jewelry in my hand and shuddered.

"Vito, do bad things really happen to former Miss Blossoms who don't leave town?"

"If they *believe* it will happen, then it does. Most Miss Blossoms *believe* they will have a good life when they leave, so they go. The curse, you see, is in what we believe."

I believed that. So did Murray McCready.

"Is there a way to break the curse?" I said.

Vito's watery eyes sparkled. "Ah, that is a good question! And the answer is yes, I think. If we crown a Miss Blossom who refuses to pose for the portrait."

"You mean—?"

"A girl who defies every gag order will cancel the effect of the curse. But she must be a very brave girl."

Just then Brady pushed open the kitchenette door.

"What smells good in here?"

"Not your chili," I replied.

The sausage vendor served Brady a bowl of his special soup and answered his remaining questions about Winimar. Brady knew most of the story already from speed-reading and reading between the lines, as well as from interviewing the LePadanni ladies.

"Tammi admitted that she hit on Dock. Not because she wanted him, but because she wanted what he could do for her," Brady said. "He promised to make sure Brandi won."

"But why would Tammi and Brandi care so much about winning the Miss Blossom competition?" I said.

"Brandi has her heart set on becoming a top model. Or the next Angelina Jolie. And Tammi's the Stage Mom from Hell. Together they took an online course called Three Steps to Building Your Modeling Career. Step One is to enter and win beauty pageants. Miss Blossom was supposed to be their easy first victory. If Dock didn't come through, they had a backup plan."

Tammi admitted to Brady that she'd never loved her husband; she'd married him for the prestige of being a surgeon's wife. At her prompting, Dr. LePadanni had agreed to lobby for Brandi's victory. He would "bribe" the judges by offering them entrée into the Magnet Springs Country Club.

I snort-laughed. "Not that panel of judges!"

"*Exactamundo*," Jenx concurred. She had joined us in the kitchenette and was now ladling soup into a coffee mug. "Hen hooted when the doctor offered her a membership in exchange for her vote. The other judges felt the same—except Rico. He has fantasies about seducing homophobic bluebloods. And Martha Glenn accused the doctor of trying to seduce *her*."

"What about the doctor?" I said. "Did Tammi kill him?"

Jenx tipped back her head to drink from her mug. Then she smacked her lips. "Not directly. But she helped."

"She let him eat too much fast food!" Vito exclaimed. "The man, he was a big fat pig!"

"True. And he was scheduled for coronary bypass surgery," Jenx said. "Tammi says he frequently got chest pains. She picked a fight before she left at around seven on Saturday. She wanted to upset him, but she couldn't have known for sure she'd kill him. The coroner thinks he had a heart attack. He was probably already dead when Brandi had her tantrum. Brandi thought he was just being a bore."

I said, "What happened to the lights at Providence?"

"Brandi was furious with her father for failing to 'buy' her the crown. So she pulled the same stunt her mom once did when she got angry: she turned off the power and stormed out."

"Why would anyone do that?"

Brady said, "The doctor knew a lot about a lot of things but nothing about his domestic life—from his wife's sexual partners to the infrastructure of his house. You might say the women in his life liked to leave him in the dark."

"And then Dock picked up Brandi and took her back to his place?" I asked. To Vito, I added, "I … uh … went looking for them at the marina."

"Nope, that's not what happened," Jenx said. "Tammi picked up Brandi and took her to a motel. Abra was in the car, too. With the crown. That's when Tammi pried out the jewels. See, the doctor had a neat little pre-nup that would have prevented Tammi from getting much cash if they divorced. Which looked like a possibility. So Tammi planned to fence the jewels. We've recovered them."

"Back up," I said. "How did Tammi get Abra to give her the crown?"

"Just as Wells suspected, Whiskey: she corrupted Abra's training. Tammi knows a lot about dogs. She figured out how to subvert The System. But Abra got away and took the stripped crown to Vestige. Tammi and Dock were back at Winimar this morning looking for her. They'd heard police scanner reports that Abra was in the area, and they were afraid she'd tip off the cops. Tammi lured her into the Hummer, but Abra jumped out at Mrs. Brewster's house and left her scat. Then Abra followed Tammi to Vito's. We can only assume your dog planned some kind of revenge."

"Or she likes Italian sausage," I said. "So who was Dock screwing Saturday night if it wasn't Tammi or Brandi?"

I hoped it wasn't Noonan.

"Dock won't tell us," Jenx said. "And not because he's a gentleman."

"Who killed Crystal Crossman?"

"We're working on it," Jenx said. "The MSP forensics unit'll run the blue paint on Sweeney's Hummer and Dock's truck. Paladino's not going anywhere anytime soon. Neither is Tammi."

A few minutes later, I left the station with Abra on a borrowed collar and leash. I was coaxing her across the street toward my car as she strained for one last look back at Roscoe. Suddenly a horn blasted, long and loud.

I glanced up in time to see a black Dodge Ram truck bearing down on us.

FORTY-EIGHT

I HAD A SPLIT second to choose: forward or back? Violently jerking the leash, I lunged ahead, and Abra flew with me. The truck sailed past, its brakes squealing. I skidded across the asphalt, embedding granules in my knee, forearm and palm. That hurt … though not as much as impact with a ton of moving metal. As I slid, I heard the crunch of steel and glass. The Dodge Ram had rammed a light pole. At least it stopped.

What happened next was disjointed. Surreal. A high-pitched scream was followed by a chorus of shouts. I rolled onto my side. Abra sat next to me, alert and unhurt. She licked my face. There was probably a smudge of Vito's soup on my chin. Jenx, Brady, and the two sheriff's deputies ran past us toward the truck. Vaguely I wondered who was watching Dock and Tammi.

A while later, Brady helped me to my feet. By then the EMTs had come for the driver of the truck. I watched the paramedics place Emma Kish on a backboard.

"Is she dead?" I said.

"No," Brady replied. "And she says she wasn't trying to kill you."

"Why would she? Isn't that Dock's truck?"

"Yeah. I don't know how Emma Kish got it. The MSP forensics team was supposed to take it over. By the way, where's Abra?"

I groaned. My diva dog was gone again. Brady wouldn't let me panic, however. We found her back inside the station, looking for Roscoe and doggie treats. Brady offered me a couple aspirins and assured me that Abra was tired of running. We could only hope.

"Emma confessed," Jenx announced, arriving with her notebook open.

"To what?" I said.

"She killed Crystal."

"She did? Why?"

"Jealousy. Before the pageant, Emma heard Dock tell Crystal he still loved her, and he was thinking about following her to Vegas."

"But Dock was doing Brandi! And Tammi."

"And Emma," Jenx said. "Dock used to be Crystal's boyfriend. She dumped him when she caught him in bed with Tammi. But Emma didn't know he was doing the LePadannis. She thought he loved her, and she freaked out when she heard him tell Crystal he still cared. That cell phone call Emma made from the stage? It was to ask Dock if she could borrow his truck. She wanted to follow Crystal out of town and give her a good-bye scare. Emma says she only meant to *tap* Crystal's bumper. But she ended up running her off the road."

"So the paint on Dock's truck *is* from Crystal's car!" I exclaimed.

"Yeah, but Dock didn't kill her. And that was Emma you heard in Dock's bed."

"She had sex with Dock after killing Crystal?"

Jenx checked her notes. "She said it made her 'hot.' Then she stole Dock's spare set of keys. That's how she drove off in his truck just now, before the MSP forensics team could remove it. Emma's been following Dock since yesterday. She finally figured out he was involved with the LePadannis. So she decided he owed her his truck."

"Man," Brady said, "she's one lousy driver."

"She's one pissed-off chick," Jenx corrected him.

I said, "If Emma killed Crystal with Dock's truck, then why is there blue paint on Sweeney's Hummer?"

Jenx said, "I guess you'll have to ask Sweeney."

And I did. The next morning. Something happened before that, however. Something momentous: I had sex.

Drum roll, please …

Abra and I went home to Vestige, where we discovered Chester and Prince Harry waiting on the front porch. They were rocking on the glider, Prince Harry happily settled in Chester's lap.

"Why didn't you let yourself in?" I asked. Chester could access my house 24/7, with or without a key. When he rang the doorbell, he was just being formal.

"Because we need to talk," he replied, sounding serious.

Abra and I sat down next to him. Prince Harry opened one eye and wagged at his mom, who ignored him. By now Abra was sufficiently detached from motherhood to view her son as one more unwelcome guest.

"You have visitors," Chester began.

"Who?" I hadn't noticed a vehicle.

"Very small but annoying visitors," he continued. That was when I noticed that both he and Prince Harry were scratching themselves. "Whiskey, you have fleas."

"I most certainly do not!"

"I mean your house is full of fleas. You have an infestation. I wouldn't go in there if I were you."

"How could my house be full of fleas?!" I sputtered and instantly knew the answer. "It's those damn cats, isn't it? Dr. David gave me fleas!"

"Fleggers dipped them before they shipped them, but they couldn't guarantee results." Chester scratched again, and so did Prince Harry.

"How did you two get fleas?" I asked.

"We were helping Deely with Cat Recreation. Harry and I rolled around on the floor, and the rest is history. Deely said she'll have an exterminator here in the morning."

"Where am I supposed to sleep tonight?"

"I have a suggestion."

Chester reached into his school blazer pocket and extracted a piece of paper. After clearing his throat, he read aloud: "'Whiskey, feel free to come to my house tonight. And bring Abra and Prince Harry. They can share the extra kennel. I'll find a bed for you.'"

"Who's that from?" I asked, but I was pretty sure I knew.

"The Judge. He called while I was here, and I wrote down what he wanted to tell you."

"Is that all?"

"He said you should bring something besides the dogs, but you'd know what it was."

My black camisole. I was wearing it.

By the time I arrived at Wells Verbelow's house, it was late, and I was sure I was too exhausted to test the camisole.

Sometimes it's fun to be wrong. And really delicious to let someone undress you.

We said little. Wells led me to his bed, where he tenderly kissed every part of my body. And, yes, he lingered extra long over the camisole.

After a whole year of living celibate, I thought making love with someone other than Leo would be … monumental. I suppose it was. But Wells had lost a wife, so he understood the transition. He made the whole process natural and sweet and not overwhelming. Although I didn't feel the volcanic passion I'd been dreaming of, I didn't feel disappointed or anxious, either. I felt desire … and desired. Also very much alive.

Even the morning after felt right. When I woke to find Wells gone, I put on the robe he'd left out for me and followed the scent of coffee to his kitchen. He was making eggs just the way I liked them: over easy with a runny, yummy yolk plus lots of thick-sliced, whole-grain toast slathered in real butter.

"How did you know?" I asked.

"I've seen you in restaurants," he said. "I pay attention."

After we ate, we fed the dogs. All four of them. Norman and Mooney vied for Abra's attention in a gentlemanly, sporting way. There was no contest, however; Norman was Abra's clear choice. To his credit, Mooney was avuncular with little Harry. They roughhoused together, Harry receiving a free drool shower while Norman and Abra played kissy-butt.

Suddenly I gasped.

"Wells—look at Prince Harry!"

He did.

"Now look at Abra and Norman!"

He did. Our eyes met.

Wells said, "When did Fenton Flagg and Norman first arrive in Magnet Springs?"

We did the math. Although Abra and Norman couldn't say so, they were telling us.

"Prince Harry, meet your father," I said.

We left them all to get better acquainted; Wells headed for court, and I drove to CMC to see Faye before her surgery.

Miss Blossom was too groggy to listen to Vito's theory about how she could break the Curse of Winimar by refusing to pose for the portrait or honor the gag orders. I'd explain it to her later. Today Faye just needed to survive the Curse of Tammi LePadanni. Fortunately, her parents were due in by noon.

While she was in surgery, I made my way to Kevin Sweeney's room. Every security guard I passed smiled at me. I almost felt welcome. It had to be the sex.

Wee Sweeney looked surprisingly well. Though pale, he was alert and friendly. Very friendly, considering all those gag orders.

I cut right to the chase. "Why were you and your Hummer at Winimar?"

"We were hijacked by Dock and Tammi."

Kevin explained that the duo showed up at his condo in Grand Rapids on Saturday night. When he opened the front door, they dragged him to his vehicle.

"Dock had already had the Schuyler Heir's Official Tour of Winimar, so he knew what was there and also the back way into the estate. He'd told Tammi everything. The man has no respect for gag orders! And she's a gold-digger. She was sure there had to be something of value in the bathhouse. So she made me open the room and the vault. She removed the hair jewelry and wrote down the lock combinations, in case she wanted more loot later. When I threatened to go to the police, she told Dock to kill me and throw me down the well."

I showed Sweeney the index card I'd found under Tammi's phone.

"Are those the combinations?"

He nodded. "Recognize the numbers?"

"Should I?"

"Only if you know what everybody knows about Winimar."

By now, I thought I actually did. I studied the digits. And it hit me.

"48-50-75—as in 1848, 1850, and 1875. The years when Schuylers were murdered at Winimar?"

Wee Sweeney nodded. "And 04-11-48?"

"The date the first Miss Blossom was crowned?"

"Think again. That was in 1847."

I recalled that Mar Schuyler did not appear at the coronation of her successor because she was supposedly sick with consumption.

"The date Mar's baby was born?"

"Exactly."

Time to find out where he'd gotten the scrape of blue paint on his bumper. Sweeney winced.

"When Dock commandeered my Hummer, he didn't see a parking post in my lot. I warned him, but he drove right into it."

I studied the diminutive attorney. "Why did you pretend to be Brady and fax Fenton Flagg's map of Winimar to Deputy Clifton?"

"Good sleuthing, Whitney. For the same reason I've been trying to subtly discourage young women from competing in the Miss Blossom contest since I took this job: It's a rotten business, and I want it to stop."

"So you knew about Fenton Flagg's project?"

"Knew about it?" Wee Sweeney sniggered. "I created the dummy corporation that contracted with him to write the book! If he can't find a commercial publisher for the finished manuscript, I'll publish it myself."

"But—you'd be violating your own gag orders!"

"It's about time. Dock's going to prison, and Vito wants this to end as much as I do. Through the law, we'll find a way to make it so."

At that moment Kevin Sweeney sounded prouder to be a lawyer than any lawyer I knew. I almost admired him.

FORTY-NINE

I was thrilled to find Faye and her parents safely back from surgery and Venezuela, respectively. Mr. and Mrs. Raffle were so effusive in their thanks for my concern about their daughter that I wanted to bolt before they realized how inept I was. All that mattered was that Faye was going to be fine. Even immediately after surgery, she looked invincible. Somehow I knew that she would be the first Miss Blossom to beat every possible curse.

I excused myself to drop in on Fenton Flagg to let him know that his companion dog was in the best of hands. That should have taken two minutes. Yet I ended up sitting in his room for half an hour.

What can I say about the man formerly known as Murray Mc-Cready? That he was around fifty years old and ruggedly handsome with flashing green eyes. Also that he wasn't weird. As the creator of the Seven Suns of Solace, he seemed surprisingly down to earth.

"I can't tell you how much I appreciate your help, Whiskey. You saved my life, and probably Norman's, too."

I demurred and then inquired about his dog's age and pedigree. As I'd suspected, the Golden had impeccable bloodlines. Finally, I asked about his name.

Fenton Flagg laughed. "You don't think 'Norman' fits?"

"I didn't say that." But it was exactly what I thought.

"Well, the late Norman Vincent Peale was my role model. I named my dog after him."

That made sense, I supposed. I asked whether he and Norman had first come to Magnet Springs about six months ago. The answer was yes. So I took the plunge.

"Do you recall if Norman … ran off during your first visit here?"

Fenton's eyes widened. "As a matter of fact, he did. He was missing for two whole days. I wondered if I'd ever see him again."

The New Age guru cocked his head, no doubt intuiting that there was more to my story. So I told it, illustrated with a photo of Prince Harry.

"I see the resemblance," he said. "Well, I guess that means we're related. How about you, Abra, Harry, Norman and me getting together to celebrate just as soon as I can leave this place?"

I promised Fenton we would and shook his warm hand, which cradled mine a little longer than necessary. So help me, I had just left another man's bed after a whole year of abstinence, and now here I was, flirting with this guy! This guy who was married—sort of—to Noonan.

That reminded me of a technical question: "I'm a little confused about the Seven Suns of Solace. My stepdaughter said the

319

First Sun is asking for what you want. But my handyman said it's doing the right thing. Which is it?"

Smiling, Fenton replied, "My belief, Whiskey, is that the first step in recovery is whatever you need it to be."

Although I didn't say so, I realized that my first step in recovery was surviving a whole year without Leo. Driving back to Vestige, I felt better than I had in twelve calendar pages.

Until I saw Avery sitting on my front porch. She was slouched in the glider, looking as sour as ever. When I pulled into the driveway, she straightened and started toward my car, her tongue flicking. Reflexively, I locked my doors. Part of me—the cowardly part—wanted to shift into reverse and run for my life. But I owed Leo more than that. So I rolled down my window.

"Hey," I said.

"Hey, yourself." Her voice was neutral.

We studied each other's facial contusions. I decided that she looked worse than I did, though not too bad. Not major lawsuit bad.

"Whiskey, it's really hard for me to say this, but … I need your help."

Who was she kidding? Avery had never had trouble asking me for help. I didn't point that out, though. I just pursed my lips and listened.

"Can we … talk in the house?" Avery said.

"Not a good idea. They just finished fumigating in there."

Avery looked as if she hadn't slept in days. Something told me that wasn't because she and Nash were having nonstop sex. I popped the door locks.

"Climb in. Let's go for a drive."

We headed north along Lake Michigan, past greening woods, wineries and orchards. I made small talk while waiting for Avery to say what was on her mind. Finally she blurted it out: "Nash wants the babies to have a paternity test! He thought he was sterile, and now he needs proof that they're his."

"Are they?" I asked.

She burst into snorting, wheezing tears. "I don't know! I think so, but I had sex with another guy that same week! A real loser I met at this bar near campus. Oh, God, Whiskey! What should I do?"

I pulled to the side of the road and offered her a box of tissues.

"Avery, I think you know what to do. If Nash wants to test the babies, let him."

"But they might not be his! Do I have to tell him about the other guy?"

"Not yet. And maybe not ever. One step at a time. Wait till you get the results."

"But … what if the twins aren't his? Where will I go? What will I do?"

Very gently I said, "Nash found *you*, remember? You had no intention of telling him he was a father. If worse comes to worst, you'll be right where you thought you were. No harm, no foul."

"But I *like* living with Nash!" she wailed. "He's so sexy!"

Though sorely tempted to tell her what a toad the man was, I said nothing. *One step at a time.* I was learning, too.

———

The next day, the first anniversary of Leo's death, dawned bright, cool, and cat- and flea-free. Before the fumigators arrived on Tuesday, Dr. David and Deely had moved all the felines to another location. Call me paranoid, but I'd required photographic proof that Yoda, the Devon rex, was living elsewhere.

Abra needed her day at the doggie spa; she had an appointment at noon. And I had one at the human spa, ten minutes later.

Before that, though, we were going to visit Leo's grave. As we headed out the door with a big plastic bucket of daffodils, my phone jangled. I almost kept going, but something made me grab the receiver on the fourth ring.

"Hey, Whiskey. You doing all right today?"

I set down the bucket. "Yeah, Jeb, I'm doing fine."

My first husband was calling from Norfolk. He knew what today was. And even though he couldn't be here to comfort me, he cared. Halfway through a tour to promote his latest CD, Jeb Halloran was due back in Magnet Springs by Memorial Day. We didn't say much because we didn't need to. Like Fenton and Noonan, Jeb and I would always be linked, whether or not we hooked up again. Jeb was lobbying to renew our carnal relations, and I was not beyond temptation. My first love still had the power to stir my insides. No black camisole required.

"Let's go," I told Abra. She grabbed a mouthful of white daffs from the bucket and bounded ahead of me through the breezeway to my car.

We were off to pay our loving respects to Leo. A year after losing him, the diva dog and I were both finally finding our way.

~ The End ~

ABOUT THE AUTHOR

NINA WRIGHT, a former actor and playwright, writes novels for adults and younger readers. Watch for *Whiskey and Water*, the next installment in her humorous Whiskey Mattimoe mystery series, as well as *Sensitive*, the sequel to her popular paranormal novel *Homefree*. Nina is a skilled public speaker and teacher. For more information about her entertaining workshops in writing and the creative process, visit her website and blogs.

Contact her at

http://www.ninawright.net

http://whiskeymattimoe.blogspot.com/

http://mrfairlessrules.blogspot.com/

http://ninawrightwriter.blogspot.com/

www.MidnightInkBooks.com

From the gritty streets of New York City to sacred tombs in the Middle East, it's always midnight somewhere. Join us online at any hour for fresh new voices in mystery fiction, book club questions, author information, mystery resources, and more.

Midnight Ink promises a wild ride filled with cunning villains, conflicted heroes, hilarious hazards, mind-bending puzzles, and enough twists and turns to keep readers on the edge of their seats.

Order by Phone:

- Call toll-free within the U.S. and Canada at 1-888-NITEINK (1-888-648-3465)

- We accept VISA, MasterCard, and American Express

Order by Mail:

Send the full price of your order (MN residents add 6.5% sales tax) in U.S. funds, plus postage & handling to:

Midnight Ink
2143 Wooddale Drive
Woodbury, MN 55125-2989

Postage & Handling:

Standard (U.S., Mexico, & Canada). If your order is:
$24.99 and under, add $3.00
$25.00 and over, FREE STANDARD SHIPPING

AK, HI, PR: $15.00 for one book plus $1.00 for each additional book.

International Orders (airmail only):
$16.00 for one book plus $3.00 for each additional book

Orders are processed within 2 business days. Please allow for normal shipping time. Postage and handling rates subject to change.